THE PIPES
ARE CALLING

THE PIPES ARE CALLING

CHIP HANNAY

ISBN:
979-8-89079-322-5 (Hardcover)
979-8-89079-323-2 (Paperback)
979-8-89079-324-9 (Ebook)

The pipes, the pipes are calling.
This book is dedicated both to those
who rise to the call,
And to those who must stay home and bide.

MAYBE SHE'S RIGHT

When Ditch Dietrick came back from his second deployment, he was off his game, and his wife wanted to know why. He thought it was performance anxiety, but Gully blamed the war.

"You probably have PTSD," she said. "It messes up everything: desire, arousal, and especially the quality of the –."

"Can we talk about something else?" Ditch asked.

He was grilling ahi steaks on the patio of their apartment in Kaneohi Bay, not far from the Air Station. A Cobra from his squadron flew over and he looked up. The evening was CAVU, so the guys up there could see all of K-Bay, the islands, and the barrier reef. He remembered a pilot adage: It's better to be down here, wishing you were up there, than up there, wishing you were down here. He didn't think that was true for him right now.

"Are you even listening to me?"

Gully sat on a chaise wearing a pair of his silkies and a white wifebeater without a bra. An uninhibited blue-eyed brunette with long legs, she'd brought a lump to his throat since the day they met. She had an iPad on her lap and was whisking the screen with her fingers.

"It says right here you're at 'an eighty-five percent increased risk for ED.' And this is an official government study."

"Oh," he said, "well, then." After a pause, he added, "Babe, I don't have PTSD, or ED, or any of those acronyms. The desire's there, but it's just become a self-fulfilling prophesy now."

"Then maybe you should do what Jenna says, and take some mycoxafloppin."

Jenna was Gully's bestie and partner in their yoga studio. She gave advice, frequently.

"Gul, I've only been home a week. I just need to eat decent food, drink beer, and chill."

"Maybe. But the last time you came back, you were always, always trying to hump me."

"When I chased you around the sofa, you weren't too pleased. You called me oversexed."

"Oh," she said, "I didn't mind it that much." She whisked to a new screen and studied it a moment. "Maybe you should watch some porn."

"That's not my jam," he said. "I feel too sorry for the girls."

"Women," she corrected. "Only misogynistic fuckwits call us girls. And anyway, you're not one of them. You actually like women, and they like you."

"I don't think Jenna likes me much."

"Oh," Gully said, "you'd be surprised at how she thinks about you."

Ditch glanced at Gully. Conversations with her were often confusingly circular, but he sensed she was coming to her point. The whole thread had begun with the question, "Do you find Jenna attractive?" Ditch thought Jenna might be trisexual – meaning she'd try anything. Anyway, she was certainly bisexual. When she adjusted Gully in her yoga poses, she had a lingering look in her eye. During his nine-month absence, how close had they grown?

"I know you think I'm dense," he said.

"You're a man, so it's not your fault," she replied.

"But I see where you're going with this."

"Just saying, a little experimentation might get the blood flowing to your nethers again."

Ditch flipped the tuna. "Babe, I'll be alright, after a little time in my Nothing Box."

"Fine, you can spend the evening there. I'm going to Jenna's to work on my crow pose."

He watched her slide into the fancy jandals he'd bought her in Thailand, and flip-flop in through the sliding glass door. She went to the bedroom to change clothes. He might go watch her, he supposed, maybe get a little frisson going, but he heard her laughing on her phone, no doubt with Jenna. She returned wearing pink yoga pants and a lemon-yellow tank top, her long brown hair tied into a single braid.

"You look beautiful," he said.

"Jenna thinks you ought to consider a threesome."

"That seems a little crowded," Ditch said slowly. "Is there anything I should know?"

"You already would," she answered, "if you were ever here."

"I'm here now."

"No," she said, "you're *really* not." She said this over her shoulder on the way to the door. When he asked when she'd be back, she cast him a glance that seemed tinged with rue.

A month later, Ditch returned to the war, after a quick, no-fault divorce. Taking the blame, he admitted to being insensitive. "And she may be right, that I never do come home."

"You think?" said all his friends.

A REPLACEMENT WOMAN

But three years later Ditch did finally come home, to Kerrville, Texas, where his widower dad was declining with dementia. The old fellow's medical bills amounted to four thousand a month. The VA paid a small portion of that, and Ditch alone picked up the rest. His younger sister was married to an out-of-work welder, they had three kids, and they were so broke they had to move back to the family ranch. Compared to them, Ditch was better off, although half his savings had gone to Gully in the divorce. To make ends meet, he stayed in the Active Reserves and took a job flying a corporate jet. Adapt, Improvise, and Overcome.

Leaving the Memory Care Home one afternoon, he stepped into the sunlit parking lot and stood a moment, taking a breath. Across the parked cars, he saw his dad's nurse, a black Army vet named Sam. They did the chin-lift greeting, fellow members of the one percent. Wearing Oakleys like Ditch, he was leaning against an ambulance, Zippo-lighting a cigarette. When Ditch walked over, he shook out the pack.

"Want one, Jarhead?" he asked.

"No thanks, Army Strong. After I made it out of Helmand, I quit."

"Yeah, I'm gonna do that someday." Sam took a drag and regarded him. "Good visit?"

"Same as usual," Ditch said. He'd spent most of it wiping pudding off his dad's chin.

"Alzheimer's," Sam said, "nature's ultimate fuck over. Did he talk?"

"Does he ever?"

"Used to, in the mornings, mostly about women: your dead mom, your sister, and your ex-wife. Said you should be out looking for a replacement woman."

Ditch smiled. "Yeah, that sounds like the old dad, a fountain of goofy advice."

"Uh-huh, but another woman never hurts. Dude, you're a Cobra pilot, right?"

Ditch nodded. "Active Reserves now, after four back-to-backs. Came home to Texas for dad, and a job flying a corporate jet. You?"

"Medic. Falluja, where you bugfuck Cobra jocks saved our Army shit more than once."

"Hey, we were all in it together, bro," Ditch said. "Two cheeks on the same hairy ass."

"Fucking A," Sam laughed.

They bumped fists, and looked around, surveilling the parking lot, which they didn't need to do, but they did, anyway, out of habit.

"It's fucking weird, isn't it," Sam commented, "feeling safe?"

"Adrenalin's harder to quit than tobacco," Ditch said. "Listen, I'm gonna be gone for maybe a month, flying out of country – but I left an emergency contact number at the office."

"Copy that."

"And thanks for looking after my dad."

"It's a privilege," Sam said. "I saw his medals from Vietnam."

"Yeah, and they thought that was a long war," Ditch said, walking to his car. "Later."

"Later. And good luck, dude," Sam called, "on finding that replacement woman."

Ditch raised his middle finger, with a laugh. Climbing into his old diesel Mercedes, he turned the key and let the glow plugs warm. Another woman? Yeah, right, like he'd go down that serious relationship rabbit-hole again. But he did remember some other advice his dad had given him, before his first deployment to war. "In combat and in life, whatever you think is gonna happen, you're probably wrong."

CHAPTER 1

September 22, 2011

THE NEXT MORNING Ditch had pre-flighted the Phenom 300, cleaned and outfitted the cabin and galley, sorted out the requisite customs forms, supervised the fueling, checked the weather, and filed the flight plan, all well before dawn. Then he waited in the civil twilight at the foot of the airstairs for the corporate SUV to arrive. He wore the required corporate pilot uniform with epaulets, in which he felt like a fraud. He preferred an honest, smelly combat flight suit, but now his job was flying an eccentric multi-millionaire around, because he needed the money.

While waiting for the corporate SUV, he had some time to think about his fucked-up marriage, which he usually avoided doing. But now, after three years, Gully had started communicating again, via a text. He took out his phone and re-read the first line: "I met one of your after-me girlfriends in the studio yesterday, and from what she said, you don't have that problem anymore, so I have a favor to ask."

He would have read more, but SUV headlights came through the gate and swung across the airport ramp. Joe

D. Grand – or Warbucks, as the personal staff codenamed him – had arrived. When the Escalade parked some fifty meters from the aircraft, both rear windows slid down and faces peered out, looking warily about. Then they retreated to have a backseat discussion before the doors snapped open and two men hurried out and across the tarmac. They both clutched briefcases and wore hats. Supposedly, this abrupt trip combined both business and a medical checkup: a defense contract deal with the Saudis, and a week at the Swiss Clinique La Prairie for Warbucks. As they crossed the fifty meters, the younger man pulled ahead. He was Lawrence Donker, the older man's personal attorney and worrier-in-chief, and his codename was Whistling Booger. A thin, nervous fellow with hooded brows over dark-ringed eyes, he saw threats everywhere. Panting, he passed Ditch and rapidly climbed the airstairs, bleating out an order.

"Our bags are in the car. Get them quickly, and don't scratch mine this time."

"Okay, Larry," Ditch said, "not this time."

Pausing halfway up, Booger shot a look back down. He was certain the insolent pilot intentionally marred his luggage. But then he thought of something more important.

"Do the passengers' names appear anywhere on the flight plan?" he asked.

"No, just the number of souls onboard. But they'll be on my flight manifest."

"Which," Booger raised an admonishing finger, "is the property of Grand Wright Corporation, and as such, is confidential. I needn't remind you of that."

"You needn't," Ditch said, and turned away to greet Warbucks.

Seeing him, Ditch realized he no longer disliked the pudgy, screwy old fart. True, as a defense contractor, he no doubt cut corners, overbilled, and offered inducements to sweeten his deals. But on the personal level, he deeply loved his wife, and he was a comical hypochondriac. Walking fast, he was shaking out his left arm, probably to see if it had grown numb, an early sign of a heart attack.

"Feeling okay, Sir?"

"What? Oh, I don't know. Is the heart monitor onboard?"

"Yes Sir, along with your blood oxygen monitor. And how many are travelling with us?"

"The usual, plus one: that new girl my wife just hired."

"The Kiwi horse trainer? Your wife mentioned she's a war widow."

"Is she?" Warbucks passed by, breathing hard. "I must've missed that."

Ditch smiled to himself, watching Warbucks labor up the airstairs. The status of war widow was a pretty salient fact to miss. Frequently, Warbucks' corporate head seemed firmly wedged up his hyper-tense ass. But his wife Louisa was the polar opposite, and she'd hired all of their personal staff, most of them vets. Their codename for her was The Saint.

Over at the SUV, Ditch saw his buddy, Hugo Perilloux, climbing out from behind the wheel. Wounded six times as an Army Ranger, Hugo was an amiable, slightly addled guy with a touch of TBI. He was Warbucks' personal driver and bodyguard. He went to the rear and opened the hatch to retrieve his kit, calling to Ditch.

"Want help with this shit, bro?"

"No thanks, man," Ditch said, walking past the Escalade's dark tinted windows. "I got to act like I'm scuffing the Booger's bags a bit."

"Roger that. That dude's an asshat. The whole drive, he's worried we're being tailed. And what the fuck is a '*subpoena duces tecum*' anyway?"

"Above our pay grade," Ditch said. "But something's hinky in the state of Denmark."

At the hatch, Ditch looked in and sighed. Warbucks never travelled light. Neither did Whistling Booger. He reached in for the heavy bags, then noticed his last passenger still in the front seat. She was talking on an iPhone in a thick New Zealand accent. Having arrived in Texas just two days ago, she was already off to Switzerland to buy Warbucks' daughter a world class horse.

"Don't spit the dummy, Moira. I weel zip you snaps as soon as I can. But you understind, the feenal decision is meen."

She listened a moment, then punched off, muttering, "Spoiled tweet."

Ditch took hold of the heaviest bag, then thought to speak. "Twit trouble?" he asked.

The woman's head snapped around, surprised. She was mid-twenties, and had curly, unnaturally black hair, thinning at the temples, tied in a ponytail. Annoyance showed in her gray eyes.

"You were earwigging me?" she said.

"If that means eavesdropping, hell, yes," Ditch said. "We staff are all but invisible, but we do get to overhear some funny shit."

She thought about that a beat. "Na yeah, all good," she said. "No wakas, eh."

She got out of the car and came to the rear. She wore a black polo shirt, chinos, and rough-cut paddock boots. She also walked with a hard limp. She was definitely on the small side, jockey-sized, plucky, compact and muscular, but pretty in a thin-haired, broken-nosed sort of way. He stuck out his hand.

"Ditch Dietrick," he said.

She shook with a strong grip while she squizzed him: tall, dark haired, and olive skinned, with a military haircut, a moustache, and a grin. He wore sunnies up on his forehead and some sort of uniform.

"Yeah na, I heard about you. You're the carpet peelot," she said.

She meant corporate pilot, of course, but Ditch played along.

"Well, it's not something I like to admit," he said. "But I do sometimes pee on the carpet, when drunk, but not a lot."

She smiled, reaching in for her bag. "You pulling my Kiwi tits?" she asked.

Ditch laughed. "I wasn't aware of their presence. And your name is. . . ."

"Rainey Gauge."

"You're shitting me."

"I shit you not. That's my married. My maiden was Rainey Day. And I'll get my own beggage," she said.

He probably started liking her right then. He liked her even more when she also carried one of Warbucks' bags. Ditch followed along with the remaining luggage, curious enough that he had to ask, "What does 'spit the dummy' mean?"

"What owl? Oh, it means have a tantrum."

"I'm gonna need a Kiwi-English dictionary," Ditch said, stowing the bags.

"Use contixt clue, mate. How long's this flight gonna to take?"

"It'll be at least three days, before Geneva."

"Crickey, that's yonks." She started limping up the airstairs. "We should've done it commercial."

Ditch followed along. "Yeah, but this way they're off the grid, and they don't have to wait in lines. And the Phenom can get into smaller airports closer to the city."

Inside, the passengers found their seats, Warbucks and Booger occupying the four center facing seats, with Hugo and Rainey Gauge stuffed in the cramped far aft, as befitted the staff.

Before Ditch had raised the airstairs, Warbucks was pumping up his blood pressure cuff, while the Booger worried aloud

5

in legalese about a forensic audit or something. Meantime, Hugo had started snoring lightly in his rear seat – while across the narrow aisle, the war widow with thinning hair, in a private moment, was staring out her side window with a sudden sadness in her gray eyes.

But within a few minutes behind the cockpit curtain, Ditch had put them out of mind, and was busily running the checklists. Soon the two Pratt and Whitney engines spooled up with pleasant, eager whines. This was something he loved, following procedures, and doing shit he'd been trained to do. And the Phenom 300 was a dream to fly. Climbing out of Kerrville at 3000 feet per minute, he contacted San Antonio Approach and was cleared through its airspace to the north. On the other side, his controller radioed to contact Houston Center on a new frequency.

"Six Juliet Golf, switching to Houston, One Tree Fife, Niner Fife. Good day."

Since the air traffic that early morning was light, the controller came back with a personal question. "Where you headed today, Ditch?"

"Goose Bay tonight. Europe tomorrow."

"Lucky man."

Ditch clicked the mike button twice, signifying agreement, because he did feel lucky indeed. After all, he'd survived a thousand plus days of war, and the crash of his marriage, unscathed – despite the contrary opinion of his ex-wife. The trick was to compartmentalize, and make sure the contents never leaked – which occasionally, inevitably, they did, making it difficult to breathe.

Back in her seat, port side aft, Rainey Gauge was in a blue funk, remembering her last night with Jack, in their duplex outside Papakura Military Camp. The pipes, the pipes were calling, and off to war he'd be, come the morning.

The moment they connected, making love, Rainey let out a little satisfied sigh.

"Sweet as," she said.

"Fully," he replied.

She was smiling broadly when he kissed her, which was good, because this would be their last sex for seven, maybe eight months. They made it last, and even when it ended, they didn't disconnect. The room was dark, but their eyes were used to it now, and they spent some time looking, studying the face in front of them, committing it to memory. Jack reached out and touched her broken nose, and then her curly blonde hair.

"You're worried." She smoothed his furrowed brow.

"I am," he admitted. "You're so pretty: while I'm gone, you'll probably turn into a Hangi Pants."

"Well, it's your fault," she said. "You've got me used to getting rooted regular."

They both smiled then, because they knew infidelity was completely unthinkable. They were so much in love, their hearts felt bruised. But he had lied, a little. He actually was worried, about the final parting scene, coming tomorrow at Zero Dark Thirty. Physical pain he could endure, but this heart-pulling pain, it was too much. He had a plan to avoid it, though.

"Even when I brass you off," he said, "you still love me, eh?"

"Until the end of my days, luv. Now go to sleep," she said, settling his head on her chest above her breast. "If we get up early enough, we might have time to root again."

Later, she woke the instant she heard him start his ute in the parking space outside their tiny duplex.

"Scarpering chook!" she shouted, jumping out of bed and running to the front door. But his truck was already fifty meters down the dark road to Auckland, where his unit was assembling to deploy. He needed to escape that last farewell scene, she knew. The emotions would've left him frayed. But he had kissed her, on the forehead, before he slipped out of bed. She remembered it on the porch, though at the time she'd thought it was a dream. And watching his tail-lights disappear around the first turn, she still felt the print of his lips.

For the next kiss, she would just have to bide, until he came home from the war.

CHAPTER 2

AN HOUR INTO the flight, east of the Ozarks, Ditch felt a breath of air when the curtains behind him parted. He pulled the headset off his right ear and turned. Rainey Gauge stood behind him with her arms crossed, studying the six-foot panel full of screens, blinking lights, and knobs.

"You understand all this shite?" she asked.

Ditch smiled. "You better hope I do. You need something?"

Rainey shifted on her feet uncomfortably. "You mind if I squat up here with you? Hugo's asleep and farting up a torrent."

Ditch laughed. "Hugo's a Cajun. They all fart a lot. It's how they communicate."

He gestured her into the right seat, steadying the yoke with a hand. Climbing in took a while, as her left leg seemed reluctant to bend. When she'd strapped in, he handed her a voice-activated headset and pointed where to plug it in. They flew silently for a few minutes, before Ditch felt compelled to break the ice.

"Your husband, what was he, over there?"

It took her a moment to speak. "SAS," she said. "Special Air Services."

These were the New Zealand Special Forces, elite operators.

"Then he was a Romeo Mike," Ditch said. "A real man. How'd he buy the farm?"

Rainey blinked, unaccustomed to questioning this direct. Most people tried to avoid the subject entirely. But she'd heard this Ditch had served four combat tours. Also, there was something about him, an ease, a simple directness, a steady honesty that relaxed her a bit.

"Rescuing hostages," she said, "in Kabul."

"Small arms, IED, or RPG?"

"A bullet." She swallowed. "To the neck. Missed his body armor by a centimeter."

"Muthafukjonson," Ditch said, sympathetically.

"Aye," she said, "muthafukjonson."

After a moment of silence, Ditch went on, "And you, what happened to your leg?"

"Crickey-dick, you don't beat about the bush?"

"Might as well get the big stuff out," he said. "Sharing a cockpit, we'll likely be friends."

She looked across the cockpit at him, then nodded slightly. She could do with a mate, espesh one who was a bit of a dag. God knows she could use a laugh.

"Na yeah. But I'm doing all the hard yakka here. What about you? I heard things went pakaru with your wife."

She could be as direct as him, which seemed fair – and even enjoyable, talking to someone as candid as he. Still, Ditch sat quiet a moment, pretending to check the instruments.

"During my second deployment," he said finally, "she fell in love with her girlfriend."

"They de facto now? That's what we call living together, in Godzone."

"Yeah, happily de facto, running their yoga studio in Honolulu. But she texted me yesterday, with her ovulation cycle."

An explanation seemed in order. Rainey Gauge waited. Ditch shrugged.

"They're considering artificial insemination. And she likes my genes, even though I'm toxic masculine and cisgender, whatever the hell that means."

"Not even, ow."

"No, the divorce and her going gay, that was totally on me. It's probably hard to imagine, but I can be an insensitive asshole."

"Inconceivable," she smiled. "But if insensitive asshole blokes caused gaychicks, there'd be heaps more of them."

He laughed. "Well, whatever direction she was leaning, I sure pushed her over." After a pause he added, "Do you think we can talk about something other than my sex life? This is getting deeply personal."

"Just saying, rough ride, mate. Jack and I, we bonked like happy bunnies."

Ditch laughed at her frankness, and looked over. "George," the autopilot, was flying, but he disengaged it now.

"Put your hands on your yoke," he said.

"Okay," she said, "now we *are* getting deeply personal."

"No, really, take the flight controls, see what it feels like to fly this bird."

She flew for some time, very smoothly for a novice. Nevertheless, something else was on her mind.

"Four tours in harm's way," she said, "seems a bit excessive. Why'd you keep going back?"

"It started out for good reasons: you know, the pipes were calling and all that shit," Ditch said. "But at the end I mostly went just to get away from my life."

She thought about that. "Na yeah. Sometimes you can't stay where the memories are. But what about you?" she added. "Some of Jack's mates came back a bit dicky."

"I'm okay."

"Hmmm," she said, changing the subject back to artificial insemination, in which she had a very vested interest. "So what you gonna do now, about this baby request?"

"I've thought about having kids – a lot of soldiers do," Ditch said. "But to make one with a magazine and a jar. . . . That," he shook his head, "may be a bridge too far."

"Tu meke," Rainey Gauge said.

"I'm gonna need that Kiwi-English dictionary."

"Cont*i*xt clues," she said, then grew thoughtful again. Jack had left a vial of his frozen swimmers at Fertility Associates in Auckland. Several men in his unit had done the same, in case something important got blown off. And more than anything she'd wanted to see Jack again, which she might, now, in a baby's eyes, if the procedure last week had been successful.

Ditch looked over. Rainey appeared to be having a conversation within herself. He knew better than intrude, but it occurred to him that Rainey, like Gully, tended to have circular conversations, because here they were, back at artificial insemination. She glanced over at him again.

"You know, mate, AI isn't that weird. It's how we breed the broodmares on our family farm. They seem to prefer it."

"They do? Really?"

She thought about that, then laughed. "Prolly not. Too true."

"Yeah, and maybe it's my mom's Spanish blood in me, but if I'm ever gonna do the baby thing, I want to do it passionately," he said, "and preferably by direct deposit."

She laughed again, and it felt good. A box of birds.

Later, over Michigan's Upper Peninsula, Ditch introduced her to the Garmin Prodigy on the panel. "You any good with computers?"

"Mean as."

"Good. Then you've got a permanent seat up here, if you want it."

"Bonza," she said. "Ta."

Context clues indicated that she was pleased.

That night the staff ate dinner at the transiting pilots' favorite Happy Valley-Goose Bay restaurant, Bentley's Beer Market. The cod tongue was fresh, the beer cold, and the decor too low rent for Warbucks' taste. He and Booger were dining elsewhere, down Hamilton Street at the European Chef.

"This is good. Have I been here before?" Hugo asked. Propped on his elbows, he was eating his way through a mountain of greasy chicken wings. Like most special operators, Hugo was a medium sized guy, tough and muscular, but not in an obvious way, and after three hard combat tours, he had trouble sometimes with his short-term memory.

"No," Ditch told him, "but a buddy recommended this place." Then, in a lowered voice, he explained to Rainey. "Hugo got blowed up a few times."

"Is he safe?" she whispered back.

"As a baby," Ditch said, "unless you're a Taliban. He doesn't like them very much."

"And," Rainey asked, "will he *be* okay?"

"Not soon. But probably. And he's getting excellent treatment, thanks to The Saint."

"Na yeah, Louisa's doing the same with physical therapy for me," Rainey said. "She's a wonderful human being, isn't she?"

"There must be something wrong with her," Ditch said, "but I don't know what it is."

CHAPTER 3

LOUISA GRAND AND her daughter were having a not so jolly family dinner, which was not unusual for them. Louisa was a handsome woman of sixty with graying blonde hair and a tan from the hours spent in the riding arena. She had her hand in many charities, too, and was a valued participant because of her intelligence, generosity, and good humor.

Moira resembled her mother only in appearance, although she still carried the twenty pounds she'd gained back in college. An indulged younger child, she often felt put upon.

"I don't know why you hired her," Moira was saying at dinner. "She's not up to scratch. Mother, are you listening to me?"

"Yes. I've hired someone else you don't like."

"And she hung up on me, after she said the 'feenal' decision was hers. Hers – as if!"

Louisa looked up from the salmon she had not been eating. She now knew who her daughter was talking about.

"Rainey Gauge knows volumes more about horses than you do," she said. "She grew up on a breeding farm, and was Mark Todd's top exercise rider."

Mark Todd was and is New Zealand's legendary Three Day Event rider, having won nearly every international event multiple times, including two Olympic gold medals.

Moira took the rebuke as she usually did, by ignoring it. But there was something different lately about her mother. She had a short fuse, whereas before, she was the soul of patience. Also, she appeared to have no appetite. Moira herself was enjoying her veal, smeared with roasted pine nut aioli. Still, she preferred Kobi beef from the Miyazaki region. It melted in her mouth. This veal she had to chew.

Her mind returned to the bossy New Zealand girl. "Yeah, but then she fell off a horse over a jump, and exploded her leg. She can't even really ride anymore, not competitively."

"She needs our help."

"She needs," Moira sniffed, "a better colorist. She's a blonde who dyes her hair black, in a sink. No wonder she's losing her hair."

"It's called Telogen Effluvium, hair loss caused by sorrow, not dye. And black is the universal color of grief. Do try to be compassionate."

Moira muttered an epithet, hoping it was too unintelligible for her mother to hear. She couldn't help it, though. Like her father, she could not tolerate anyone not up to scratch.

"You know what your trouble is, Mom? You're always meddling in other people's problems so you don't have to look at your own."

"Excuse me," her mother said, rising. "I need to use the facilities."

"What? Again?"

Without answering, Louisa walked out of the ridiculously large dining room. The two of them should have eaten in the kitchen, but Moira always vetoed that. She claimed the staff listened in on them, which was probably true. According to Louisa's jogging companion Ditch, eavesdropping was the staff's chief form of entertainment. Louisa smiled as she hurried to the closest downstairs bathroom, thinking of Ditch. He often made her smile, and it was medicinal, what humor could do.

Nevertheless, all this recent bloating, post-menopausal bleeding, and burning during urination: she probably had a urinary tract infection again – perhaps masked by the estrogen hormone replacement therapy, which complicated everything. But with her time of life, when the vaginal walls were thin, and Joe D. as sexually needy as lately he'd been, HRT seemed the remedy. And it couldn't hurt, according to Dr. Washburne.

Settled on the toilet, Louisa had time to think about her daughter and what she'd said.

"Meddle," she said aloud. The word meant to interfere without right or invitation. Was that what she did, helping people? No, of course not, she thought. Okay, maybe she had meddled a bit when she'd contrived to get Rainey on this European jaunt. She just had a feeling about her and Ditch. In quite different ways, they'd both lost spouses in the wars – the wars that Joe D. had profited so much from. And how could it ever be wrong to help the wounded to heal?

However, on the toilet Louisa did wonder if her focus on others served to distract her from her own problems, such as her selfish daughter and her erratic husband. Given their deficiencies, Louisa thanked God for her son, Dan, who favored her in looks and temperament.

Dan had escaped his father's world of the cut-throat defense contracting business. Dedicated to science, a confirmed bachelor with a doctorate in entomology, he lived in Antarctica now, where he studied mites, or fleas, or something. Whenever he explained his work to Louisa, she understood it while he was speaking, but the moment he stopped, she had no idea what he'd just said. They communicated solely by infrequent email. And so she was left alone with Moira and Joe D.

If Louisa were not a deeply committed Catholic, she might have given up hope for them. But. . . but there was always hope, hope for redemption, hope for growth.

However, when she returned to the dining room, she wasn't feeling particularly hopeful or patient. She had, in fact, heard the epithet Moira used to describe Rainey. To quote Ditch, it royally and truly pissed her off. She sat down and glared at her daughter.

"Rainey Gauge has suffered greatly in a world you will never know. And despite that, she's a fine person, as well as an experienced equestrian. If you listen to her, and listen to your body, you will grow a partnership with a horse like nothing you've ever felt before. And if you ever again call that young woman a loser, I will slap the mouth right off your face."

Her mother never, ever spoke to her like this. Moira sucked in her breath so sharply that she inhaled a piece of veal. She coughed to get it out, which worked, luckily – luckily, that is, because her mother didn't appear in the mood to perform the Heimlich Maneuver.

The staff finished their dinner much sooner than the wine cork sniffing Warbucks and the Booger, so they waited in the shadows outside the European Chef to escort the boss back to the Hotel North. Rainey was unfamiliar with all the code-names, and asked, "Why do you call him Whistling Booger?"

"Because he's an irritation you can't get rid of," Ditch said.

"I've never had a whistling booger," Hugo said.

"Na yeah, mate, you snore them all out. You know you fart when you sleep?"

"How would I? I'm asleep."

The three of them stepped forward to check through the restaurant window. Booger was leaning across over his half-eaten plate, whispering to Warbucks as he glanced at the other patrons, making sure they weren't listening in. Meantime, Warbucks had removed his glasses and was repeatedly tapping his face with his fingertips.

"What's he doing?" Rainey asked.

"Harmonic Meditation," Ditch said, "where you tap the facial pressure points to stimulate vibrational resonances in the brain."

"Grand," Rainey said. "The bloke who signs our paychecks is up the boohai."

Ditch smiled and repeated one of his dad's goofy aphorisms: "It would be nice to believe that the world is run by people who are not fucked up."

At the table inside, Booger suddenly leaned forward with greater urgency. Warbucks gave up on his resonances, and tucked deeply into his third bottle of Chateau Pontet Canet.

"He'll be getting rinsed, for certain," Rainey said. "Do that often, does he?"

"Yes," Hugo said, turning away with a shake of his head. "Rainey needs a background brief, bro. You do it, while I run the route back to the hotel."

Hugo stepped off, surveying Hamilton Street: doorways, alleys, windows, rooftops, and pedestrians. Was this necessary? Probably not, Ditch thought. Warbucks had legions of people who disliked him – disgruntled subcontractors, not to mention the competitors he'd underbid – but these weren't Hollywood movie villains, just businessmen who were more likely to key his car in the country club parking lot. Nevertheless, Warbucks liked – what was the word he misused? – liked the "ambiance" of an ever-present bodyguard.

While Hugo surveilled, Ditch and Rainey watched through the restaurant window. Booger was waving his hands, even more agitated now.

"I'm guessing he's wobbly, too," Rainey said. "Paranoid?"

Ditch laughed. "There ought to be a stronger word. Not that he shouldn't be. With the wars winding down, mid-level defense contractors like Warbucks are getting looked at closely."

"How'd he make his money?"

"He and his buddy invented CHUs." When she didn't appear to understand, he explained. "Containerized Housing Units, CHUs, made from converted overseas shipping containers. I've lived in a few: not too bad, better than a tent in the sand."

Ditch went on to explain that Grand Wright Corporation, privately held, was a genius idea from the start. With a minimum number of employees, Warbucks was the procurer and salesman, his partner Jonny Wright – codename Castle-builder – was the constructional engineer, while the actual construction was sub-contracted out. From CHUs they'd diversified into pre-fabricated buildings, Porta-Shitters, mobile radar containers, concrete security barriers, and tilt wall concrete bunkers.

"Warbucks was selling mobile homes to enlisted servicemen during the Persian Gulf War, when he noticed that General Schwarzkopf was planning the largest invasion since Normandy from a tent. He figured there must be a better way. He called up his college buddy, and together they made history and a shitload of money."

Hugo returned and took a quick look through the restaurant window.

"Good. They're finally paying the bill."

"Then I'll leave you to it," Ditch told him. "I got to take the courtesy car back to the airport to check weather and file tomorrow's flight plan. Want to come?" he asked Rainey.

"Yeah na."

Because Hugo seemed confused by this answer, Ditch explained, "She means no. Kiwis always say what they really mean last." Then he said to Rainey, "You do look knackered."

She flashed a smile. "Now you're catching on."

As Ditch walked away, he turned back to glance at her, and saw that she was watching him. If this were a movie, he thought, the shared look would've signaled the beginning of something – but everybody knows that movies are mostly bullshit.

Inside, Joe D. put his glasses back on, stood up unsteadily from the table, and announced, "I need to micturate."

He weaved his way across the room, bumping into chairs, thinking about the odd word "micturate." He'd learned it from his wife, which reminded him to call Louisa as soon as he got back to his room.

Rushing to the urinal, he fished around in his boxers. "Come on out, Little Friend. I'm taking you to Switzerland to get fixed again."

Peeing, mostly on his shoes – Christ, now he had to take Viagra just to keep his shoelaces dry – he stared at the tiled wall, and thought about his state of affairs. Not good: trouble was in the offing, he knew. The government was trying to subpoena his financials, which was bad enough, but worse than that was his health: myocardial infarction or coronary thrombosis, his best guess. At least that's what it said on Google. But about the government, he had a plan, a get-out-of-jail-free card to play. All he had to do was not die first.

Shaking off and zipping up, he stepped over to the sink to splash cold water on his face. He needed to sober up a little before he called Louisa. Drying off with a paper towel, he studied his red eyes and fleshy jowls, trying to see in them the grease-streaked face of the young roustabout on his father's oil rigs, the kid saving up to go to college, which in the Permian Basin was pronounced "collich." For some unknown reason, Louisa had fallen in love with that kid.

God, did he love her. Lately, he found himself thinking about her constantly: her face, her voice, the way she lifted her chin, and the way, too often, her eyes saddened when she shook her head at his behavior – they were all constantly on the periphery, reminding him of what had become of him. And now here he was, practically a fugitive, trying to put together one last deal, while in a last-ditch effort to shore up his health. His own father, after a string of dry holes, had drunk himself to death at fifty-nine. The autopsy put the cause as a heart attack brought on by influenza, but everyone in Midland knew it was the booze.

Joe D. needed to get to Switzerland fast. But more than that, he needed to talk to Louisa. She was the only human being who really knew him, and she always spoke the truth. Without her, he didn't know who he was.

CHAPTER 4

UPSTAIRS IN HER room in Hotel North, Rainey took a quick shower, then slipped into her night shirt, one of Jack's old rugby jerseys. She checked her watch: 2100 here, which meant 1300 tomorrow in The Land of the Long White Cloud. Her dad would've finished lunch and gone back down to the barns, so a good time to catch her mum alone and fill her in. But before she could talk, her mum jumped ahead with her usual question.

"Is there anyone new in your life?"

"Abso-not," she said. "Matter fact, I'm ringing about Jack."

"Yes?"

"You remember, I'd been thinking, if I couldn't have him, I could at least have a slice."

"Oh," her mother said, not enthusiastically. "You mean, Dr. Allsgood?"

"Na yeah, so I pressed on and had the procedure done. A few days back, right before I left Godzone."

"Can't hear you, luv: the reception's not too good," her mum said. "Where are you?"

"The top of the world, mum. And I know you heard what I said."

Her mother was silent a moment, thinking. Her daughter never could be easy.

"And what are the chances, luv?"

"A roll of the dice. They couldn't be sure about the timing, but they thought it was worth a shot."

"Well, fine then," her mum sighed, "if it's what you want. It's just –"

"What, mum?"

"It's just you leaving, going so far away. And now this. It's all coming rather fast, isn't it, luv?"

"Na yeah, mum, but I've been in slow-mo for over a year and half. Time to get something cracking."

After a moment's pause, her mother came back and said, "I'm very glad I'm not young."

"It's good to hear your voice, my lovely," Joe D. said. "But you sound tired."

"I am," Louisa said, "a little. What about you – you sound like you've had a few."

"Not at all. Not at all," Joe D. said, which he always said when she suspected him of drinking too much. He made a mental note to change his denial pitch.

"Maybe you should dry out with Jonny. You're picking him up in London?"

Joe D. nodded. "And I'm getting rid of Donker there, sending him ahead to Riyadh, before he gives me a stroke. That guy takes foreboding to a whole new level."

"Maybe he should," Louisa sighed. "Two Federal Marshalls dropped by this morning. Are they the reason behind this sudden trip?"

Joe D. answered with a deep sigh of his own. "Partially," he admitted. "But I'll take care of it when I get back. I have a plan." Then he fell silent for a moment. He was lying on his hotel bed, still in his dress shirt and Italian slacks, staring with curious horror at his bare feet.

"What are the symptoms of toenail fungus?" he asked.

At the other end, Louisa smiled. "I'd be more worried about hypochondria," she said.

"No, I'm serious. I see old men's feet in the club locker room. Hideous things, with veins and curled yellow toenails. And mine are beginning to look like them."

"If you don't die, you get older every year," she said.

"Not you. You haven't changed since the day we met."

"Now I know you've been drinking," she said. But truthfully, she had aged well. Still thin, toned from riding, jogging, and doing an hour of yoga a day, she never felt tired, despite all of her charity work – at least, not until recently.

"Is anything wrong?" he asked.

"No, nothing, just a little infection, I think. And Moira and I had a tiff again. I think I'd better go to bed."

But Joe D. didn't want to get off the phone quite yet.

"See Washburne tomorrow. And tell Moira to behave herself. She's twenty-four, so we can legally throw her out."

"Yes, that's likely to happen," Louisa said, and he could tell she was smiling.

Making her smile had lately become important to him. He knew how to do it again.

"Before you tuck in, check your phone. I'm sending you an intimate picture."

"Please don't," she laughed, and said good night. After she hung up, Joe D. kept the phone to his ear, thinking of other things he should have said to her. He would. When he returned, he'd tell her all the things that had recently come to light in his heart. But for now, he would just send her a picture of his feet.

Rainey had a greater than usual number of restless dreams that night, mostly about Jack, but also about horses, jumps, and falls, and one strangely enough about flying, which she'd never had before. She was probably trying to work something out, something deep, but she wished it would stay wherever the fuck it was supposed to be. She'd grown accustomed to her private misery.

Her last dream, though, was really odd. She couldn't remember it entirely – it was dream-plot incoherent – but at the end she was leaning over Jack on the rubble strewn streets of Kabul, trying to stanch the bleeding in his neck. He wasn't looking at her, though, but rather up at the sky. He seemed to see something up there, but he did know she was kneeling beside him. When he spoke – directly to her, which was a rarity in her dreams – his words were difficult to hear.

"What is it, luv?" she asked. "What do you see?"

"A chariot," he croaked, "coming out of the clouds, to take me away."

Then his eyes shifted to hers – God, his eyes were so blue – and about the chariot he said, "Presumably, we'll be ascending."

Which was utterly bloody ridiculous, because Jack never would've used those words. Sometimes dreams are complete and total bullshit. Nevertheless, when she woke, her pillow was wet with tears.

CHAPTER 5

ACROSS A LENGTHY stretch of the North Atlantic, aircraft have no radar coverage, which necessitates position reports along the route. After Ditch taught her how, Rainey made the HF calls, but in the intervals between waypoints, she had time to look out and think. The ocean below was cloud shrouded, but the sky above was pale blue: nothing but space between them and the stars. Last night's dream kept replaying in her head. She turned to Ditch, with a question.

"Do you," she asked hesitantly, "believe there's an afterlife?"

They were just south of the tip of Greenland, at Flight Level 240 – 24,000 feet – which Ditch hated. The fuel burn at that lower level was nearly twice the rate for a higher flight level, but the North Atlantic Air Traffic Corridor was packed today. Still, they should arrive at Keflavik, the Reykjavik airport, with over ninety minutes of fuel in reserve. The weather there was bad, with a current ceiling of a thousand feet of stratus, but on the ILS approach they should punch through, land, re-fuel, and take off on the final leg to London City airport on schedule. Warbucks had already been up to the cockpit three times to ask if they'd arrive on time. He had an important dinner meeting with a Prince, the Saudi Minister of Defense.

So with all this on his mind, Ditch struggled to under-stand Rainey's question.

"Believe in Heaven? Hell, I don't know."

She seemed embarrassed now and turned away, looking out the right seat side window, but not before Ditch had seen her wince.

"Sorry," he said. "I'm just preoccupied. But I'm really glad you're helping me up here, even if you do ask impossible questions."

A couple of minutes later, she turned and asked him again if he believed.

"Not in my rational mind."

"But in the other part of your brain?"

"I don't know. I don't use that part much anymore. It may have withered away."

They flew on, Ditch obsessively monitoring the fuel flow. But the withered away part of his mind was still considering Rainey's question.

"You know, I guess I do," he said finally. "I believe in a lot of things I can't see or understand, but just feel."

"Like what?"

"Like true love."

"True love – na yeah. Me, too," Rainey said, then added, "One more question?"

"It'd better be easier."

"Is Hugo pissed up large? He's all smiling and squirming around in his seat sweet as."

Ditch guessed she was asking if Hugo was drunk, which was not likely. Hugo had just received his bronze two-year sobriety chip. And he had another reason for acting so giddy.

"I told him this morning: I booked us a couple of tickets for *The Phantom of the Opera* tonight. Albert Hall. I bet we can get another one, if you'd like to go."

"Yeah na. I'm visiting old friends in Langley, Buckinghamshire. But wait a tick: Hugo likes musicals?"

"Likes," Ditch said, "is *not* the verb."

She laughed at this surprising facet of Hugo, then looked over at Ditch. "You're a right good mate," she said.

Leaving the stupefying three-hour meeting of the hospital board, Louisa fell in step with her friend, a big boned gynecologist named Eva Hoffsteader.

"So go the days of our lives," Eva said. "I could actually feel my cells committing apoptosis."

When Louisa said nothing, Eva turned to look at her. Louisa had been unusually quiet through all the proceedings, not even speaking up when they discussed cutting the budget for the Children's Care Center, a subject closest to Louisa's heart. And today she did not look well.

"You okay, Louisa? I don't like your color."

"A little urinary tract infection," Louisa explained. "I'm seeing Dr. Washburne tomorrow."

Eva Hoffsteader sighed. "Not him again. I know Joe D. trusts Washburne –"

"Our family doctor since time began."

"Not anymore," Eva said. "You come see me, right now."

"I can't. I'm due at Church for Alter Guild."

"Then tomorrow?"

"I'll check my calendar," Louisa said.

Beryl Gauge sat with her friends having tea in the 20th Lounge of the Royal Wellington Golf Club. At these afternoon teas, Beryl always presided, being the wife of a prominent judge on the Court of Appeal. She liked to think she knew everything that went on in New Zealand, at least with the people who mattered. But across the table young Shaye Timmons had surprised her with a question.

"What's going on with your daughter-in-law?" she'd asked.

"I'm sure I don't know. I've had no contact with that girl since, since Jack was taken," Beryl said. Using that phrase caused her to flinch internally. Jack, her only child, their only child, their heir. But her face betrayed no emotion as she dismissively looked away and out the window toward the golf course. She liked putting greens because they were so trimmed and so clean.

But young Shaye pursued her with a follow up comment. "Only I saw her last week in Auckland, at Fertility Associates."

"Oh," Beryl said, a bit nonplussed. She covered her surprise by continuing, "And was she dressed in men's clothing, as usual?"

"In moleskins and chambray, yes. Curious, though, why she'd be there at all."

"I'm sure I don't know," Beryl said, but thoughts began turning in her head. Later, at home, she would have to call Rainey's mother Meg. Not an interrogation, just a courtesy call, checking in on her widowed daughter-in-law. They were still related, after all.

Meantime, she continued to smile pleasantly at her friends while sipping tea. It tasted somewhat bitter. Perhaps an apricot thumbprint tea cookie? Young Shaye seemed to be reading her mind and was already passing her the biscuit tray.

Jonny Wright watched his friend leap out of the cab in front of The Dorchester and run up to hug him on the curb. Lately, Joe D. was semi-decrepit, but at the scent of a big sale, he could always rally. He got off on the selling; he truly believed in their product; and with a client, he could be charmingly antic and funny. Energized tonight, he seemed solidly on his game.

"Thank God you're here, Jonny. That nutjob Donker was driving me insane."

"Oh, that's what's doing it?" he said, smiling as they stepped into the hotel. In the lobby, at the entrance to The Grill, Jonny lagged behind.

Joe D. always made quite an entrance when he was pitching a sale to the Crown Prince. Just inside the door, he stopped and crouched into a gunfighter's stance. The priggish British diners looked up from their Yorkshire pudding when he bellowed across the restaurant, "Paladin, you dirty dog, I'm calling you out! Stand up and draw!"

Seated at a corner table, the robed Prince motioned to his bodyguards at the next table to stay seated. Then he grinned and leapt to his feet, his trigger finger twitching beside the imaginary holster on his hip. They both drew finger-pistols, and shouted, "Bang!"

Laughing, Joe D. trotted over for the customary embrace which ended in customary kisses on both cheeks. Joe D. stepped back and took a look at the Prince as he sang: "A knight without armor in a savage land."

They both laughed and sat down. Jonny followed across the room making a smoothing gesture to the patrons, explaining. "They're old friends, old friends."

Which was true. Years ago Joe D., making some minor sales to the Saudis, had met the young Prince and told him he looked just like Richard Boone, the star of the old *Paladin* TV show. Afterwards, he sent the Prince the whole series on videocassettes, addressing them to Salman bin Abdulaziz Al Saud (aka "Paladin"). The nickname had stuck, and the Prince became, as he said, "the world's Number One Paladin fan." He was also the new Minister of Defense.

As usual, the Prince wanted to get the business talk done immediately, so it wouldn't spoil their dinner and drinks. The subject concerned three new bases on the border of Yemen.

"We can have the mobile radar containers," Joe D. said, "on site and functional in three months. And the pre-fab structures, too – but they won't protect your troops from rocket attacks. For that, Jonny can design you tilt-wall concrete bunkers."

"No," the Prince said. "The Houthis are Zaidi savages: they are lightly armed."

"So far," Joe D. said. "But they'll have Zilzal rockets, once Ahmadinejad sends them."

These were the improvised rocket-assisted munitions (IRAMs) favored by Iran. The Prince considered this as he sipped Wild Turkey. Ancient hatred for the Shia darkened his brow. He nodded thoughtfully. "We will add the concrete structures to the contract."

"Okay, but let's do this quick. I have the government breathing down my neck about something else, but they'll back off, once the Saudi government is onboard with Grand Wright."

"At least," Jonny said, "that's the plan."

The Prince shook his head sadly. "Your government can be so hypocritical."

Jonny smiled. Here was the Crown Prince of one of the most repressive authoritarian regimes on the planet – in which drinking alcohol was punishable by up to 500 lashes – enjoying a whiskey and shaking his head over the hypocrisy of a democratic republic. Sometimes, Jonny wondered how he'd gotten into the defense industry. He'd been happily designing homeless shelters in San Francisco when Joe D. had tempted him into the CHU business. No wonder he drank like a fish. Finishing his glass, he tuned back into the conversation, noting that it had turned to him.

"Tell Jonny about La Clinique. He's a skeptic."

"Oh, my friend, do not be. When I was young –"

"Hell, Paladin, you're only forty-nine now."

"Much younger, yes," the Prince said, "with women I had some–" he searched for the sufficiently vague word "– some difficulty."

"But now you have a wife," Joe D. said, "and four kids."

"Sadly, only two of them are sons."

"It's your scuba diving," Joe D. said. "I've told you before. The pressure crushes the male sperm in your nuts."

The Prince laughed. "You are such a repository of medical knowledge."

"Of course I am: I'm a hypochondriac," Joe D. said. "Now let's all have another drink."

"So what's this carpet peelot like? You mentioned him a couple of times. He's not a bad boy, is he?"

"Not even, ow," Rainey said.

Naomi went back to stirring the lamb stew, while taking quick looks at her friend. In the past two hours they'd caught up on old, mutual friends, what horses they were riding, where they were competing, and so on. Naomi and Rainey had been mates for yonks, since back at Waikato Technical Institute, though since then, their lives had taken different routes. Naomi had married a Brit and moved back to his family farm, The Old Pile of Bricks. They ran it as a layup facility for injured steeplechase horses. Meantime, Rainey had pursued her dream of being a world-class Three-Day Eventer, until she fell arse over tit for Jack – a great guy, too true, but he was dead.

"Peelots are supposed to be handsome," Naomi said. "It's a requirement, I think."

"Isn't that stew ready yet?"

Naomi turned off the range in the old farm kitchen, went to the cupboard, and took out three large bowls for the adults, and three smaller ones for her and Fred's kids. While ladling out the stew, she said, "I'm just saying, you could use a good root."

Rainey laughed. "That's your solution for everything, and the reason you have three ankle-biters."

Naomi smiled and gestured up to the ceiling with her hands. "Thank you, God, for the gift of sex."

"Well, it's not happening," Rainey said. "I dried up and grew shut."

"Eat some stew." Naomi handed her a bowl. "It'll right warm you up."

CHAPTER 6

IT DIDN'T START with a snog in the hotel corridor, but rather at an Italian restaurant in Lausanne after a two-hour hike along Lake Geneva. After three days of sitting, Ditch said she needed to work her leg, which was probably true. At the restaurant they both ordered spaghetti carbonara, sipped a glass of Chianti, and talked. Rainey had changed from her hiking chinos into a black V-neck cashmere dress. She was curious about his fucked-up marriage.

"I knew going in, Gully wasn't run of the mill. But I liked her for that."

"And for her bum?"

Ditch laughed. "Yeah, there was sure that, too. But my dad had a goofy theory back then, that I have a soft spot for oddballs, like you."

"Rack off. I'm not odd."

"No? You're a short, muscular, gray-eyed, broken-nosed, extremely loyal blonde who dyes her hair black and grieves for her Romeo Mike. On a lighter note, you also love everything about horses, even their manure. Nope, nothing unique about you."

Hearing this, Rainey felt two impulses. One was to ball her fist and hit him in his saucy moustache. The other was to say, thank you. It seemed, somewhat, somehow, like a compliment.

Across the table, Ditch studied the girl. He thought he knew her remarkably well. After all, they'd spent three days together in the cockpit, where you got some insight into the person beside you, and they'd talked for hours about their lives. But there was something more: he felt he'd known her much longer than he had. Anyway, he knew what she was thinking now.

"Go ahead," he said. "You can punch me if you want. But I bet you grew up with older brothers."

"I deed," she said, a little surprised. "Twins. How'd you suss out that?"

"I just twigged you deed."

"Quit poking me accent," she said.

"Oh, come on. You grew up getting teased. But I am curious: what do you see happening in your future life, without Jack?"

The directness of his question took her breath away. She sipped Chianti and stared at the candle on the table. Her future without Jack depended on the success of the procedure, but Fertility Associates had an excellent track record, and tonight she did feel a stirring down there, didn't she? She wouldn't mention any of this to Ditch, of course, although he was grouse to talk to. He had very honest, greenish-brown eyes, which she noticed for probably the first time. She returned to the question about a life without Jack.

"I dunno. But I keep going back to one pipe dream. We bought some land, before Jack deployed, sort of our escape hatch. It's an old macadamia nut farm on Bream Bay near Waipu."

This was a small town north of Auckland, settled by Scots in 1853.

"I love macadamia nuts," Ditch said. "You go, girl."

"Get stuffed," she said, but she said it with a smile. She looked again at Ditch across the table. Okay, she'd noticed his eyes before, but not notice-noticed them until now. And she liked the easy way he teased her; he'd probably done the same with Gully. He was a cracker mate, no pressure.

"What about you? What do you see ahead?"

"To quote you, I dunno. I've stayed in the Reserves, to pay the medical bills, but I may not be the career military type, except in values and standards of behavior and all that shit. And eventually I might start my own charter outfit. I've got all kinds of ratings, from twin engine jets to choppers, gliders, and even seaplanes."

Because he seemed quite enthusiastic, especially when he mentioned "seaplanes," she raised her glass of Chianti. "You go, fly-boy," she said. She took a sip and studied the glass. Still half full. She decided it would be unwise to finish it. A clear head, and all that shite. Also, she might be up the duff. So when the waiter brought their food, she asked for a bottle of cold mineral water.

That same night, before the full cure could begin, Joe D. and Jonny slipped out of Clinique La Prairie for one last, old-fashioned emetic drunken binge. As usual when they drank heavily, they argued about their different approaches to life.

"I'm not such an idealist," Jonny said, defensively. "I mean, I am, but back in my younger days, I was also an unprincipled animal. For instance, I tried to seduce Louisa."

"I know. She told me," Joe D. said. "And if it wasn't for her, I might've taken a crack at one of your wives."

"Which one?" Jonny demanded. He'd had three wives. A handsome, balding ladies' man, he had just a twist of hair on top, which he arranged into an elaborate comb-over.

"They were all beautiful," Joe D. said. "But I really liked the middle one the best."

Jonny's anger subsided as quickly as it had come on. After all, it was all water under the bed, or wives under the bridge, or however the saying went. He was on his fifth aquavit.

"Yeah, Elena, I did, too," he admitted wistfully. "Good ole, funny Elena, she deserved every penny she took from me."

"I told you a hundred times," Joe D. said. "An iron clad pre-nup."

"I can't help it. I'm a romantic. Besides, you never had a pre-nup with Louisa."

"Never wanted one: she's the love of my life."

"You're a one-woman man." Jonny clasped him on the shoulder drunkenly. "Very admirable. You're really more a romantic than me."

"The fuck I am. But this legal crap, it's made me think: at my age, I either have to turn a corner in my life, or go around the bend. And so do you, old man."

Jonny sagged. He did feel terribly old. Joe D. sought to cheer him up. "Lucky for you, my ole, soon-to-be lusty friend, there's that lovey Thai masseuse."

"What? That sadist?" Jonny said, shocked. "This morning that crazy woman nearly pulled off my arms and legs."

"All part of the Revitalization Program," Joe D. counselled. "And wait until Wednesday, when you get your first injection."

"Livers from fetal lambs, shot into my buttocks. I must be crazy, doing this with you."

"It's all medically proven. Charlie Chaplin had it done, and so did one of the Popes. I'm telling you, you'll feel passion like you never felt before. You'll be your old animal self again."

"Oh, boy," Jonny said, doubtfully. "Oh, boy. Horney as a Pope, I bet."

Later, after considerably more recreational drinking, they staggered out of the hotel bar. It was still early yet, but they had to get back to Clinique La Prairie before their binge escape was noticed.

Hugo waited beside the rental Mercedes at the curb, opening the doors for the drunken men. Watching them laboriously climbing in, he repeated the Serenity Prayer in his head, thinking, Thank God, I was just a drunk and not a drunk idiot.

Remembering himself back then stirred up a storm of regrets, not only about himself but about his wife. Nan had followed him into the bottle, but hadn't, yet, followed him out. As a public-school music teacher in Baton Rouge, by fifth period every day she was drinking "coffee" from her thermos. He prayed rock bottom was not far away. Then, on her own, she had to admit she was powerless over alcohol, and that her life had become unmanageable. He'd already enabled her enough.

Meantime, in the back seat his passengers continued an exuberant conversation about the government having to back off, now that Grand Wright was hand in glove with the future Saudi King. In fact, Joe D. began to sing "Happy Days Are Here Again," and Jonny Wright joined in.

Hugo stuffed in his earbuds. As soon as he dropped them off at the Clinique, he'd drive back to Lausanne, to the staff's modest accommodations in the Hotel de Manche, where he'd write a letter to Nan and watch Swiss TV in French. It was French-French, but being Cajun he could understand it, sort of. And maybe he'd have a cup of really sweet tea. And some Swiss chocolate, too. It seemed as if it was going to be a very pleasant, quiet evening.

"What do you think she's playing at, leaving the country and such?" Beryl asked her husband, the Judge. "Remembering what I told you, about where Shaye Timmons saw her at the fertility clinic in the city."

"Can we discuss this in a moment," he replied. "I'm trying to sink this bloody long putt."

Beryl, seated behind the wheel of their golf cart, frowned at his use of coarse language. The Judge was the model of probity, sobriety, and decorum everywhere except on the golf course. As his golf partner of fifty-five years, Beryl had long ago closed her ears to this. She'd had to give up playing herself at sixty-eight, due to arthritis in both knees, but she still accompanied him because she enjoyed the immaculate landscaping. Now she watched him complete his usual hip wiggle before settling into his putting stance.

He took the putt, and missed.

"Bloody hell," he said.

"I told you," Beryl said, "it would break to the left. Now, what do you think that girl is doing?"

"You talked to her mother?" the Judge said.

"Yes, and very evasive she was. Broke the connection quite quickly, saying she had to tend a mare in distress."

The Judge climbed into the cart, remembering the Day's breeding farm and their one and only visit there, to drop some of Jack's things the girl had asked for. Why she wanted all of his old rugby jerseys, he didn't know. At any rate, Beryl had been disgusted by the untidiness of the farm, the mounds of steaming manure and the like, and talked of nothing else on their drive back to Wellington. "I'm very glad," she'd said, "we won't have to see her or her family ever again." But now here she was, thinking of nothing but that girl.

"I'm sure you'll uncover the truth," he said.

"I'm sure I will. Meg Day did mention the name of her employer, in Texas," she replied. "Now move over: your elbow is touching mine."

CHAPTER 7

SPONTANEOUS COMBUSTION OCCURS by internal self-heating, followed by a thermal runaway and auto-ignition.

"Yeah na?" he asked as they breathlessly pressed themselves together in the corridor of the Hotel de Manche. "Or na yeah?"

"Na yeah. Yeah," she said. "Pash me quick."

He didn't know exactly what she meant, but context clues connected pashing to passionate kissing, which he did, complete with darting tongues and all, until he pulled back to catch his breath. They looked at each other. They were panting so hard, they breathed in each other's garlicy breath. This was their moment to decide.

"Don't," she said, "stop."

"I won't," he said, "stop."

She reached up, put her hand behind his neck, and pulled him back down to her face. Because she was much shorter, he was bent over in the shape of a question mark. He hadn't known what he was doing, he still didn't know what he was doing, nor did he know who he was, or where he was: he would've flunked the military intelligence test. But. . . but he knew exactly what he wanted, right now, immediately: to pash this girl. He was living exclusively through his lips, like some kind of suckerfish. And he sure didn't need to worry about getting it up.

But for Rainey, there was something like anger in the pash. She didn't know exactly what she was mad at, but it wasn't Jack. He'd only been trying to save his mates. Probably she was just fucking furious at fate. And at herself. Because even though he was dead, and she'd grieved with every atom for the last one year, nine months, and twenty-seven days, she still had longings, which came out now, like a blast of scalding steam from a vent.

With their lips still attached, Rainey pushed hard – she was very muscular – propelling him across the corridor to the far wall with a bang.

The only resident aroused by this noise was Hugo, who'd arrived a half hour earlier and was lying in bed watching *Law and Order*, Season 7, Episode 11, in French. He rose and crossed the tiny room to the door – all rooms in moderately priced Swiss hotels were tiny. He turkey peeked out, saw them deep kissing, and pulled back into his room, saying, "Oh, shit. Oh, shit." Behind him on the TV, Detective Lenny Briscoe said, "Cher chez la femme."

Outside, Ditch pushed back, aiming Rainey toward the door to her room. She reached for the door handle. Luckily, she'd already inserted the key card, and the door lock was, miraculously, still flashing green. Green: Go!

They entered together, still attached at the lips, her backwards, him kicking the door shut. He'd flown many, many missions, and knew how to bank the bird, almost inverted, toward the target – in this case, the tiny bed.

They hit it going hard, and clinked teeth. No matter. Nothing could get in their way. It was voluntary and completely consensual, hot, sticky, and mad in all extremes. She did, pulling her dress off over her head, hit him on the chin with her elbow, which he hardly noticed, shucking off his jeans. They fell on each other, kissing, moving, gasping unintelligible utterances. Neither of them had any kind of control. But they were both sober adults, in a private room, doing nothing that hadn't been done in it before. Yet. . . yet it felt important, imperative, to put everything else out of mind. Nothing else existed but the two of them, right here and right now.

However, afterwards the past and future rushed back in – but not at first. They rolled apart briefly, awash in a wave of peace and sweet release. Then they returned for a post-coital kiss, and a deep look into each other's eyes. Something happened in that look – or rather, something happened in Rainey's gray eyes. A look of realization, a stab of instant regret.

They rolled apart, onto their backs, staring up at the perforated ceiling. After a beat, Rainey rolled farther away, onto her side, covering herself with the sheet. Ditch looked upwards with a deep breath. What the fuck just happened?

Presently, Rainey got up, still covering herself with the sheet, and limped to the bathroom. Ditch heard the door lock click.

In the bathroom Rainey leaned on the sink counter, not facing the mirror, and waited. Two minutes later, Ditch came to the bathroom door and spoke through it, in a hoarse voice, "I, I don't know what got into me. It was all my fault. I'll leave right now if you want." He listened for her response. She said nothing. After a minute of silence, Rainey heard the room door swing open, then fall shut, the lock tongue snapping into the receiver with a metallic *snick*. Within seconds, she was weeping, sobbing, heaving – trying, but failing, to empty herself and go dry.

Out in the corridor, naked Ditch dropped his clothes on the floor and sorted through them, pulling his jeans and shirt on with shaky hands. Damn, he'd forgotten his shoes.

He'd obviously and unforgivably lost his mind. And what the fuck just happened?

Ditch tried, but failed, to sleep, and eventually swung out of the rack at 0630, shaved, showered, and went down the corridor to Rainey's room carrying his flip-flops. He didn't wear them because of the silly sound they made. He put his ear to the door, heard nothing, thought to knock with knuckles raised, then chickened out and slinked off, putting on the flip-flops only after he got to the stairwell. Their stupid sound echoed off the walls as he descended.

Hugo sat at the hotel café's far table against the wall, facing the door, as usual. Ditch flip-flopped toward him and took the opposite seat.

"I got you an Americano. Should still be hot," Hugo said, pushing a cup toward him. "I thought it might clear your head."

"Thanks, bro." Ditch took what he hoped resembled an innocent sip. "You seen Rainey?"

"Yep, about 0330. She stopped by on her way to the train station. I went with her, to make sure she got there safe."

Ditch nodded as if there was nothing at all unusual in this. Watching him, Hugo smiled. Ditch was one of the most honest guys and worst liars he'd ever met. So it was perversely enjoyable to see him try. Hugo watched him, waiting for the next attempt. And sure enough, here it came, Ditch trying to act very casual.

"So, did she say where she was going?"

"Yep. Zurich. And then by car on from there, to look at that horse."

"But I thought she wasn't leaving until the day after tomorrow."

"Must've changed her mind. I wonder why."

Ditch drank his Americano, looking around, with an attempt to appear nonchalant. Almost off handed, he asked, "Did she say when she'll be back?"

"If she likes the horse, never. She decided to fly back with it, not us."

Ditch let the air out with an audible groan, and slumped in his chair. Meantime, Hugo reached down to the floor and brought up a pair of Keen hiking boots, plopping them on the table. Ditch stared at his shoes, then brought his eyes up to his friend's. Hugo shook his head.

"Dude, you royally and truly stepped on your dick."

Ditch opened his mouth to offer some defense: consensual sex and all that shit. After all, in the civilian world of the millennials, casual hook-ups happened all the time – but not, really, for their special one percent. Their military standard of behavior harkened back to a time when war widows were sacrosanct. Nevertheless, this morning he didn't feel any real shame. He'd sussed it out in the middle of the night. Christ, he was even beginning to talk like her.

"I don't know how it happened," he confessed, "and I may have fucked it up – but this girl, Rainey Gauge, she has something. . . and when I'm with her, I can breathe."

Hugo rocked his head back, hearing that. Ditch was one of those vets who never really came home. He'd spent almost all of his twenties leading the simpler life of war. But something about this Rainey had snagged him, made him think of another possible future.

Hugo considered Ditch's predicament briefly, then came to a decision.

"Put on your shoes, dumb-fuck, and come with me."

"Where?"

"Got an AA meeting down the street, at 0800."

"But I'm not –."

"No, but you'll be in a room full of people who've all been tempted, and slipped. We're pretty experienced at making amends."

Ditch followed along, thinking about the word "amends." It meant something like, to correct a mistake that you've made, or a bad situation you've created. Making amends was something he absolutely had to do, because the words he'd blurted were absolutely true. Out of the blue, Rainey Gauge had woken up some part of him, with her gray eyes and plucky, sorrow-filled soul. She might just be his ticket home.

CHAPTER 8

RAINEY GAUGE RAN her hand over the 15.3 hand gelding
in crossties, a six-year-old seal bay Einsiedler named Aladdin's
Lamp. Behind her, Jurgen Kundig watched with folded arms.

"You saw the x-rays, Sunshine," he said. "Everything is
quite in order."

"Too right, Jurgen. I would never doubt the word of
someone trying to sell me a horse."

Jurgen grinned. This was the game the seller and buyer
always played. He watched her work over the gelding. She'd
come a long way from the crazy Kiwi barn girl he'd met
when she was a sixteen-year-old groom. He'd always called
her Sunshine.

Satisfied with his hooves and tendons, Rainey stepped
back to take in the whole horse again, his confirmation,
the way his parts fit together. The gelding turned his head
slightly to watch her. His neck was well set, arched gracefully;
a good sloping shoulder, prominent withers, a flat back, and
the slightly descending croup that was typical of this Swiss
warmblood breed. She'd seen the gelding two years ago in
England, at Burleigh, already competing as a second level
dressage entry – and she'd thought, when she watched him

extend his trot, that's a bloody bonza horse. The only reason the gelding hadn't sold since then was that Jurgen's prices were impossibly high.

"How would you describe his temperament?"

Jurgen pursed his lips thoughtfully. "He is not a prima donna. He is, how shall I say, patient."

Hearing that, she went to stand in front to look at his face. He blinked, completely confident, and sniffed her hair.

"What's his barn name?" Rainey asked. All horses at this level had paper names, reflecting lineage, and barn names, based on personality.

"We call him Snorkel," Jurgen said. "Wait a moment and you'll see why."

After sniffing her hair, he raised his muzzle straight up toward the high arched barn ceiling, and drew back his lips. He resembled the snorkel air intakes that Kiwis put on their 4x4 trucks.

Rainey laughed. "Right then, let's see him work."

She and Jurgen walked out to the arena, while Marsha, the exercise rider, threw a saddle on. Jurgen was one of those thin, nimble horsemen who never seem older than fifty, but probably were, although their sexual age was never more than twenty-one. He followed along behind, checking her out.

"Still off on your left, Sunshine. But you do look, shall I say, comely in breeches."

"Jurgen, quit humping my bum. You don't have a chance."

"Nevertheless," Jurgen persisted, "there is something about you today: a luminescence."

Rainey blushed. Did getting rooted last night really show? Or was it a pregnancy glow?

"Let's talk about something else. I'm looking for just the right fit. My rider, she's inexperienced, overconfident, and impatient."

"Oh," Jurgen said. "An heiress."

At all levels, but especially the upper ones, the horse world depended on the largess of people with money. In fact, Rainey had often thought the dressage judges didn't need to see the contestants ride. Instead, medals could be awarded based on descending levels of trust funds. But that was unduly cynical: the truth was that a talented rider, with some good luck, could rise up. But those riders had to fight for it, and that's what she herself had done. Nevertheless, the imbalance made her think, sometimes, of a less complicated life, say on a macadamia nut farm in Waipu.

Later, watching Marsha put Snorkel through the elementary paces, Rainey squizzed on something.

"Marsha's not carrying a crop or wearing spurs."

"Snorkel doesn't need them. He does everything asked."

"Yeah right. I think I'll take a ride."

Marsha brought Snorkel over and hopped off. Rainey adjusted the stirrup leathers, two holes longer on the left. She mounted from the off side, which was unusual enough that Snorkel bent around and looked back. He settled when she gingerly threw her munted left leg over, found the stirrup bars instinctively, and lowered into the seat. The gelding felt it, felt her seat bones connecting to his spine. He relaxed even more when she took up the reins, which run like a nerve between the rider's hands and the bars of the horse's mouth. Her touch was firm, but light. She moved, and he knew what she meant, what she asked, and because she was kind, he responded. He obviously had a finely tuned sense of fairness, and would not tolerate being treated unkindly. Hence, his aversion to spurs. Rainey liked that: he might be able to teach Moira to ride.

Jurgen watched her work the horse, sucking on his briar pipe. Even with a shattered leg, she was a rider's rider, albeit no longer a competitive one. He pointed at her with his pipe stem and said to Marsha, "She still has the seat, does she not? I call her Sunshine because that's what shines out of her –"

"I get the picture, Jurgen. You are *such* a pig."

"Yes, I am a pig, but a pig who today will sell a horse."

He began thinking of how to arrange the transport, the pre-export testing and licenses, health certificates, blood sample, and micro-chipping. He and Sunshine would have to work closely the next week, which made him smile. And, yes, today she did have a glow.

"Ditch left this number," a man's voice said, "as an emergency contact. I'm Sam, from the Memory Care Home."

"What is it?" Louisa asked. "Is anything wrong?"

"Yes ma'am. Ditch's dad, early this morning, he passed on. But it was painless, and quick." He added that the cause was pneumonia, known at the Home as The Old Man's Friend.

Louisa was sitting in the waiting room of Dr. Eva Hoffsteader's office, waiting to get a D&C.

"Oh, I'm so sorry," Louisa said. "God bless his soul."

"Yes ma'am. I'm calling to see if you can contact Ditch."

"Of course. Immediately. We'll have him home on the next available flight." Louisa thought a moment about how to do this, then asked, "Are arrangements being made?"

"Yes ma'am. His sister's taken care of that. They're planning to bury him day after tomorrow, on the ranch beside his wife."

"We'll have Ditch home by then." Louisa said.

At that moment the nurse opened the door and called her name.

"Look, Sam, I have to go. You keep my number, let me know if there's anything I can do. And is this your number, are you calling from your cell phone?"

"Yes ma'am."

49

Louisa paused. This young man was so polite, she had to ask, "Sam, are you a veteran?"

"Yes ma'am, I am."

"Thank you for your service," she said, "I'll call you soon."

"Louisa, this is going to be unpleasant. Are you sure you don't want me to perform an endometrial biopsy? It's much less invasive."

"Yes, but you said it's hit and miss. Let's do the full scrape, and find out what's really going on."

Eva Hoffsteader snapped on her blue latex gloves. "Feet in the stirrups, please."

She administered a local, as per Louisa's request, then waited for it to take effect, while reviewing Louisa's charts. The asshole, pill-pusher Washburne had put her on straight estrogen. Didn't he read any of the literature? This did not bode well. She checked her patient's progress with the anesthetic. Satisfied, she pulled her rolling stool into position and began by inserting the speculum.

"How long before you receive the results?" Louisa hissed.

"For you, I'll expedite. But it will be some time."

Louisa lay back on the examining table taking deep, supposedly relaxing, yogic breaths. They were utterly useless.

CHAPTER 9

UNDER A GROVE of live oak trees on a hillside overlooking the Guadalupe River, they put his father in the ground beside his beloved wife, Carla Zavala Dietrick, among the many graves of their ancestors dating back to 1854. Ditch's sister, Ingrid, and her family attended the service, along with the whole Zavala clan including Ditch's cousin Rudy, who was the assistant to the Texas State House minority whip, the youngest ever. He walked toward Ditch shooting his cuffs.

"Condolences," Rudy said, "on Uncle Reiner's demise."

His wordiness and sharp clothes made Ditch smile, despite jet lag. "You look smooth, cuz, straight out of *GQ*," he said. "How much did you pay for those shoes?"

Rudy laughed. "My cousin, the mercenary. You're still such a bastard," he said.

"*Yo se, pero yo te amo, hermano.*" He gave Rudy a hug, purposely messing up his suit.

"Bastard," Rudy said, straightening up the suit. "You still working for Joe D? I hate that son of a bitch."

"Of course you do. He's a Republican."

"Worse than that. You know the DCAA is investigating him?"

This was the Defense Contract Audit Agency, overseeing corruption in defense contracting, where lavish gifts, over-billing, and fraud were not uncommon.

"They probably should," Ditch said, "but I like his wife. Come on. I'm gonna introduce you to one fine lady."

Louisa Grand was standing back, under a two-hundred-year-old live oak tree. She was gazing at its twisted, massive limbs when Ditch walked up, with Rudy hanging a little behind.

"Ditch," she said, hugging him. "His soul is at rest."

"It is," Ditch said. "According to Rainey, he's now with mom."

"How is Rainey?"

"I," Ditch said, looking down, "don't really know."

Louisa considered this. She'd had that feeling, an intuition – okay, maybe a deep wish – about the two of them. Instead of addressing this, she turned and put a hand on the big oak. "This is a magnificent living being, isn't it?"

"Yes ma'am," Ditch said. "And it's been fertilized for a hundred and fifty years by my family." He gestured around at the many graves. "We're like Jobe Plant Spikes."

Louisa looked at him and laughed. "I've missed you," she said.

"And I, you. But I have someone here you ought to meet. My cousin, Rudy Zavala."

He motioned Rudy to join them.

"I know you," she said, shaking his hand. "Or I know your work. I like everything about you, except your position on third term abortions."

"I know," Rudy said. "As a Catholic, I feel pretty lousy about that."

She smiled and took his arm. "Walk me to my car. Let's talk." Maybe his was an opinion she could sway. "I'll call you later, Ditch, about your flight back."

Ditch watched them walk up the hill. Louisa didn't look the same, maybe even a little wobbly, which was quite a change. When they jogged, she could always outrun him – and, hell, he was a Marine. But she couldn't outrun him today.

He went over to his sister and talked about what would happen to the ranch. There was legal stuff to get started, and he wanted to get back to Europe fast. He had amends to make.

More than a year earlier and half a world away, at a different funeral, rifles were fired, bugles were blown, and Rainey, her family and Jack's, walked behind the hearse across the tarmac. His regimental unit came forward to greet their dead brother, with the traditional Maori funeral haka, a passionate warlike dance of grief, postures, and chants – very courageous and defiant and proud, like Jack. That was the first day she'd dyed her hair black.

When she now thought about him, though, she didn't remember the funeral as much as the way, whenever they entered the room at party, he always put his hand on the small of her back. And she remembered the way he frequently glanced at her – he was only a little taller than she – and smiled. He was gap-toothed, and had a reddish-brown cowlick that fell sort of funny across his brow. She also remembered the way he often began a sentence with her name. "Rainey and I were thinking. . ." like they were joined forever, even grammatically. And, God, his eyes were so blue, so full of laughter and life.

How could he be dead? How could she live without him? And how could she do what she had done?

CHAPTER 10

RAINEY PUT DOWN the old landline phone in Jurgen's barn office.

"The transfer of funds has gone through. Check your account on the computer."

Tapping keys, which was difficult with a broken middle finger, Jurgen asked, "Who was that you were conversing with, Warbucks?"

"Yeah na, Whistling Booger. Ditch says he's an irritation you can't get rid of."

Jurgen tapped some more keys, clicked the mouse, and squinted. He should put on his glasses, but he was vain, especially in front of young women. Sunshine had mentioned this Ditch a few times, which made him wonder.

"How was the fellow awarded that curious given name?"

"He was born in a ditch, on the way to hospital."

Jurgen smiled. "Texans are quite peculiar."

"Na yeah, not like the Swiss, who run around their mountains yodeling in lederhosen. Do you see the funds?"

He squinted harder. "Ahh, yes, but I am still rather disappointed with the amount."

"Quit whinging, Jurgen. I'm not a sook."

Jurgen didn't know what "sook" meant, but he reflected that Kiwis were also peculiar.

"We shall celebrate. I shall take you to dinner, Sunshine." He stood up.

"No wine for me. I'm off the piss. But I'm warning you, if you get sauced up and try something with me again. . . ."

Jurgen raised his hands in surrender. "No, please. I have had enough!"

Rainey joined him at the door. "On the way, tell me what you've arranged for transport."

Ditch stood in the boarding line at Houston Intercontinental. United had a flight direct to Geneva. Louisa had purchased for him a ticket, First Class, which he felt guilty about. He should be sitting in an economy seat, instead of lying fully reclined like a maharajah. While he waited in line, he pecked out a long text.

"Hi, Gully, it's me. But you know that. I wanted to let you know my dad died. He liked you, and talked about you a lot, and I know you liked him. It was quick, and a friend's convinced me he's now with mom.

"But I'm also writing you about something else: your last request. Yeah no, but sorry, I can't donate to your pregnancy. I can't do it that way. I'm sure you'll find a suitable donor. Fact is, I can't move forward, looking back. My best to you and Jenna. Hope you're safe and well. Over and out, Your First Husband."

This peck texting took a long time, but when he looked up, the line hadn't budged a bit. Across the velvet rope, the next boarders had queued up. Closest to him a very old lady was patting herself down, searching feverishly for her boarding pass and passport while glancing at the overhead monitor.

Ditch spoke across the rope. "Apprehensive about flying?"

She startled, and looked at him. He smiled, trying to resemble a nice young man.

"Yes, yes," she said. "I don't like flying over so much water. And my feet swell horribly."

"It's the shortest path possible, ma'am. The Great Circle Route."

"Oh," she said, not understanding. "I see."

"And come through." He lifted the rope for her as his line moved forward. "You're about to be upgraded to First Class."

"I am?" she said, slipping under eagerly. "What a stroke of luck."

"Yes, ma'am."

At the boarding desk, he arranged with the attendant Jeff to switch their seats. He didn't need First Class. After all, he was a Marine. Later, he reflected that it was true: no good deed goes unpunished.

"There's something you're not telling me," her mother said. "I know there is. You never could lie to me."

Which wasn't strictly true. Rainey had lied to her mother heaps, like any girl, and her mum never knew. Her dad did, though. He was a big bloke, with a craggy face and extremely shaggy eyebrows, like a Cairn Terrier. In contrast, her mum, short like Rainey and a redhead, always acted positive and cheerful, to counter-balance her husband, the family skeptic and lie detector. So Rainey was glad it was 0630 tomorrow in the Land of the Long White Cloud, and he was already down at the barns.

"Too right, mum. I didn't tell you I've flown to Switzerland to buy a horse from Jurgen."

Her mother knew Jurgen, and disliked him intensely for the free use of his hands.

"Humpf!" she said. "He even felt up *my* bum."

"Well, you are a looker, mum. Anyway, I broke his middle finger."

Her mother laughed, "Good on you." After a moment's pause, she added, "Is there anyone new in your life?"

Rainey was sick of being asked that.

"Abso-not," she said. "But there's something else I need you to do, has to do with Jack."

"Oh," her mother said, not enthusiastically, "about that, Beryl called a few days back, asking all kinds of questions about you."

"No way. She was only too chuffed to see me gone. Scratched me off the books the day after the funeral."

"She's changed her tune now, for certain."

"Bugger all," Rainey groaned. "Anyroad, would you please give Dr. Allsgood a jingle and tell her all good so far? But if it doesn't work, would she begin arranging sending them here?"

After a moment's hesitation, her mum said, "Yes, luv. If it's what you want."

"It is. Now I've got to fly, literally. Ta, mum."

She hung up hurriedly, before her mother could pry any more.

Outside, on the wet tarmac, she joined Jurgen and the transport company rep supervising the hydraulic loading of the three-horse containerized stall, into the cargo bay of the freight Airbus. Horses are the second most frequent flyers in the world, and along with Snorkel in the container were two racehorses from Dubai.

Watching, Rainey hugged herself in the cold Zurich drizzle. She hadn't known where the unexpected impulse about Jack had come from, but back in Auckland, over a year and a half after his death, his mates had drifted away, she'd broken her leg ending her competitive riding, and she was alone, trapped in widow weeds, upended. But now, now she felt something was changing in her life, albeit slowly, like the first tentative movement of a tidal shift. And she wondered where the new tide would take her. Somewhere with a purpose, she hoped. She was tired of feeling alone and adrift.

Meantime, the company rep came over.

"You don't have to travel with him," he said. "We have our man onboard."

"Na yeah. But he's my charge," she said, because caring for Snorkel was her purpose for now. Also, flying with him, she'd avoid, at least for a while, another encounter with Ditch. She cursed herself for the sex that night. For certain it complicated the fuck out of things.

CHAPTER 11

"GOD MUST HAVE put me beside you, another veteran like my daughter. Have you been to the war? You have? But you don't seem insane."

"I hide it well," Ditch said, reflecting that a worried, chatty lady seated next to you was an airline passenger's worst nightmare. It'd started as a steady stream, mostly about her hometown in East Texas and her husband Ralph, who, she believed, sometimes tuned her out – but once she discovered that Ditch was a vet, the floodgates opened.

"And you still have everything. Poor Daphne, she came back from Iraq without a foot."

Shocked, Ditch looked over at her. "Ma'am, maybe you better start at the beginning."

"Of course, of course. Ralph says I jump into the middle of stories. Daphne," she said, "she grew up with us, but she never really fit in. Unlike the rest of the family, she was always such a mess. Her closet looked like Fibber Mcgee's. And once she even stole a car. But the Army straightened her out, and she became a different person. Very. . . ."

She searched for the word. Ditch filled in. "Squared away?"

"Yes. Exactly. She worked with those dogs, the ones who can smell bombs."

Shit, Ditch thought, Military War Dog Handlers had one tough job in the Sand Box.

"And when she was over there, we heard hardly a word. Never called, rarely wrote."

"She probably had her hands full," Ditch said.

"No, it was more like she'd joined a different family. Even Ralph noticed it, and he hasn't noticed much in years. Anyway, I wrote her that she cared more about those other soldiers than about us, her own flesh and blood."

"The bonds of war are very strong," Ditch said, "and unique."

"Well, she's certainly unique now. A bomb blew up, and nearly killed her, and it did kill the dog. She got a medal, and so did the dog, and I didn't even know they did that, for dogs.

"She was in Walter Reed for months before she even called. That's when she told us she was an amputee. But – and this really flabbergasted me – after she got a prosthetic foot, she volunteered to go back again. I mean, is she crazy? I told Ralph she has PTSD."

Jesus, Ditch thought, this story keeps getting worse.

"Of course, the Army had the good sense not to send her, but when she finally came home, supposedly on leave, you've never heard such cursing in every sentence. I cannot abide profanity. Pastor Stevens says the Lord frowns on blasphemy."

Fuck Pastor Stevens, Ditch thought.

"You don't want the Lord frowning on you, I told her. I won't tell you how she responded to that. Even Ralph's face turned red, and he curses, too, when he hits his finger with a hammer. Anyway, I told her she'd changed."

Don't do that!

"Sure, she was wild as a teenager, but pretty. But, I told her, she's different now, all hard in the face."

Oh, great. That didn't piss her off, I bet.

"At home she just holed up in her room. And as for her old hometown boyfriend, Bill – well, he was never very suitable, was he? He works as a car mechanic, and drinks. But I told her she should go out with him. It might bring her out of her stupor."

Yeah, fat fucking chance she'd connect with a civilian.

"She didn't even get dressed up for her date. Wore cutoff jeans and an old Army T-shirt. I mean, in our small town, that is considerably underdressed. And she didn't put a shoe on that mechanical foot, either. That is a breach of etiquette, I told her. After all, this *is* East Texas! She went out anyway, poorly dressed, and came home drunk. Totally inebriated. I'm sure you know how Pastor Stevens feels about that."

Fuck Pastor Stevens, again.

"She was so drunk she had to hold on to the back of the sofa to stand up. That's when she told us she wasn't home on leave. She'd been discharged, medically. I told her good, now she can get a real job, and settle down with a nice local boy. Honest to Betsy, I've never heard a door slam that loud before."

I love you, Daphne, my war-sister, Ditch thought. He checked his watch. Six more hours of worried yammering to go. He looked out the window, and wondered if he could fit through it. Civil twilight was falling outside, and up ahead he could see the Labrador Trough. Also, like any pilot, he scanned the sky for air traffic, and sure enough, a thousand feet above them an aircraft was passing, headed west. It looked like an Airbus. He wondered who was onboard.

Rainey Gauge started chundering halfway across the North Atlantic. When she used up all the barf bags in the cargo bay, Corky, the company in-flight groom, went up to the cockpit to fetch more. Then he dug around in his flight bag and retrieved the tin of digestive biscuits he always carried. Giving three to Rainey, he ate one himself.

"I hate being airsick," he said.

"I've never been," Rainey said, wiping her lips, "crook before. Flown horses thousands and thousands of kilometers."

She chewed a biscuit, thanking Corky. He was a fortyish black bloke, wiry, with a full, slightly graying beard. He'd told Rainey he'd grown up in Kentucky racehorse barns, where his father was a farrier.

"I can't believe your dad shod Secretariat. What was he like?"

"A fine fellow. Secretariat, not my old man. He was always grouchy, because of his back. Died of a painkiller overdose, in his Lazy Boy. I decided to take a different route, and ended up with this gig."

He paused, to watch Rainey hurl again. He thought he'd seen this before. He and the missus had two kids. To give her privacy, he moved on to the small exit door window, and looked out. An aircraft passed below them, headed east. He wondered who was onboard.

Between this bout of nausea and the next, Rainey checked on Snorkel. He had plenty of hay, and he drank water from a bucket she held. She pinched the skin on his neck, pulled it out, and released it. The skin snapped back elastically, which meant his hydration was bang on. Next, she looked into his eyes. Horses have the largest eyes of any land mammal, just the kind of eyes you can speak your heart to.

"You're a patient man," she told him, smoothing his forelock. "I wish I were more like you. But I couldn't wait, and I had this thing done back home. Then up here, I made a mistake with a bloke, and I'm worried I may have cocked it up, and knocked the egg loose."

Snorkel blinked and affectionately snuffled her hair.

Then a wave of nausea rose up, and she returned to her canvas seat and her friend, the airsickness bag. But it wasn't airsickness, she thought. It was those bloody mussels she'd eaten at dinner with Jurgen. Why had she ordered mussels, when Switzerland was so far from the sea? But she'd chosen them because of Jack. He was a seafood hungus. She wondered if their baby would look like him. Probably. They say that most babies favor their fathers, for evolutionary reasons. Dads prefer babies who look like them, and not like the bloke in the next cave. She smiled, thinking about that, and then she began to spew again.

In Geneva, when Ditch stood up to de-plane, she was still talking. He used his command voice to shut her up. "Ma'am, stop speaking, please."

"I beg your pardon?"

He held out a piece of paper. "When you talk to your daughter next – and do it soon – give her this phone number. The lady at the other end will be Louisa Grand. She's helped a lot of veterans."

The lady took the paper and stared at it. Then she looked up, tears in her eyes.

"Oh, thank you, Captain. I will tell Daphne. Tonight. I'll call home. Thank you so much. You see, God did put you beside me for a reason."

"I'm sure He did," Ditch said – but he thought, God, if He exists, is sometimes a cruel son of a bitch.

CHAPTER 12

A FLY LANDED on the Director's nose. He quickly brushed it away. Rationally he could not blame the abundance of October flies on the Texan, but all the same, he did.

"Mr. Grand, you complain that the treatment is not working?" he said. "You understand, it often takes months to rebalance the body."

"I don't have months," Joe D. said. "And it's always worked by now before."

"But, Sir, you are now well into your sixties, when incipient impotence is not uncommon."

Joe D. screwed up his face. He had a feeling that the phrase "incipient impotence" was going to haunt him.

"What about Cialis, or something even stronger?"

"Sir, an erection that lasts four to nine hours cannot be healthy."

"Why not? It didn't hurt when I was seventeen."

"Perhaps when you were seventeen. But the side effects – priapism, the risk of permanent blindness, loss of hearing – as well as the unknown consequences to other organs, such as your liver. I mention your liver because your bloodwork and urinalysis reveal some damage. Which brings me to the subject of alcohol."

"Okay, okay, I drink a little too much sometimes, because I'm impotent."

"Perhaps you are impotent because you drink too much."

Joe D. grunted and looked down at his shoes. "You're talking chickens and eggs. That's all you've got?"

"I am only providing relevant information about the effects of your lifestyle. Highly stressed, driven Alpha personality types can – what is the phrase your American marathon runners use – 'hit the wall.'"

Joe D. looked up from his Italian loafers. He did, in fact, feel like he'd slammed into a wall, and not only because of his legal problems. After all the treatments, the nutritious diet, the herbs, the vitamins, the massages, the injections, the spa, the sauna, the icy baths – and still he felt like shit warmed over. His body was a traitorous hunk of meat, stealing from him his life. All he wanted was to be fixed, so he could go home and make love to his wife, really make love, really talk to her, tell her what she meant to him. Also, he had to explain how he'd gotten into this legal turmoil. But now he was going to die soon. He was certain of it. His Appointment at Samarra could be tonight, could be tomorrow. He would call Louisa the moment he got back to his room.

But the Director wasn't finished with him yet. "Next, shall we address the issue of your sarcopenia?"

Louisa was taking a lesson from Rainey on the new horse Snorkel.

"You're still a wee bit behind him, Louisa. Balance in your irons, and talk to him with your hips. You shouldn't even need the reins."

Frustrated, and not feeling well, Louisa brought Snorkel to a stop in front of Rainey.

They were working in the jumping arena, with a straight line of three jumps, then a bending left line to a wide oxer.

"I'm cooked for today," she said, sliding off and passing Rainey the reins. "But would you please show me how it's supposed to be done."

Rainey unclipped the reins from the bit. She wouldn't be using them. Lengthening the left stirrup leather and shortening the right, she mounted from the off-side, which Snorkel was accustomed to now.

"He'll know what I want, what I'm asking, by listening to my hips, the same way it works in bed with a bloke."

Louisa laughed and stepped back to watch. Using her weight and knees, Rainey guided Snorkel around, squeezing him from a trot into a canter, and with her hands on her hips, she aimed him, ears perked, toward the first jump, a ramped, three-foot oxer – rising, folding, dropping her heels – a sweet leap with heaps of bascule. Then came a slight hip-rock back, to shorten his stride approaching a vertical triple-bar in-and-out, one stride between it and a liverpool. With each jump, Rainey folded to his neck, his mane flying in her face. This was something she did and did well, and her smile was broad when he landed over the liverpool in the left lead, perfectly pitched for the last, very wide oxer on a graceful bending line. Snorkel picked his spot, a little too close, so Rainey adjusted it, leaning back a nibble, then up, over, and across, folding, soaring, perfectly together, beautifully in sync. Louisa spontaneously clapped. Rainey trotted over and halted in front of her, still with her hands on her hips.

"That was downright amazing," Louisa beamed.

"Yeah na." Rainey slid off and stroked Snorkel's neck. "I was better before the leg, but it still feels sweet as, to talk to a horse with your hips."

"And you say they work the same way with a man?"

"Not exactly," Rainey laughed. "But there are *some* similarities."

"Not in *my* house," Louisa smiled. "In bed Joe D.'s always in quite a hurry."

"A question of training," Rainey said. "But some men don't need teaching."

"You're talking about Jack?"

"Na yeah. Of course I am."

They continued talking, walking Snorkel to the barn, but Rainey was also thinking. When she'd said some men don't need teaching, she'd actually been flashing on Ditch. She couldn't forget their sex that night, no matter how hard she tried. Fact was, she'd even dreamed about it a couple of times since, waking up woozy and embarrassed. The guilt of it, she decided, was the cause of her feeling so crook. Worser, she may indeed have knocked the egg loose, because she was a wee bit spotting now, a prelude to a deluge, perhaps. She might not be preggers atall.

Later, Louisa walked slowly up the hill to the house, thinking about Joe D. Maybe he could be trained; maybe she'd give it a try. Joe D. had grown into someone quite different from the handsome, ambitious, passionate, penniless boy she'd married thirty-six years ago. Nevertheless, she still saw, within him, two struggling men, one of whom she did love terribly.

But for now, she just felt very tired. The test results still weren't in. She needed – what would Rainey call it? – a good lie down. Rainey herself had gone up to her apartment to do the same, saying she felt a wee bit off, too. Thinking of Rainey, Louisa smiled: she dearly treasured that short, tough, funny, gifted girl.

Joe D. left Jonny and the Thai masseuse in the lounge of La Clinique, where they were canoodling over glasses of lemon water and wheat grass. At that moment, Joe D. hated his friend. The treatment had worked for him. He bounced around everywhere on the balls of his feet. He claimed La Clinique was the fountain of youth. And he wanted to marry the masseuse.

Making his way down the corridor to his suite, Joe D. muttered "incipient impotence," and then "sarcopenia." First, his dick, dead, and now the remainder of him was rapidly turning into a puddle of mush. His muscle fibers were wasting away. Definitely, he was around the bend, over the falls, circling the drain, one foot in the grave. Of course he'd known that someday he would die, but he knew it only in a theoretical sense, an event occurring on a far, far distant day. But now its presence cast a shadow so deep that even imprisonment didn't seem so bad.

Entering his suite, he went directly to the closet where he'd stashed several bottles. He began with two glasses of red wine with a French label, then he sat down and checked the pulse in his throat: far too fast, and was. . . was that an irregular beat? Atrial fibrillation? As his mind jumped from fear to fear, it snagged on another Louisa's quote from the Bible: "Those of high degree are but a fleeting breath, On the scales they are lighter than a breath."

Pouring a third glass, emptying the bottle, he called Louisa.

"Where were you?" he asked, vexed. "I missed you yesterday, and I phoned three times today."

"I was just watching Rainey give Moira a dressage lesson, and my phone's on the blink. Also, lately it's been busy here. Ditch's father died, so he came home for the services, but he's back there now."

"Our pilot's father? How old was he, eighty or something?"

"No, he was a Vietnam veteran. Which makes him your age."

Joe D. walked over the bed and flopped down on it, stretched out, and looked at his horrible feet. At one time they'd been wonderful feet, complete with a bone spur that enabled him to dodge the draft. Louisa thought he didn't understand irony, but he did see it: a former draft dodger later makes several fortunes off of war. He reached for the wine glass on the bedside table.

"Do you ever wish," he said, taking a gulp, "that you hadn't done what you'd done?"

"Joe D., what's going on? You really shouldn't keep me in the dark."

"Sweetheart," he sighed, took a breath, and confessed, probably because he was already half in the bag. "I, I haven't always been strictly up front with you, about all my business practices. I haven't done anything really horrible, only what's common in the defense industry. But the Feds are looking to make an example of someone. Don't worry, though. I've figured a way out."

"Oh, Joe D.," she said, with piercing disappointment in her voice. "What did you do, and not just to yourself? Think of all our staff. Their daily bread depends on us."

"I know, I know, but let's not get ahead of ourselves: it probably won't amount to anything, thanks to this Saudi deal. We'll be too big to fail."

"And poor Jonny, too," Louisa went on worrying. "What have you gotten him into?"

They both fell silent for a moment on the phone. To change the subject, Joe D. asked, "How are you feeling, with that urinary tract thing?"

"Fine," she lied. Eva Hoffsteader had called to tell her that the lab had fouled up the test results, and would have to start over again. After another long pause, she said, "We'll talk about this when you get home. And now, I'm going to bed, Joe D. Goodnight."

She hung up abruptly, before he could reply. He held the phone to his ear, thinking of things he should have said. He also thought he never should have confessed. Now he would have to live with the disappointment in her eyes. Given that, he knew he'd never get to sleep tonight, unless he did something.

He gulped the last of his wine, then went back to the closet and the liquor cache. He plucked out a bottle of Cutty Sark. That should do the trick. If not, he'd drink the Jim Beam, too.

CHAPTER 13

LOUISA NOTICED JONNY Wright standing at her den doorway, but she held a finger up to him, to signal she was busy just then on the phone. Jonny watched her on the daybed. Louisa did not appear to be well, something Jonny might not have noticed two weeks ago. But since those miraculous injections, his powers of observation had grown. Not that his powers were anything like those of Kohsoom, his fiancé. She claimed she could see a person's individual aura, and he believed it. For instance, she said an aura of dirty brown surrounded Joe D., which meant afflicted by fear. He wondered what she would see in Louisa.

"Daphne, I'm so glad you went to the specialist in Houston. I thought he might help. No, no, don't worry about the expense. And about that other offer, yes, we do have a place for you here. I've been investigating something new, where you could be a great help: training emotional support dogs, for veterans with PTSD. . . .You would? Then start looking for a dog for our bodyguard. He's from Louisiana, if that helps. Let me get back to you when I firm things up. . . . Yes, certainly, within the week."

She hung up and turned to Jonny.

"Louisa, you look so – I don't know how to describe it," Jonny said, coming to take her hands as she rose from the daybed.

"So dreadful," Louisa said. "I'm a bit under the weather. Cedar fever."

During late October in the Texas Hill Country, the male cedar trees begin blowing out tons of pollen. Red eyes, runny noses, puffy faces, and fever aches were not uncommon.

"But, Jonny, you look at your peak. And what have you done to your hair?"

"Kohsoom told me the comb-over didn't work. Now I'm just a bald guy. But you know, baldness is caused by an excess of testosterone."

Louisa laughed. "Yes, I could feel your testosterone from across the room. Where is this Kohsoom? I want to meet her."

"Come with me, and you shall." He crooked his arm for her, gallantly.

"Jonny, I don't think I've ever seen you like this before," Louisa said.

"If you had, would my attempt at seduction have been more successful?"

"No," Louisa smiled. "But it would have been a lot more fun."

Dotty people never think they're weird: it's always the other people who are. Certainly, this was true of Joe D. In the foyer he watched the kooky Thai masseuse follow the head maid Hortensia up the broad bending staircase. Joe D. was pretty sure Hortensia was a transsexual, or transvestite, or whatever they were called. Anyway, she had a very large Adam's apple. Following them was the butler, a wizened old black Korean War vet named Harold, a chronic smartass who always wore a Martin Luther King button on his lapel. Joe D. might have been displeased by the staff, but his wife had hired all of them, and he loved her beyond measure. However, he was going to disappoint her today. He'd prepared for it by getting a little lit.

Meantime, Moira swept past them on her way down. Seeing her, Joe D. smiled. He and his daughter were allies, kindred spirits, and they both were a little thick around the middle.

"Daddy, you won't believe the horse."

"You won't believe what he cost."

"Well, you won't believe how he moves. He's just amazing. He completely fills my seat."

"Where are you going? I just got home."

"Out. I have a date."

"What? With a real person? A man?"

Moira most often dated virtually, on social media, though occasionally she "hung out."

"A real man, yes. Rudy Zavala. Now, Daddy, don't get mad, but Rudy is a Democrat."

"What?"

"But he's so handsome – a little plump, but not too much, like me. And you'll appreciate, he's a very successful politician."

"A Democrat?"

Moira laughed with unusual gaiety, and breezed past. Joe D. spun around to watch her, feeling his personal life was out of control. He was being replaced, in his daughter's heart, by a Democrat. That alone was cause to drink.

At that moment, Louisa and Jonny entered the foyer. Joe D. hurried toward her, but stumbled to a halt as he took her hands. "Sweetheart, you, you look terrible."

"So," she said, "do you. Is that liquor on your breath?"

Jonny sought to intervene. "Louisa has cedar fever," he said.

"Or it might be the flu," Louisa said. "To be safe, you probably should stay – ."

But mentally Joe D. had already started to back away. His father: the flu: heart attack: death. A very simple equation.

His wife was contagious, covered in germs. He felt his heart beating, hard and far too fast. Also a sudden ringing in his ears. This might be the big one, the heart attack, or myocardial infarction, or coronary thrombosis, or whatever they're called on the Death Certificate.

But, with effort, he overcame himself. "If you're sick, of course, I'll stay home and nurse you."

"But you were planning to go away again?"

He nodded. "Jonny and I should stay on the move. He has to design some things, and I need to talk to the DoD about getting the DCAA off our necks."

"Then, go," she said. "I'll be fine. And remember, all our staff depends on you."

"Kohsoom will nurse you." Jonny patted her arm. "As a healer, she has extraordinary powers."

"You two, both go," Louisa repeated firmly. "I'll be fine."

Watching as Joe D. hurried off down the west hallway to his home office to make some calls, Jonny commented with a groan, "'No man on his deathbed ever said, I should have spent more time in the office.' Who am I quoting, Louisa?"

"Someone," Louisa replied, "very smart."

"Rainey," Ditch pecked in his text. "I just got home, and it looks like I gotta turn around again. Warbucks wants to return to Austin, then on from there to who knows where. But I'd like to see you as soon as I get back. I need to start making amends. A change is happening in me. I told Hugo, and he explained it with a line from some Sondheim song: 'I'm dazed, I'm pale, I'm sick, I'm sore, I've never felt so well before.' So, please, let's get together so I can set things right."

Rainey responded immediately, because two words didn't take long to type.

"Naff off."

Louisa stood at Snorkel's stall door, stroking his neck for a very long time. Maybe there was something to this emotional support animal information she'd been reading about. Anyway, she certainly felt much better, standing here with him. He had such large, dark eyes.

Behind her in the barn aisle, Rainey dropped the phone back in her pocket, then turned to watch Louisa and Snorkel. Snorkel liked her, trusted her. He dropped his head a little, to snuffle her abdomen.

"Would you like to ride him? I can throw your Stubben on."

"No," Louisa said. "I'm not at all up for that. But I do have a request."

"Anything."

"Would you drive me into town? I don't want anyone else to know."

Rainey cocked her head. "Our secret," she said.

A few minutes later they pulled out of the barn in the ranch truck, down the incline to the lane. Most of the staff lived down the hill from the Grand Manse (which the staff referred to it as the Gland Manse) in a row of tidy staff cottages that looked across the outdoor arena toward the glinting river. At one end lay the horse barn, where Rainey lived in an upstairs apartment, while at the other end sat the hangar, where in an upstairs apartment Ditch lived. The route along the lane to the front gate ran past the hangar, where this afternoon Ditch was moodily wheeling the Jet Ranger helicopter back out of the hangar again.

"Joe D.'s beating a fast retreat," Louisa explained. "Legal troubles, and he's petrified of the flu. Poor Ditch. He doesn't look too happy, does he? Let's stop and cheer him up."

Rainey pretended not to hear, her eyes straight ahead, pressing down a little on the accelerator. With a puzzled look, Louisa's gaze drifted from Ditch to Rainey, then back to Ditch.

"Where we going?" Rainey asked, turning onto the highway to Kerrville.

"Medical Arts. Dr. Hoffsteader, the gynecologist."

"The gynie? I could use an appointment there."

"I'm sure Eva can fit you in. Care to share?"

"Just a bit of spotting," she said, which was partially true.

"It's probably nothing, but good to get it checked out," Louisa said. She sat quiet a while, her hands in her lap. Finally, she sighed. "I'm going to find out if I have endometrial cancer."

Rainey's head snapped around.

Louisa shrugged. "The answer could be no."

Rainey stared straight ahead, gripping the steering wheel. "Too right," she said.

Fact was, she had her own endometrial worries. First, the spotting, then late, when she was always clockwork, dead on. And other little things. . . . What were those stupid words in Ditch's stupid text? "I'm sick, I'm sore, I've never felt so well before." And bugger those dodgy home tests: she needed a professional one. She should feel flash hot, over the moon – possibly preggers by Jack – but the untimely root with Ditch had flushed that plan down the gurgler. Better that she wasn't, and then she could give it another go, using only the right bloke's swimmers this time.

So they drove into town, both with the hope of no.

CHAPTER 14

DITCH WAS NECK-DEEP flying the rest of that day – first to the helo pad at Austin corporate headquarters, then back to K-ville to pick up the Phenom and ferry it to Austin International for the flight tomorrow to D.C. And he was grateful to be kept too busy to think. Hugo flew along with him, and helping him button up the bird on the Austin ramp, he commented on how many things needed to be done.

"I always thought you pilots were lazy ass POGs." A POG is a Person Other than Grunt. "Where you going now?"

"Fixed Based Operations," Ditch said, "to check weather tomorrow and plan the flight."

"Good," Hugo said. "I can catch some Zs on their couch." As they walked, he observed,

"Without your dad's medical bills, you don't have to stick it with this shit anymore."

"Yeah na," Ditch said, then thought, Christ, I'm still talking like Rainey. After a moment flashing on her, he added, "But I'm gonna hang in here for a while. I'm starting to care about these people. And Louisa needs us to overwatch Warbucks."

Hugo nodded. "More like babysit. But I'm beginning to soften on him. He's just a fucked up, scared little shit. When he's not freaking out about indictments, he's hyperventilating and taking his pulse."

Ditch agreed. "We were lucky. We got shot at every day for years."

"Affirm on that. Death ain't the worst that can happen." Hugo thought about his wife, who by this time of the afternoon might be three sheets to the wind in Baton Rouge. This reminded him of Ditch's own fucked up love life. "You ain't said shit about Rainey."

"Nothing to say." As they entered the FBO, he took out his phone, punched messages, and handed it to Hugo. When he returned from ordering fuel, he took the phone back and deleted the text.

"I guess," Hugo said, "she means fuck off. Is that what you're gonna do?"

"Unless I want to turn into some weird stalker dude. Get some sack time, bro. When I'm finished here, we'll go hunt down some grub. I know a place with gumbo as good as yours."

"I fucking doubt that," Hugo said. Then he stretched out on the couch, closed his eyes, and like all infantrymen, fell instantly asleep. He dreamt of gumbo with sausage and shrimp.

Rainey Gauge climbed back into the truck cab, slammed the door hard, and after a moment's hesitation began pounding the steering wheel with her palms, cursing, then whacking the truck ceiling so hard that dents popped up on the roof.

"Fucking simon wu, kui uwha, Hangi pants, shoulda kept a peg in it, let Jack's swimmers do the job, but oh no, had to go hot and heavy, those bloody green-brown eyes, spread the yoke for a bloke who made you laugh. And does the randy shelia say, 'how 'bout slipping on a johnnie, sweetie,' before they bonk, no, no, can't wait for that, can't even think, doesn't have the fuckwit to know what nine times nine is, just give it to me, jump on the lust boat and hump away, no worries, mate. Damn it, fuck all, now bloody rooted beyond all focking recognition."

At the end of this roof pounding rant, Rainey became aware of Louisa standing in front of the truck with her mouth open. Okay, okay, settle down. Put it in the chilly bin. With a deep breath, she calmed enough to throw up her hands in a gesture of defeat. After a moment's pause, Louisa came around, opened the door, and slid in.

"I take it, not the news you wanted?"

Rainey nodded. "Na yeah. And you?"

"The same."

"Oh, Louisa, I'm so sorry."

But Louisa, typically, looked on the bright side. "Uterine cancer is probably one of the easiest types to beat. But what were you doing, shouting?"

"Cursing up a torrent. It's very therapeutic. I've tried her before."

Partially listening, Louisa put her seatbelt on. She took a deep, yogic breath. It was utterly useless, of course. Cancer. *Cancer!* Cancer should always be italicized and followed by an exclamation mark. Since deep breathing did no good, she cast about and opted for therapeutic cursing instead. And what a previously unknown pleasure it was, cussing a blue streak. She pounded the dash and kicked the floorboards with her feet, beginning with a curse she'd learned from Ditch.

"Muthafukjonson! Muthafukjonson! Damn selfish, hypochondriac son of a bitch, gotta keep doing it, no matter what, because if you don't, you aren't a fucking man. And me, I go along, doing my wifely shit, even when the walls thin and the penis flops, even go to his fucking, son of a bitch, pill-pushing doctor who says, estrogen, no problem, except of course it fucking well is. Motherfucker, cocksucker, jerk off, son of a bitch, bastard, dickhead, asshole, jerk off, son of a bitch, muthafukjonson!"

Meantime, Rainey had joined in, putting more dents in the truck roof. "Drongo, fuck-knuckle, munter! Donkey-fuck, nek minnit, drop kick!"

Out of one ear, Louisa heard her, and had to stop cussing to listen in. "Drongo, munter, fuck-knuckle?" she asked, surprised to find herself smiling. "I'm going to visit New Zealand someday, after I have my uterus removed."

Rainey looked over, panting. "Is that. . . what happens next?"

Louisa nodded. "After more tests, at MD Anderson in Houston. Then, if the hysterectomy's successful and it hasn't spread, I may not need chemo or radiation."

"Crickey, Louisa. Talk about a rough ride. Our women parts, they're so bloody complicated. Don't you sometimes wish you had a simple cock and balls?"

Louisa smiled. "No, not at all. Not with all the trouble they cause."

"Na yeah," Rainey said after a moment's thought. "Too right. And I wouldn't want all those tender bits dangling about."

They sat silently a moment, submerged in their own thoughts about what was in their uteruses. It was time for Rainey to confess.

"I, I'm up the duff," she said, then translated: "Preggers."

Louisa's head turned. After a pause, she reached over and put her hand on Rainey's shoulder. "That's. . . that's wonderful," she said.

"Is it? Anyroad, I gotta suss out what to do about it."

Louisa cleared her throat and smoothed her skirt over her knees. "We obviously need some time to think," she said. "What do you say to Francisco's? They serve pretty good tea."

"Sweet as. I could murder a strong cuppa," Rainey said, starting the truck and putting it into reverse.

They exited the Medical Arts parking lot, crossing the river and into town. Louisa was the first to speak.

"For now I want as few people as possible to know. Joe D.'s already scared witless over this investigation, and he just thinks I have the flu. Cancer could send him around the bend."

Rainey nodded. "Mum's the word – for the both of us, please. I need time to sort this pig's breakfast."

"Of course. But your condition won't stay hidden long. And isn't there someone else who should know?"

Rainey shook her head, adamantly.

"You don't have to tell me," Louisa said. "But it's Ditch, isn't it?"

Rainey said nothing, which said a lot. After a moment, she amended the silence: "Most probably, very most probably, it's Jack's. I got myself inseminated before I came here."

"Oh," Louisa said. "Oh. That certainly complicates things."

"But if, *if* I keep it, I'm saying it's Jack's, full stop. There may have been other swimmers in the race, but they got started a week late. And at the clinic they told me Jack's were very motile."

Louisa looked at her questioningly. Rainey went on to explain about the deposit Jack had left at the Auckland bank. She said mayhaps he'd had a premonition. Also, a couple of months before he deployed, he asked if she would have her IUD removed.

"Actually, he said, 'Luv, maybe it's time we pull the goalie.'"

Because Louisa didn't appear to understand, Rainey explained, "Jack was rugby, through and through."

"Oh, 'pull the goalie,'" Louisa said, with a laugh. "I would have liked Jack."

"Na yeah, a grand man. Choice. Never another like him, not in this hemisphere or the other."

81

Louisa remained silent. But she thought, poor Ditch, always to be measured against a saint.

Rainey went on, "I never put the goalie back in the game. No reason to: I was done with sex, I thought. I'm *such* an eejit."

They arrived, parked, and a few minutes later sat over a steeping pot of tea at a corner table. Louisa wondered if Rainey could really erase Ditch from this equation. But she did know personally about artificial insemination.

"I conceived both Dan and Moira via AI. Joe D.'s sperm count is very low. But mine was in vitro, and yours must have been in utero."

Rainey nodded. Yes, in utero, she thought, and in one case, very deeply in utero, and made by direct deposit. Crickey, she was such a fucktard. Nevertheless, sipping hot Earl Grey, she thought again that she'd never forget the sex that night, no matter how hard she tried. She remembered the way he'd tenderly tickled her when they moved together, with his moustache, on her eyelids, her broken nose, and in her ear. The ear snuffling really drove her a little mad. Fact was, she'd wrapped her legs around him and pulled him even further in. Good idea, that. What a fuckwit I am.

But this wasn't the first-time reckless acts got her in Dutch, after Jack died. Darkened by grief, she hadn't focused proper, taking a green horse over his first trakehner. He balked at the ditch-rail combo, and off she flew. Four surgeries later, she had three pins and a plate in her bunged up leg. Lost the love of her life and her career, all in less than a year. And now. . . now this clump of cells in her uterus.

Louisa made her situation even worse. "To be safe, you should stop riding."

"I don't see why."

"In romantic novels, whenever the pregnant heroine climbs on a horse, a miscarriage follows," Louisa said, then added, "And, no matter about the father, you don't want to lose this baby, really, do you?"

"No, I don't," Rainey said instantly, then realized it was true. She sucked in her breath. "Too right. I will be careful," she said, and she meant it, in a way she'd never expected. She began to think of this thing, this baby, differently, like she'd never thought or felt about anything else before. "It" was a baby, a "pepi" in the Maori tongue – entirely dependent on her. Her pepi, her charge, a little clump of cells in her uterus – growing, dividing, and growing some more – forming a face, a heart, and a soul. They changed everything, they changed everything in the world for her.

And at the table she began to weep with fear and joy.

"I, I don't know what's happening to me." She wiped her face with a flimsy napkin. "I'm turning into a bloody sook."

Louisa reached across and took her hand. "Darling, it's about to get even worse. You're just at the outer bands, of the hormone hurricane."

CHAPTER 15

WHEN THE PHONE rang in his office at HMLA (Helicopter Marine Light Attack) Squadron 773, the Colonel was in a Black Dog mood. The Budget Control Act signed last August, 2011, cut nearly 500 billion dollars from the defense budget, the largest chunk coming from the Reserves. This meant for the Colonel's Detachment A, Belle Chase, Louisiana, very limited funds for recurrent pilot training, even less for aircraft maintenance, but, with the continued surge, an increased demand for overseas deployments. For the Colonel the math was simple: less money equals less preparedness, equals more dead Marines.

So he picked up the ringing black desk phone, a relic of the 1960's, with a new-normal gruffness in his voice. Holding the antique, crackling receiver to his ear, he growled, "Lt. Colonel Glubczynski. I'm listening."

"Colonel Glub, Ditch Dietrick here."

Ditch heard the Colonel's ancient desk chair rock back with a loud squeak. Nothing but the best for the Reserves. They'd served together in Helmand, 2007 and 2009. In fact, the Colonel had written Ditch up for a special commendation.

"Ditch, how's it hanging?" the Colonel said, switching to his jovial voice. "You'll have to make up time for the Drill you missed last week."

"Yes Sir. Work. I was in Riyadh. And now I'm up in DC."

"Oh, ferrying Warbucks around," the Colonel said. "And is the war profiteer making a killing?"

"I overheard something like twenty million."

"Shit," the Colonel said, "ain't war hell. What can I do you for, Ditch?"

"Fill me in on the scuttlebutt, Sir. How likely is another deployment?"

"You've been watching the news?"

Lately, network news channels all concentrated on the recent setbacks in Goat Country, as well as the rise of ISIS in the Box. Something had to be done, and at the Pentagon, plans were being made. Battle-seasoned pilots like Ditch would be essential to the Spring Offensive. The Colonel shouldn't hint at this, he knew, but he liked and respected Ditch. Even though he didn't yet want to make it a career, Ditch was a hell of an attack pilot, very aggressive, and a high-value squadron Captain. Withholding information from him was not something the Colonel could do.

"Don't," he said, "make *any* plans for the spring, Ditch. But keep that on the down low,

"Yes Sir," Ditch said. "It's down and low."

After he punched off, Ditch sat awhile in the lounge of the Washington Executive Airpark FBO, thinking. Ordinarily, he'd have been all down with another deployment. At least it was a place to go, a place where he was needed, doing something he was good at. But now. . . .

When Hugo plopped down beside him, Ditch filled him in. Hugo listened, thought, and shrugged. "It's been in the back of your mind all along, ain't it?" he said. "An exit strategy?"

"Yeah, sure," Ditch said. "But if I had a shot with Rainey. . . ."

"Dude, you don't," Hugo said. "She told you to naff off."

"Uh huh, but maybe," Ditch said, "I can change her mind."

"Negatory. She's already had one man pink-misted downrange. What're the chances she'd risk that again?"

"Okay, then, but they can't send me back if I resign my commission posthaste."

"Bro, you know it'd take months for that letter to make it up the chain of command, and even then, 'needs of the service' always wins."

Ditch said nothing for a minute. Then he made his Rubicon decision.

"Since I may not get deployed, I'm gonna keep it under my hat for now. It's only a small lie of omission, and I can live with that, because I might still have a chance."

Hugo thought about it. He'd known guys like Ditch before, guys who got their juice – in Cajun parlance, their *raison d'etre* – from their time in the shitstorm of war. Hell, he'd been one of them himself, turkey-peeking over rocks, finger on the trigger, safety off, looking over his shoulder at his bros, cracking a grin as he gave them the one, two, three hand signal that would change a quiet hot afternoon into a world whipped by spinning hot lead and sharp steel.

Until he got blown to shit, that is. And it was in a coma vision thing: he'd been drifting, like on a pirogue, toward his wife, Nan, the woman who loved him despite all the cinderblocks tied around his neck. In the coma he clung to her. He would never let her go: she'd saved his life; she'd led him out of war; she was his *raison d'etre*. So he knew what was at stake for Ditch.

But Ditch's predicament reminded him of a lyrical line from the musical *The Rocky Horror Show*: "The sword of

Damocles is hanging over my head, and I've got a feeling someone's gonna be cutting the thread." Nevertheless, it wasn't his business: never interfere on another man's watch. So when Ditch asked him if he was onboard with keeping his lie of omission on the down low, Hugo responded, "Hooah," which is the phonetic pronunciation of the acronym HUA: Heard. Understood. Acknowledged.

"Dearest Dan," Louisa typed on her new Gmail account, "I've been thinking about you quite a lot. I miss your sweet face. Do you still have that Antarctic beard? How handsome you are. And I know you're on the verge of summer down there – your busy time with the bugs – but things have been happening here, and I would really love to have you home briefly for the holidays. It would mean so much to me. And it's probably time to mend fences with your father. As usual, he's manic, and becoming more so. He drinks far too much, and grows more fearful every passing year. The day of reckoning is near.

"Moira's mood, on the other hand, has improved dramatically since she fell in love. During this visit, you may not try to strangle her. And all the staff would be cheered to see you. We have new faces among them, some of the finest young women and men you'll ever meet. Okay, I've run on and on, and probably showed too many of my cards, but please do consider a visit, however brief it needs to be.

"All my love, darling son,

"Your Only Mother."

Louisa clicked the send button, and *whoosh*, it flew into cyberspace. She knew she'd been a little heavy handed with the "Your Only Mother" bit. Nevertheless, she smiled, closing her laptop, reflecting that guilt is a tool frequently used by mothers. It is also a tool useful to wives, and for that reason she'd copied Joe D. the email. He'd gone dark, and she hadn't heard from him in over ten days. She had a deep premonition that his legal troubles were closing in.

In those ten days, Ditch had flown himself silly, back and forth from coast to coast seven times, with occasional sorties to Houston to ferry lawyers to and fro. From what he'd overheard, Grand Wright corporate records had been surrendered to the DCAA's forensic auditors. There were also worries that a squirrelly Donker, if offered immunity, just might flip. And the DoD might not be able to offer any protection from prosecution. The order had recently been promulgated from the top. In a recent Rose Garden ceremony, President Obama had said, "I reject the notion that we have to waste billions of taxpayer dollars to keep this nation secure."

Ditch overheard this, but he couldn't concern himself that clusterfuck. It, like his possible redeployment, was an If and When. And he had another flight to plan.

So that evening, Ditch sat hunched over his EFB (Electronic Flight Bag) at the table of his room in the Washington, DC, Hyatt, figuring weight and balance, and fuel. Hugo had gone out, to bring back pizza from a place he knew.

Sounds of DC traffic drifted up from below. The fuckers who ran this country, Ditch thought, were all going home tonight, fat, dumb, and happy. In a foul mood he got up, went over to the window, leaned his forehead against the cool glass, and looked out. He hated cities; he hated hotel rooms; he hated politicians and bureaucrats; and he hated the way Rainey had blown him off. Maybe he should write all this down in a list: a Shit-List.

But instead he sat down again and pecked out another text.

"Hi from DC, Kiwi-girl. I want to say this: it was a bolt out of the blue that just happened to strike us. Won't happen again. Lightning twice, and all that shit. But we're sensible people. And we can't just chuck our friendship. That would be catastrophizing (is that even a word?). I miss talking to you. I miss your face. And you got to admit, there's something between us, Kiwi: we click; we fit."

Ditch finished and studied the text, then hit Send. Next, he called Flight Services to request an advanced weather briefing for his flight tomorrow to LA. When he finished, he checked his messages and found she'd already sent one.

"No more texts or calls," she wrote. "I have you blocked."

Hugo returned a quarter hour later, to hear Ditch taking a long hot shower. He put the pizza on the table, saw Ditch's phone open to messages, and read the last.

"Shit," he said, "that's harsh."

At that moment, Ditch's phone rang. Hugo saw that it was Louisa, so he answered it.

Rainey saw she had no choice. She had to nip this whatever in the bud. True, she was pregnant, with the remote, very remote chance of him being the father. But he wasn't to know, for his own good. It wouldn't do to trap him this way, taking up with a woman who couldn't truly love him. He'd already thrown his heart over the wrong fence once before. Better to cut his head off with one swift blow, than to kill him with a thousand tiny cuts.

Nevertheless, limping up the steps to her barn apartment that evening, she thought she might be going bi-polar or skizo, or maybe it was just Baby-brain. In Godzone, they called it mumnesia. Anywho, she was always, lately, of two minds. In one she hated herself: she was weak, lacking any moral resolve. She'd given way to attraction and lust, and had betrayed her love for Jack.

But in her other mind, when she dared to think about it, she found herself queerly missing Ditch. She felt she'd known him yonks, and, for certain, they did get on, they jibed. Not love, not like how she felt about Jack. Just she enjoyed his company, his good humor, the way he looked at her like she was a riot. It made her feel stoked again, the way he joshed her about. And getting clean of him would be easier if he were, like Naomi said, a bad boy – but no, he was "staunch." That was her dad's favorite word for someone you could count on.

Thinking of that word made her think of her dad, and her mum, and suddenly she became homesick something terrible. In her apartment, she checked her watch: 5:30 pm today, which meant 12:30 pm tomorrow at home: a good time to call and hear their voices. The oldies always ate lunch sammies together, watching old "I Love Lucy" re-runs. And she had some news they ought to know. It was appropriate, too, that today down under was Guy Fawkes' Day, a day when New Zealanders traditionally blow things up. She spooled out the whole story, omitting Ditch – AI, Jack's baby – and despite her mum's initial reservations, she was thrilled.

"Don't jump the gun, mum. It's early days yet."

"Nonsense. You'll be right. But I'll wait till you tell me, to give Jack's family a buzz," her mum said. "They'll be happy as Larry with this news."

Rainey's dad had a less credulous reaction. All he said about her story was, "Hmmm."

CHAPTER 16

THEY FOUND HIM in the Hay-Adams hotel bar, obliter-
ated. Louisa, sensing he'd gone off the cliff, had called Ditch
to ask him and Hugo to mount a search.

"Oh, 'llo, boys," Joe D. said, draining his glass. "Sit down,
buy you strong drink."

"No thanks, Sir. Let's get you up to your bed."

"But I doan, doan," he said, "wanna go. Fucking DoD
idn't gonna put the brakes on this."

Ignoring his protests, Hugo got on one arm, Ditch on
the other, lifting him to his feet.

"Stop. Wait," he said. "I gotta figure some way to proteck
Jonny. Louisa'll never forgo me if I doan."

"Worry about that later, Sir," Ditch said as they guided
him toward the door.

"No, Jonny, a gud man, my best bud, years. And you
know, together we did do some gud for you fightin men."

"Yes Sir, you did," Hugo said. "But now you got to work
on yourself."

"How ezactly I do that, Hugo my man?"

"Begin by going to a meeting with me tomorrow morning."

"I can't 'morrow. I half lawyers then."

"Fuck the lawyers," Ditch said.

Joe D. stumbled along between them. "Yeah," he agreed. "Fuck all lawyers."

Upstairs, they got him onto the bed and pulled his shoes off.

"Doan take off my shocks," he said. "I doan wanna see my feets."

They rolled him on his side, so he wouldn't choke on his own vomit, and wedged him there with a pillow. As they left the room and turned out the light, he was muttering, "What'm I gonna tell her, what'm I gonna say?"

Hanging up after talking to her oldies, Rainey fixed herself a simple tea – a cuppa oolong along with two packs of Tim Tams and one of Pineapple Lumps – standard junk food in Godzone, and a meal tasty and easy to chunder back up. The Tim Tams, technically an Ossie snack, were two chocolate biscuits sandwiching chocolate mousse and coated with creamy milk chocolate. To eat them, she first bit the ends off the biscuits, then stuck one end into the cuppa, and sucked the tea up through the cookie until it was saturated. Only then did she pop the whole delish mess in her mouth.

This absorbing procedure almost took Rainey's mind off her mum's last words: "They'll be happy as Larry with this news." Jack's old and very Victorian parents were the only thing wrong with him. His father, Sir Grey George Gauge, was a senior judge on the New Zealand Court of Appeal, and his mother frequently mentioned her "descendancy" from a "barony back home." They'd given Jack a proper rark up when he dropped out of uni, then enlisted, and then ran off and wed "that horse-girl." The fact that he was happy doing something he loved, with someone he loved, made no matter.

"You won't believe them," he had told her. "They're some kind of throwbacks, and asexual, sure enough."

That sounded something weird, considering Jack being as sexual as he was.

"And they're your oldies?"

"I must've been switched at hospital," he said. "Only explanation I think of. It's like they're afraid to touch: the closest they get is sitting together in a golf cart. Some boys cry when they go off to boarding school – but if I did, it was for joy."

He looked over at her in his car. It was an old MG convertible, and the wind was blowing her curly blonde hair. They were driving to a meet-the-parents at "the Club," in what promised to be an unnerving encounter. Rainey didn't have many dresses, but she picked the most formal one she could: a colorful Indian embroidered pullover that fell to just above her knees. Worse were her shoes: off the rack open-toed sandals.

"You think this is nice enough?" She smoothed the dress fabric over her thighs. Never one of those girls always seeking to please, though not as big a rebel as Jack, truth was, she didn't suffer disapproval well. When she had a job, she liked to do her right.

About her question, Jack just laughed. "It'll never be nice enough. Disapproval is their default. I spilled ink on a carpet once when I was three, and they're still whinging about it."

And, of course, the dinner did not go well. Mother and Father – that's what Jack called them – had the long look of embarrassment pulling on their faces throughout. They finished as quickly as they could, even skipping their usual demitasse of decaffeinated at the end, in an effort to hurry them out and be seen by as few other cronies as possible.

On the drive back from Wellington to Auckland, Jack had proposed. She often wondered if he would have done, had they approved of her. Didn't matter, though: she and Jack were arse over tits in love.

And now, how would they react to the news that she was carrying Jack's child?

Thinking this, Rainey thought, for the first time, that she may have made a wrong turning, writing Ditch out of the pregnancy equation. But what were her choices really, still being in love with Jack, and pregnant either by him or by a onetime roll in the clover. The omission seemed such a small price to pay. And anyway, it was done and dusted: no turning back now. And she was certain Jack was the dad. Abso-certain. His swimmers were very motile.

To calm herself, she began the process of eating the second Tim Tam.

Louisa sat in her bedroom late in the morning in front of her laptop again, fingers above the keys, as usual not thinking about herself, but others. Her heart broke for Rainey, and for Ditch. She'd wrestled with this decision all night, but should she do it? No, probably not. This was definitely meddling. But she wouldn't email Ditch that he was possibly the father – that would be a breach of trust. Instead, she would just inform him that Rainey was "up the duff." Jack's baby, AI back in Auckland, arrived here pregnant. He deserved to learn at least that much. But if she knew Ditch, he would come to Rainey's aide. In another age, he would have been a knight.

"Dear Ditch," she typed, "I have some very happy news about a mutual friend. . . ."

When that was finished and sent, she opened a new window on her Firefox browser, and began to research laparoscopic hysterectomy, as well at the M. D. Anderson Cancer Center, where Eva Hoffsteader was sending her for tests, and the scheduling of the surgery.

She was still researching an hour later when her phone rang. The woman on the other end had a New Zealand accent, although less pronounced than Rainey's. She began talking immediately.

"Am I speaking to Mrs. Louisa Grand, employer of Rainey Gauge?"

"You are."

"I am Beryl Gauge, the girl's mother-in-law."

Louisa sat back in her desk chair with a smile. "Then you've heard the happy news?"

It took a moment for Beryl Gauge to respond. "Yes," she said slowly, "but I wanted to confirm it with you."

Without thinking she was meddling at all, Louise went on, letting the cat out of the bag.

CHAPTER 17

MEG DAY CLIMBED off the Mahindra tractor and headed to the house. She'd spent the morning spreading manure on the southwest paddock, so she sniffed herself as she went into the mud room and kicked her gummies off. Not too bad, she thought. She paused, hearing her husband's voice from the kitchen. He was talking on the phone, which she knew he hated doing.

"Uh yes, Beryl," Stormy was saying. "I, uh, yes, I do. But here, you talk to Meg."

He was already passing her the handset, covering the mouthpiece with his big hand. He whispered, "Take care, luv. She's on a tear."

With reluctance, Meg put the phone to her ear. She and Beryl weren't cut from the same cloth.

"You need to bring her to see reason," she was saying. "This cannot be her plan, truly."

"What plan is that, Beryl?"

"Oh, it's you now," Beryl said, "is it? Good. Your husband is impossible to talk to."

Meg smiled and winked at Stormy, who'd gone to lean against the farm sink. "Yes, he can be a wee bit taciturn. Now what plan?"

"Your daughter's. I talked to her employer, Louisa Grand, and she thought I would know about the pregnancy."

Meg groaned, she hoped not audibly, and leaned against the kitchen counter. Stormy came over, bending down to put his ear against the receiver, too.

"Do you know she plans to stay there, in Texas?"

"Na yeah, Beryl, I thought she might. She has a good job there, and mates. Anyroad, what else would you have her do?"

"Come home with our grandchild, of course."

"She might do," Meg said, "someday, to live on that farm on Bream Bay."

"What? Out in the bush? Why ever would she do that?"

"She's a farm girl at heart, Beryl."

"Yes, but alone, without financial support, with a child?"

"With her job, her Survivor's Grant, and her Surviving Spouse Pension, she'll be right."

"Nevertheless, it can't be allowed. We'll be happy to have her and our grandchild here with us, or near to us, and she wouldn't have to perform manual labor."

The Gauges lived in a large old colonial house in Wellington, and the only time Meg and Stormy had visited, Stormy sat in an antique chair, which splintered and collapsed under his weight. Storm was a big bloke, a towering man, and the chair was designed for the smaller people of the 1700s.

"Oh," Meg said, "that's generous, for sure, but we'll just have to wait and see what she decides. She's an independent girl with her own mind, and she's Scotch with money like us."

While Beryl rattled on in protest, Meg balanced the handset on her shoulder and set about helping Stormy make their lunch sammies: ham and cheese and dill pickle. Finally there came a pause long enough for Meg to say, "Na yeah, ta for your input, Beryl. G'day."

Later, when they sat down for sammies and coffee, Stormy looked at Meg with a shake of his big head and a smile.

"Our girl," he said, "does love to poke the brown snake."

Meg smiled, too, but she had to add, "Sometimes, luv, that's a mistake."

In yet another hotel room, this one not far from Reagan International, Long Beach, Ditch checked and read his email from Louisa. Rainey had arrived in Texas already pregnant by Jack? He thought back: she did seem to know a lot about AI. But how could she know for sure exactly when she became expectant? The insemination and their sexual escapade could hardly be far apart. Not that he wanted the responsibility, but it was a questionable state of affairs. He needed time to think this through. He paced the room.

Later, when Hugo returned from his AA meeting, they went out to eat at a Mexican restaurant. Over enchiladas, Ditch spilled the beans, including the doubts he had.

"I don't know how she can be so sure."

"Women," Hugo said, "know a lot of shit that we don't have a clue about. They have an extra brain down there, in their uteruses or ovaries or fallopian tubes."

It surprised Ditch a little that Hugo even knew the names of those organs. But, then again, it was only his short-term memory that was impaired. It made him curious about something, though. Hugo and Nan had been married over a dozen years.

"Did you two ever want kids?"

Hugo stirred his meal around and changed the subject. "Why the fuck does California put sour cream on enchiladas? Are they fucking nuts?"

But on the drive back to the hotel in their rental car, he addressed the question.

"We did want kids, both of us, real bad. And when she got pregnant, we were happy as clams for a couple of months, until she had a blighted ovum miscarriage."

"Sorry, bro. That sounds tough."

"Na yeah, she followed me into the bottle after that."

"But you quit."

"Somebody had to be on dry land, to pull the other one out. And it looks like she's started. Got a letter from her. Three weeks sober, and going to meetings. I've been writing her every day since."

"Why don't you just call or email or text."

"Nan likes letters. Likes the feel of the paper in her hands."

When they parked back at the hotel, Hugo got out and asked over the car roof, "What're you gonna do, about the pregnant-Rainey goat rodeo?"

"I'm going along with her story, for now. But when we get back home, I need to talk to someone smarter than me or you."

"Oh." Hugo nodded and knew who he meant. "Harold," he said.

Up in his hotel room that night, Ditch paced the floor thoughtfully, then sat down and wrote a letter on his laptop, most of which was true. Afterwards, he replied to Louisa's email.

"Louisa, I'm sending you this email with an attached letter for Rainey. I can't call or text her anymore: she has me blocked. If you could print it off and give it to her, she might actually read it. Thanks, and I'll see you home in a couple of days. I hope you're feeling better after the cedar fever or flu or whatever. Tu amigo, Ditch."

Then he added the attachment that read, "Dear Kiwi, I just heard the news, and I couldn't be happier for you, and for Jack. I don't know much about pregnancy, but I do know you'll be a bonza mum.

"About you and me, that night, I never would've, if I'd known you had a pea in the pod, or a bun in the oven, or whatever you would say. But I called my sister – she has three kids – and she says it's not harmful to have sex during pregnancy. For the fetus, I mean. As for her, she said she enjoyed it an awful lot.

"But I digress. You're always on my mind. And now you, with Jack's baby, I can't think about anything else. I'm so happy for you. Will you let me talk to you when I get home?

"Finally, I have to admit, you scare me, Kiwi. And I've been scared shitless a hell of a lot. But this is different. I don't want it to stop. And anything you need, I'll help."

Rainey found Ditch's letter in an envelope slipped under her barn apartment door. It was unaddressed, so she'd opened it and started reading before she knew what it was. Halfway through, she wandered into the kitchen and sat in her chair at the table. When she finished, she lay it down and put her face in her hands. She'd fretted that he'd ask more parentage questions, but no, he trusted her. Easier to get shunt of him, if he wasn't such a bloody staunch bloke. She tried to stop the inevitable, but still the tears fell through. They rattled down on the paper below, like rain falling on dry leaves.

In their apartment above their new yoga studio, Gully sat at one end of a leather sofa, her long legs intertwined with Jenna's at the other end, though they weren't looking at each other. They both had their heads bowed, studying the Fertility Friend app on their phones.

"What's yours say?" Gully asked.

"Ten days till peak. That puts it what, over Thanksgiving weekend? Good, because he has an at-home game then. The egg will get the full court press."

"He" was Winston, the University of Hawaii at Manoa assistant basketball coach, and he had everything Jenna wanted in a sperm donor: tall, handsome, muscular, intelligent, and not interested in a relationship. He was also, like Ditch, not the kind of man who would consent to jerk off into a cup. No, he liked sex far too much. He and Jenna had been a brief item, back in their undergraduate days, though he was mostly interested in doing it with two women at once. That's when Jenna discovered she preferred women to men, sort of.

"Don't act like you're looking forward to it," Gully said. "We're only doing this to have a family of our own."

"Of course, dumpling," Jenna said. "When's yours?"

"Sooner. I have to get there this week." She started to punch in the Travelocity number to check on reservations.

"Wait." Jenna crawled forward toward her on the sofa. "Let's do the nasty first."

"You're such a naughty girl," Gully said, taking Jenna's face lovingly in her hands.

"Yes," Jenna said, "I am."

Truth was, the thought of three days of sex with Winston was making her really hot.

CHAPTER 18

AFTER HUGO DROPPED him off after their afternoon AA meeting, Joe D. went up to his suite, opened the mini-bar, and stared into it. He hadn't yet said the words at a meeting – "Hello, I'm Joe D., and I'm an alcoholic" – because he didn't believe he was. After five days without a drink, sure, he'd had weird dreams, but he hadn't seen pink elephants, or felt delirium tremens, or anything. Hugo, however, said that was mostly bullshit.

"I had to get sober so I could throw a rope to Nan," he'd said. "She was in trouble, and you got to be there for the people you love. It's more important than life, or even drink."

Well, whatever, Joe D. thought, closing the mini-bar. He'd wait to get soused until after he called Louisa. He wouldn't tell her about his failure at the DoD. But he knew how to get her off the track.

"What's wrong with me?" he asked immediately.

"How much time do you have?" she replied.

He smiled for the first time that day. He'd been scowling continuously for eight straight hours, so it took his facial muscles a moment to adjust. He walked to look out the suite window.

"Last night," he said, "I dreamed I turned into a dung beetle."

She laughed. "Sometimes I don't think you can surprise me anymore, and then you do. So, you had a Kafka dream?"

"It was a horrible, very vivid nightmare. I woke up checking to see if I had six legs. And why, a *dung* beetle? I hate those damned bugs. They're always crawling around your riding arena."

"I know. But I delight in them," Louisa said.

"What? They stand on their hind legs rolling a ball of shit to their underground den."

Louisa laughed again. "And they always treat it as if it's such a treasure."

"They do!" Joe D. agreed. "But despite my feelings about them, I make a conscious effort never to step on any."

"Bad luck," Louisa said, "if you do."

"I know, but I still hate them," Joe D. said, "for their attitude."

"Their attitude? We are still talking about dung beetles, aren't we?"

"Yeah, they act like they're *so* important," Joe D. said. "Their work is *so* significant. I mean, it *is* a ball of shit."

Louisa paused, then said, "Now I think we're getting somewhere. You identify, on some level, with dung beetles?"

Joe D. sat quiet a moment, holding the phone to his ear.

"My lovely," he said, "sometimes talking to you is not a great comfort." But after a moment, he had to ask, "You think I'm a dung beetle?"

"What do you normally do all day at work?"

"Mostly meetings. Making money."

"Which means, rolling balls of shit to your underground den."

Joe D. Grand groaned as he turned from the window and went back to open the mini-bar. He picked out a little bottle of Harvey's Bristol Cream and wandered off to flop on the bed.

"I am a dung beetle," he said finally. "Thank you for telling me. What about you? How're you feeling? Have you gotten over the flu?"

"Joe D., brace yourself. I don't have the flu. I have cancer of the uterus."

The phone fell out of Joe D.'s hand. He scrambled around in the duvet to find it. When he did, he held it to his mouth, but his voice came out as a squeak.

"Cancer?"

"I'm talking to you from M. D. Anderson. They've been running tests on me all day."

"Oh, oh, oh," he said. "I'll get home as quick as I can."

"No," she said. "You have something else to do for me first. You have to take my place at a charity event."

"Oh, oh, oh," he said, or at least he tried to say it. The words got clogged in his throat.

"What's going on with Warbucks?" Ditch asked at the foot of the airstairs. Hugo stood beside him watching the old guy climbing up with shaky legs. "He looks scared shitless."

"Well, he's not drunk, so that's something," Hugo said. "But he and Jonny were talking real quiet in the back of the car. Then Jonny started hugging him."

Hugo preceded Ditch up the airstairs, checking messages on his phone. Ditch followed along, ragging him a little.

"Heard lately from your new friend Daphne?" He knew they'd been texting the last few days.

"Dude, I never even met her – but she's training me a dog. A Catahoula Leopard Hound."

Ditch laughed. "Outstanding! A Cajun dawg, just like you."

"His name's Pierre," Hugo said, "and he came from Baton Rouge. How long before we get home?"

Ditch filled him in: home late tonight, finally, after one stop this afternoon in Dallas for the Warrior Open Golf Tournament, hosted by George W. and Laura Bush. She and Louisa were old friends.

For the concluding ceremonies at the tournament, Joe D. sat at a table behind the dais, in Louisa's place beside Laura Bush. A sea of men and women wounded warriors and their families surrounded them. Most of them bore obvious damage from the wars: prosthetic limbs, wheelchairs, plates in their heads, and scars from deep burns on their skin. And yet they were here, with their loving families, either playing golf or watching, having a pretty good time. Laura kept getting up and going to talk to people, but Joe D. remained in his chair. When she came back from one outing, she sat down looking at him.

"What's going on with you, Joe D.? You'd normally be at the open bar."

"I know," Joe D. said, "but I'm just sitting here feeling. . . I don't know what. I mean, these people, they've given so much."

Laura Bush completed his thought. "And asked so little." She took another look at the jerk she'd known for many years. She'd never understood what Louisa saw in him. No one did.

"Are you okay? Do you need a bottle of water?"

"No, I'm fine, thanks, Laura," he said, looking out at the men and women, feeling something strange. Maybe it was empathy, or sympathy, or whatever it was called. Anyway, sober, whatever he felt for these people, it pierced him in a way he'd only ever felt for Louisa before.

He blinked, and Laura Bush noted that his eyes were glistening. Maybe, she thought, there was more to Joe D. than met the eye. Maybe, to quote "Bushy," she'd misunderestimated him.

When Joe D. finally got home, late, he stripped down to his boxer shorts in the darkened bedroom, and slid under the sheets with his beloved wife. He hugged her gently from behind.

"Joe D.?" She lifted her head.

He tried to say something that would make her smile. "Yes," he said, "it is I, your husband, the shady, besotted hypochondriac, always on the brink of death."

She smiled as she rolled onto her back and turned to see him better in the dim light.

"You're more than that," she said.

"Only you see it."

"No," she said, "you'd be surprised how many others do, too. But you sound different."

"I'm dry," he said. "Only a week. But I'm not going back. I'll be with you, fully, every day I can." After a pause, he quoted Hugo, his AA sponsor. "Because you got to be there for the people you love, and that's more important than life. Or even drink. My job is to throw you a rope, in a stormy sea."

She smiled again. He could see it in the dim light.

"Throw me a rope, in a stormy sea," she said. "Sober, you can be almost poetic. I'd forgotten that."

He gave her shoulder a gentle squeeze. "How do you feel? Do you hurt? Is there anything I can do? What happens next? I'm scared for you."

"I know you are, sweetheart. None of us knows what will happen next. Now, tell me about this investigation."

He put his nose to her shoulder and inhaled the smell of her skin. The forensic audit could take over a year, and the legal wrangling even longer than that, unless he did something his lawyers advised him not to do. But with his arm around his ailing wife who, against all odds, still thought the best of him, he knew what he had to do: throw himself on the grenade.

"I've decided," he said. "I'm gonna cop a plea. I'm going down solo on this federal rap. That's how we criminals talk, I think."

Hearing him use that slang, she smiled, in spite of what might lay ahead for both of them. She looked over at Joe D. in the dim light. She searched for the word that could sum up their state of affairs. "Crucible," she thought: a situation where concentrated forces interact to cause change.

"Then," she said, "we both have trials ahead."

But then she let out a little laugh.

"What?" he asked.

"Oh, it's just so strange, and so completely eccentric, like you: man has an epiphany, in his underpants."

He looked over at her in the dim light. She still had a smile of laughter on her lips. And, in spite of what lay ahead, he felt he'd never been so rich.

CHAPTER 19

DITCH WORKED UNDER the spotlights from the hangar, performing the post-flight check, but he kept glancing up the lane toward the barn and Rainey's apartment. The cottage closest to the hangar belonged to Harold, the butler. The November day had been warm, but the night was much cooler, so Harold was out in his vegetable patch hoeing around his collards and cabbage.

When Ditch finished and wheeled the helicopter back inside the hangar, he walked over. Harold saw him coming and stood up, leaning on his hoe. He was very black with white hair, and somewhere over eighty years old. He'd driven ammo trucks at the Battle of Chosin Reservoir.

Ditch began the conversation immediately, because they were friends.

"Harold, you're old, so that means you're wise, right?"

"Not," Harold said, "necessarily. But I am. You got a question, Marine?"

Ditch hesitated, embarrassed now. "No, it's probably too personal."

"I'm a Baptist deacon," Harold said. "I don't take confessions, but I do answer hypothetical questions."

"Okay," Ditch said, pausing to organize his thoughts. "Let's say there's a young man who falls for a girl, but has sex with her way too fast. She turns up pregnant but says it's not his. She was already pregnant, she says, by her dead husband, artificially. He goes along with her story, but he still has serious second thoughts and doubts."

Harold raised his chin, thought a moment, then picked up his hoe and resumed chopping up clods. Doing so, he glanced down the lane toward the barn. He chopped on, thoughtfully.

"That's okay, never mind." Ditch turned to leave.

"Stand down, Marine," Harold said. "I'm just deep thinking. You're wondering if this hypothetical young man should confront the girl about his suspicions?"

Ditch nodded.

"The answer to that is apparent. He can add to her troubles, or subtract. If he takes her at her word, he garners her trust. Truth will out, eventually, and whichever way it goes, he'll be standing tall on that rock of trust."

Ditch thought about that. "And if the young man voices his doubts?"

"That young man," Harold said, "is fucked."

Ditch laughed. "I knew you were a wise man," he said.

"Wait, boy, before you go: one more question. What does that young man remember most about that night?"

Ditch answered instantly, "Her smell. Or the smell of her ear."

Surprised by this, Harold laughed. "Then he is a strange young man," he said, but as Ditch walked away, he rubbed his chin, recalling the fragrance of his own wife's ear. They'd been married fifty-three years, and Pauline's smelled like tangerines. He put his hoe down and headed inside to see what she was doing.

Over his shoulder, Ditch called back, "Thanks, Harold, and Semper Fi."

"Semper Fi, Marine."

The parentage question on the back burner, at least for now, Ditch climbed into his solitary rack, turned out the lamp, and buried his nose in the pillow. It smelled the way it always did, when it needed washing; it smelled like him. But he remembered that other smell, from that night in the Lausanne hotel, the *odeur* of Rainey's ear. Somehow as they'd made love, he ended up there, inhaling her deep, rich, inner fragrance. But what was that fragrance exactly? He rolled over onto his back and thought. Avocado. . . mixed with salty macadamia nuts? That was Rainey's personal inner odor. Or was it?

He got out of bed, went to the kitchen table, cut an avocado in half and sprinkled some macadamia nuts on it. He lowered his nose to the table and inhaled. It was nearly her. He slowly drew in another breath, then became self-conscious and sat up and looked around. If anyone had seen him through the window, they'd think he was crazy. And he probably was, because of her.

Admittedly, he had a limited idea of the depth of Rainey's grief – an abyss, a bottomless chasm, he guessed. But he did have an inkling of it. After all, he'd spent a third of his life in the wars, and had lost close friends. There's guilt and grief attached to that, surviving when brothers had not. And even though they were dead, they were still kicking around in his head. As for Jack, Rainey's true love, KIA, how much more piercing for her must that be?

The fucking war: like any soldier, Ditch hated it. He hated the deprivation, the danger, the destruction, the death and dismemberment of friends, so far from home – and nobody bitched about louder it than him. But he also knew that, given the choice, he wouldn't want to be in any other place. In the thick of it, he had a purpose, as a part of something big, fighting for what he believed, being needed. In fact, when he wasn't there, he sometimes wished he was.

They, the wars, had driven a wedge between him and Gully, perhaps as much as her sexual needs. She thought he never really came home. But that wasn't true. Okay, okay, maybe it was, sort of. At home, he'd felt restless all the time, irritable, without a mission. What was he supposed to do, just sit around indulging himself? But then his dad's Alzheimer's had impelled him to transfer to the Active Reserves and take this job. And here, he met people he came to care about, or maybe even love. A window of opportunity seemed to be opening up in his life.

Rainey Gauge: the way she'd looked at him with those gray eyes, the way she watched him doing things in the cockpit, the way she laughed at what he said, the way she called him out on his bullshit – not to mention her frank, plucky, indomitable spirit, and her salty, sorrow-filled soul – he fed off all that. And her pregnancy made it all the more poignant. It made him feel he could be important here. It made him forget the wars.

Later, at the kitchen table, he pulled up Word on his laptop, and wrote and printed the formal letter resigning his commission. He put it in an envelope, but decided not to mail it right away. Why send it, he thought, if Rainey wouldn't even talk to him now? But sitting at the table, eating avocado and macadamia nuts and drinking a Shiner Bock, he began to devise a strategy. Naturally, he thought about it like a military man: Ends, Ways, and Means.

The Objective was to get her talking to him. The Way was to make her laugh again. And the Means, well, that would take some thinking. Around 0300, he came up with a plan.

"He's been back for days, and you say you don't want to see him," Daphne said, "but you're always making me look for him up the lane."

"That's so I can dodge him. Go on now, mate, take a squiz out the barn door."

Daphne was helping Rainey muck out the stalls, and they actually made a pretty good team, Rainey with a munted left leg, and Daphne with a bionic right foot. As a mate, Daphne was honest, blunt, and adept at detecting bullshit. She came back from the barn door with a smile.

"What is it?" Rainey said.

"Something you need to see for yourself." Daphne passed Rainey the manure fork and exited out the rear, saying, "You're right, though. He's one strange man."

With reluctant curiosity, Rainey went to the barn door. And there was Ditch, coming toward her down the lane – and the sight did make her laugh. He was riding on a massive, very placid cow, its head bobbing and ears flopping lazily in the rising morning heat.

"I thought you might finally talk to me," he explained, "if I rode up astride a handsome steed."

Smiling despite herself, Rainey leaned on the manure fork at the barn door, and limped down the incline to the lane. Fact matter, it was hard to pack a sad, when he was looking at her with those bloody green-brown eyes. And though she would never admit it, she felt chuffed to see him again, which she covered by saying something cross.

"Only a very, *very* strange bloke," she said, "would break a cow to ride."

"You don't know cattle, do you? Technically, Rowdy's a steer."

Ditch pulled his mount to a halt in front of her. He rode bareback with a war bridle, a loop of leather around the steer's lower jaw. He slid off and came around to where Rainey was petting Rowdy's face and studying his eye. The steer had a kind, pampered look about him. And at the sight of Ditch within range, Rowdy swung his head and licked him on the face. Ditch grinned, wiping off with a sleeve.

"He's an affectionate old fellow. And we have a long friendship," he said.

Rainey continued to study Rowdy's eye. There was a softness in it when he looked at Ditch. He loved the fella, in the way only a cow can love a man. Ditch scratched under his chin.

"He was my FFA project, but when it came time for the Stock Show, I couldn't sell him. I mean, they were going to murder him and eat his flesh, for God's sake. That was the end of my career as a rancher."

Rainey rolled her eyes. "Yes, it would be. I say again. . . ."

"I know, I know." Ditch ran his hand lovingly down the wrinkly skin of Rowdy's neck. "But you got to go with the feelings you have. Which brings me to the subject of you."

Rainey tucked her chin down, an odd gesture, like she was trying to cork something in. Ditch considered her. Her roots were definitely growing out, maybe a half inch now.

"Look, I'm not trying to jump start anything. And I really am happy, for you, and for Jack. But I miss my copilot, my mate," he said. "You're under my skin."

"Like a splinter," she said.

Ditch ignored that and pressed on. This was his chance.

"And," he said, "besides the chemistry between us, there's something more: feelings I'd forgotten how to have."

"Give 'em time; they'll go away."

"I don't think so. I don't roll that way. And neither, I think, do you."

Rainey tucked her chin down even further. It didn't completely work. Truth was, ever since she'd heard the helicopter landing the other night, she felt as scratchy as a teenager again.

Hormones, no doubt, and abso-no room in her heart for any but Jack. Abso-none. Still, she did feel an undeniable pull, a draw, an undertow. The heart was a wobbly organ at best. She raised her chin and tugged on Rowdy's forelock. She actually did know something about cattle. He was a Santa Gertrudis, liver colored, good with the heat. They'd been imported to Australia and New Zealand a few years back.

"What're you gonna do with him now?"

"I was hoping to keep him somewhere here. If I leave him at the ranch, my sister will eat him."

"That'll never do, mate. Come with me. We'll get him sorted in the far paddock."

Ditch led Rowdy and followed along. Did he squiz Rainey's bum in the moleskin jeans, or the outline of her brassiere under Jack's old rugby jersey? Hell, yes, he did. After all, he was a man. But from now on, strictly platonic. His mission was to look after this woman and her child.

Rainey said over her shoulder, "And it's fine with me, if you pop 'round time to time for a yack. But only as a celibo-mate, understand?"

"Too right. Mean as. Bonza," Ditch said, touching the envelope in his shirt pocket, the formal letter of resignation. He would definitely mail it now.

As she walked on, Rainey shook her head and smiled. Ditch was a numpty with Kiwi slang. But she'd teach him, if he could be taught. She owed him that much, and she did like his company something fine. Something fine, and no pickle in that, was there?

CHAPTER 20

"YOU SEE," DAN Grand explained to the attendant on the flight to Santiago, "the belowground world of Antarctica is really the empire of the wingless midge *Belgica antarctica*. But what's of utmost interest is that this midge has taken the genome down to the bare bones."

"Oh," the attendant, Isabella, said, looking into his dark brown eyes. She'd never seen lashes that long before. She'd sat down next to him, claiming there might be turbulence ahead, but really the turbulence was in her chest, which swelled in repeated heaves.

"Down to the bare bones," she repeated, as if they were the most beautiful words ever spoken.

He went on, demonstrating with his hands.

"The subsoil is an extraordinarily complex ecosystem, interlocking, each element dependent of the others. In a recent paper, I likened it to a geodesic dome."

"Interlocking," she said. "A dome." He had, she thought, the handsomest, sweetest face she'd ever seen, combining masculinity (the abundant blonde beard, the strong chin) with a sensitivity (those huge, luminous brown eyes). And his hands, his fingers, not to mention his thighs. . . . She'd seen Michelangelo's David in Florence, and it hadn't affected her this way.

"I wonder," he asked, "could you get me another club soda?"

"I'm not married," she answered. "And I love bugs."

"Oh," he said. "Yes. . . well. . . the club soda?"

"Club," she said, "soda." To her, the words were poetry. She stood up and drifted off toward the galley. A couple of other passengers were madly signaling her with raised hands, but she didn't see them.

Dan rested his head back on the seat cushion, thinking, Oh, damn, I'm headed back into the world again. He'd seen this dazed look before, many times. It was so distracting. In fact, as an associate professor at Princeton he'd had a raft of woozy female graduate assistants following him everywhere – his colleagues called him The Pied Piper of Coeds – and those assistants were of no assistance whatsoever. Hence, his prolonged sabbatical in Antarctica. At the bottom of the world, there were very few women, and those few tended to be serious, and they had to wear very heavy clothes. He'd finally been able to get good work done.

But. . . but now he'd been summoned back to the world. Up here, he would keep his protective beard, which might have a deleterious effect on the opposite sex. And perhaps he would wear sunglasses, too.

When he sensed the flight attendant returning, he rolled his head toward the window and feigned sleep. Still, she sat down beside him. Even with his eyes closed, he could feel her adoring stare. I hate the world, he thought. It was so fucking distracting.

Jonny was intrigued by the change in his friend, so he'd observed him carefully over the past few days. Despite Joe

D.'s impending indictment in Houston, and the plea bargain he was trying to negotiate, he'd stayed off the sauce, entirely preoccupied with Louisa's surgery ahead, intent on researching a cure.

And Jonny caught him that afternoon in the library. This was the vast room with bookshelves that reached up to the twelve-foot ceiling, complete with rolling ladders, and deep, leather reading chairs in the center. Joe D. typically only used the room as a place to take afternoon naps, among the thousand, silent books he never cracked. Today, however, Joe D. was perched on a ladder with an open book in his hands, his half reading glasses on his nose.

"What the hell are you doing up there?"

Joe D. startled and nearly fell off his perch. Clinging tightly, he climbed down.

"Nothing," he said. "Only lately I've gotten curious about Sigmund Freud, and bugs."

Jonny looked at him with his mouth open, so Joe D. explained.

"Did you know that one of Freud's earliest books explored the meaning and uses of humor?"

"You don't say."

"Yeah, but Freud's horrible to read. What I got from him is, it's good to laugh. You get around the ego. But this book, by Norman Cousins, is easier. You know, he laughed his way out of a fatal illness. They gave him five months, but he lived almost another thirty years. Anyway, I'm gonna make Louisa laugh a lot more now, and I'm gonna do it, too."

To demonstrate, he said, "Ha. Ha. Ha. Ha." He stopped a moment, then started again.

"Ha, ha, ha, ha! Ha, ha, ha, ha! Ha, ha, ha, ha! Ha, ha, ha, ha!"

At the end, he was laughing involuntarily, and so was Jonny, contagiously. They laughed for several minutes, occasionally pausing to smack each other on the back. Finally, they collapsed into two side by side leather chairs, out of breath and wiping their eyes. And then they started laughing again.

It began when Jonny said, "Bugs?"

"Yes! Dung beetles! Ha, ha, ha, ha! Ha, ha, ha, ha! Ha, ha, ha, ha!"

Hortensia heard the commotion as she passed down the hall to the west wing, and looked in. The rich men were apparently going insane. Nevertheless, as she moved on, she found herself laughing a bit.

"Ha, ha, ha, ha!"

Rainey Gauge stepped out of the shower, where she'd been hurling her dinner, then stomping the large bits down the drain. At the sink she brushed her teeth for the umpteenth time that day. She worried about the effect of stomach acid on tooth enamel. To be fat and puffy faced was bad enough; she didn't want to be toothless, too.

Drying herself off, she wiped the misted mirror and examined her naked body. Oh, Crickey, she thought. Scarce more than a month in, and her shape had already begun to chunk up. Her knobbies, formerly small and perky, were larger, as was her lower belly. She sucked, but it would not suck in. She was morphing into someone she didn't recognize. Still, she smiled, somehow pleased. The tide was taking her, and she'd go where it went.

In her bedroom she put on a fresh set of her normal barn clothes, but she didn't button the moleskin jeans at the top. Too much pressure. Then she pulled on a chambray shirt, tail out, and went out the door down to the barn. Evening feeding time.

As she hauled buckets to the stalls, she listened for the sound of the helicopter returning from Austin. But instead she heard someone, a woman, outside in the lane calling, "Ditch? Ditch?"

She went to the barn door to see who it was.

CHAPTER 21

"HARRY, IT'S GREAT to see you," Dan said in the entry hall.

"Masser Dan," Harold said with a grin.

"Cut that shit out, Harry," Dan said, hugging him. "How's Pauline?"

"Doing pretty good, but she'll be better when she sees you. Boy, I believe you could steal my wife. You got something with women."

"It's a curse."

"Maybe, but if you could bottle it, you'd be richer than your dad. Here, let me get your bag."

"The hell I will, Harry. You're eighty something."

"Dan!" His mother's voice rang out in the foyer, almost echoing. She hurried down the bending staircase, her hand on the rail.

Dan beamed, seeing his mother, even though she didn't look well. They hugged, and Harry melted away with Dan's bag. Then Joe D.'s voice echoed down from above.

"Oh, Danny-boy, the pipes called, and now you're home! Ha, ha, ha, ha!"

Dan looked at his mother.

"He's gotten even nuttier. He's treating me with laughter therapy. Come into the sitting room and I'll explain."

"Wait!" his dad shouted, hurrying down. "I want to ask you about dung beetles, the *Scarabaeinae*."

"He's also been studying bugs," Louisa said. "He's being indicted on criminal charges, so he's passed control of the corporation to Donker, with orders to sell it off, piece by piece. From now on, he's dedicating his life to us."

"God have mercy!" Dan said.

She smiled and patted his arm as they went into the sitting room. There she would tell him about the cancer, and the hysterectomy, too.

Joe D. caught up and followed them in, saying, "I'm fascinated by their life cycles. Ha, ha, ha, ha!"

Earlier that evening, Ditch had flown to Austin to pick up the son Dan, who climbed in the back and didn't talk, didn't even put on a headset. He seemed pretty depressed about coming home. Ditch dropped him at the ranch pad, then spent an hour post-flighting the bird, before he could beat feet to Rainey's door, to yack a bit. Lately, they spent all their free time together. But when the door opened. . . .

"Gully, what are you doing here?"

"It's wonderful to see you, too," she said. "I came for a little post-connubial visit. And I was wandering around, looking for you, when your friend Rainey took me in."

Ditch saw Rainey over Gully's shoulder. She did not look at him. She concentrated on pouring steaming water from a kettle into a teapot.

"So," he said, "you and Rainey met."

"Yes, sweetie." Gully gave him a kiss, aimed at his lips, but he turned in time to take it on the cheek. "She's been telling me all about getting pregnant, via in utero AI."

"Oh, really?" Ditch said, trying to sidestep Gully. She grabbed him by the arm and forced him to look at her while she looked at him.

"No visible bullet holes, yet, but not for a lack of trying," she said. "So how long you staying this time, before you cut and run, and get yourself deployed again?"

"No chance of that," he said, glancing at Rainey, who was definitely earwigging them. He changed the subject quickly back to Gully. "And you, you've become. . . even more you."

"Yes. It's all really happening for Jenna and me. Our careers have taken off. We have our Ashtanga classes on DVD, and we're on the internet now, with a half million followers online. And since we went on *Ellen*, people recognize us, like we're stars."

"You're a telly celeb then?" Rainey asked. This Gully looked the part. Dressed in a tight purple tank top and cream-colored yoga pants, she was tall and slender, with legs, cheekbones and breasts.

"No, no," Gully laughed about being a celeb. "Okay, sort of, as much as a yogi can be."

Compared to this Gully, Rainey felt extremely small and mousey. But apparently Ditch didn't think so. He sidestepped Gully again and came to her side.

"I'm making a cuppa," she said. "Want one?"

"Na yeah, I could murder a cuppa," he said.

She smiled, and they shared a glance. Gully noted it and came over, inserting herself between.

"Ditch, come with me," she said, "and show me where I'll be spending the night. Also, I rented a Prius in Austin, and don't know how to plug it in. Oh, and there's my box of organic produce from Whole Foods. What do you smell like?" she asked, dragging him out.

"My usual fragrance after flying a helicopter," Ditch said, "sweat and hydraulic fluid."

He managed to wrench himself away long enough to call back to Rainey, "We still on for the bonfire tonight?"

"Sweet as," Rainey said.

"Chur," Ditch replied, as Gully levered him down the barn apartment steps.

Out in the lane, he shook her off. "What's really going on, with this sudden visit and the charm offensive?"

As they walked, Gully thought she might as well be direct. That's the way Ditch operated.

"I'm ovulating," she said. "And since you won't do it AI like a civilized man, we have to do it manually, two or three times tonight."

"So much for the charm offensive," Ditch said. "Now you're just being offensive. And," he added, "I'm not screwing you."

"If you don't, then I'm screwed in another way," she said. She shook him by the arm, pleading. "Oh, come *on*, for old time's sake. I want a family; I need a family, to hold Jenna and me together. We're starting to drift apart."

Ditch stopped and looked at her. All her pretenses were gone. She was the old, nutty uninhibited Gully, the one he'd loved. And still did, sort of. He would have told her that a baby can't bind people together, but given Rainey, her baby, and Jack – not to mention the way he felt about Rainey and the baby – he wasn't certain about that. He was almost convinced now he wasn't the father, though the baby did seem to be holding them all together. So what could he say to comfort Gully?

"I feel you," he said, putting his arm around her as they walked. "Even though I'm not screwing you. But you're pretty resourceful, and I'm sure you'll figure something out. Don't they have, like, catalogs, at the sperm bank?"

"Sure, *if* you believe them. With my luck, I'd end up impregnated by a short, fat congenital liar grad student with schizophrenia in the family. No, I need a known quantity."

"Well, my tadpoles are staying home tonight. Sorry, babe."
She sniffed back tears, and something else. "You *do* smell
like hydraulic fluid," she said.

Louisa was folding clothes for the trip early tomorrow to
Houston and M. D. Anderson, for surgery in the afternoon.
Hortensia helped her pack the bag. When Louisa finished,
she sat down exhausted on the bed. Hortensia looked at her.
Louisa had something to say.

"Sometimes, Ten," she sighed at length, "I give in to fear."

Hortensia came over and sat down beside her, reaching
over to put her arm around Louisa.

"Of course you do. But you're putting up a very good
pretense, and it's fooling everyone. When you're out of the
room, they all talk about how amazingly strong you are."

"Fake it till you make it," Louisa said. "I think it was
Aristotle who said to be virtuous, you must act as a virtuous
person would act. I'm role playing, but sometimes the mask
doesn't fit."

Hortensia squeezed her shoulder. "Won't you let me come
with you?"

"No," Louisa said, then added, looking her in the eye.
"You know, you are a good friend, and you've been through
a difficult operation yourself. But when I get back I'll have
a personal nurse, that young man Sam from the Home. And
while Ditch is flying the family to Houston tomorrow morning, I need you and Harold here, to arrange the Thanksgiving
dinner Joe D. has planned."

"Speaking of your husband," Hortensia said.

"I know. I'm astonished, too," Louisa said, with a wan
smile, remembering a quote from *Othello*: "How poor are
they who have not patience! What wound did ever heal but
by degrees?" The words offered hope for her and the surgery,

and for Joe D. and his sobriety, and even for Rainey and Ditch. Who knew what would happen next?

This reminded her of a quote from Ditch's dad: "In combat and in life, whatever you think is gonna happen, you're probably wrong."

CHAPTER 22

ON THE WAY back down the lane to the bonfire, with Gully solidly attaching herself to his arm, Ditch caught sight of traffic merging from the right in the dark, a male figure walking toward the fire saying, "Ha, ha, ha, ha!" Ditch knew who it was.

"Hey, Dan. It's Ditch. I'm the guy who flew you home. What are you doing?

Dan tilted a beer bottle up and took a drink. "Oh, nothing. I'm just saying, Ha, ha, ha, ha! It's something my crazy father started, and now they're all doing it, all over the house. The whole place has gone mad. But my mom told me about you. You got the DFC."

"Yeah, well," Ditch said as they approached the fire. "Oh, this is Gully, my ex-wife. This is Dan, Dr. Grand, professor of something at Princeton. He's been in Antarctica for years."

Gully had dropped Ditch's arm, and was now staring at Dan. He was an Adonis. And a PhD. She didn't know what to say, but she was ovulating, so she said, "Ha, ha, ha, ha!"

He laughed. "Ha, ha, ha, ha!"

Then they both started laughing, for real – and Ditched backed away, chuckling a little himself. Contagious laughter, it really was a gift. Once he was away, he looked for Rainey among the staff seated on hay bales around the blazing fire. She was there, sitting next to Hugo, Daphne, and a dog. When their eyes met, they both smiled. He sat down next to her.

"Hiya, gray-eyes. It looks like I scraped Gully off of my shoe."

On the far side of the roaring fire, Gully and Dan had occupied a bale, and Gully was gesticulating, in a way that emphasized her breasts. Dan had taken his sunglasses off, at least for tonight. After all, he was a little drunk, and he had been a celibate for over two years.

"Ha, ha, ha, ha!"

"Gully, she's very," Rainey said, "beautiful. You didn't mention that."

Ditch smiled, reached over, and squeezed Rainey's hand. It was amazingly muscular.

"You kick her ass," he said. "Anyway, it looks like I need a place to bunk tonight. How's your spare room?"

Rainey smiled, and felt as fine as feathers. A box of birds.

"Wide open," she said. "But no hanky panky."

"How about just a bit of panky?"

She smiled and shook her head. "What," she said, "is a DFC?"

Ditch changed the subject quickly. "New Zealand girls, according to Google, are the most promiscuous women on earth: an average of twenty-two lovers."

"Crickey," she said, "I better amp up me game." She stared at the fire for a moment, watching the hypnotic licking flames. But she was thinking about Ditch and what Gully had said.

"If you're in the Active Reserves, does that mean you'll have to go back again?" She looked up so she could squiz his face.

"No, I'm getting out. I resigned my commission in a formal letter," Ditch said.

She studied his face a long moment, then nodded. "Good on you."

On the next bale over, Hugo listened in and slowly shook his head. The resignation letter might or might not get Ditch out. The needs of the service always trumped the needs of the soldier, so Ditch was lying by omission again. Understandable, though, because Rainey had taken him in as a "celibo-mate." Never-the-fucking-less. . . . Hugo reached down to pet his dog.

"Bro, is that Pierre?" Ditch asked.

"Yeah, ain't he fine?"

Hugo looked lovingly down at his Pierre, who was looking lovingly up at his Hugo. Beyond them, Daphne was smiling at both of them. Her face didn't look so hard anymore. Doing something good for someone was doing something good for her, as, no doubt, was Louisa's plan. And everybody already loved Daphne, and the way she didn't cover up her bionic foot. Fuck it, that's the way it was: they all had their battle scars.

"We're all gonna hike by the river tomorrow," Hugo said. "Figure it'll take our minds off of Louisa in Houston. You can't come?"

"No, got to fly early to Houston for Louisa's surgery. But take Rainey with you. She needs a good, long tramp."

"No worries," Hugo said. "We asked her long before you, and I only did that to be polite."

"Nice to know where I stand," Ditch said, squeezing Rainey's hand again. "Make sure you ask the new guy Sam to go. He took good care of my dad."

"Wilco."

Rainey looked at the faces around her in the firelight. Probably because she was chocka with hormones, she felt almost euphoric tonight. She might be a widow, with child, in a foreign land, but she was not alone. She was not alone.

DFC: Distinguished Flying Cross, awarded for heroism or extraordinary achievement while participating in aerial flight.

It was a simple, single bird over-watch sortie, making sure they were safe on the road below, when the IED blew the first Humvee into the ditch. Then small arms fire poured in from the hills on both sides, pinning the platoon down. Radio chatter erupted. Ditch, in the front seat, the H2P (Helicopter Second Pilot), managed the weapon systems, the Hydra rockets and 20 mike-mike Gatling cannon. In the backseat, then-Major Glub, did the flying. In short order they cleared the hillsides, but on the ground one Marine had been hit the worst. In shock, he was bleeding out through severed legs. Medical help was an hour away. He would die in Afghanistan.

"Land it," Ditch said, and at the steely sound of his voice, the Major did.

Ditch popped the canopy and leaped out. He carried the wounded Marine back and put him in the front seat. Tourniquets had been applied to his legs.

Ditch hooked his helmet back up to the cord and told the Major, "Take off. Get him back to Bastion. I'll hang onto the skids."

And the Major did. He followed the Lieutenant's orders, and saved the life of the Marine. But he didn't take the commendation. He wrote Ditch up for the DFC. If anybody ever deserved it, Ditch sure as hell did, dangling from the skids at sixty knots above hostile territory. However, Ditch didn't see it that way. He'd never been so terrified in his life. Shit-scared beyond belief, so much so that he may have pissed himself. Someone had snapped an iPhone photo of him back on the flight line, hanging for dear life to the skids, and eventually, the picture got onto the Internet. It was supposed to be inspirational, but when Ditch looked at it, he only noticed his tan flight suit soaked dark around the crotch. So much for "heroism while participating in aerial flight."

Jack's war photo, enlarged, hung on Rainey's bedroom wall beside the door. Wearing helmet and BDUs, his Steyr slung over his shoulder, barrel down, he grinned gap-toothed at the camera and held up two fingers, not in the victory sign, but the reverse, palm toward him, in a gesture that meant "up your bung." Rainey loved that snap: it showed Jack's true brave and stroppy heart.

But it was shocking, the pain she still felt. Daphne had explained it medically: phantom pain, felt by amputees in the part of them that had been removed. Your mind simply refused to acknowledge the loss of a limb. Often, standing beside Jack's snap, a stab of phantom pain rose up from her chest to her throat, and the tears literally squirted from her eyes, some of them landing on the picture frame.

Half-awake pre-dawn, Rainey heard Ditch up already, shaving in the dunny. After he finished, she waited another minute or two before she hurried in for her morning wee. Sitting there, she sniffed the air. Amazing how acute her sense of smell was these days. The dunny definitely smelled of a man, and at the scent, something softened within her, or some hormone was released in her blood. . . anyroad, she felt amazingly at peace, despite not having a bowel movement in nearly a week.

When she came out, she checked the spare bedroom, noting that the bed was tightly made, then heard Ditch through the kitchen door. Fixing her brekkie, he was barefooted, in jeans without a shirt. He turned and smiled to see her as she sat down in front of her plate.

"Blueberries, prunes, and Bulgarian yogurt, topped with macadamia nuts. Impaction should not be taken lightly."

"Na yeah. I tried those suppositories you got me," she said, "but I don't like the way they taste."

Ditch laughed, called her a hard case, and looked at his watch. "Shit, I better rattle my dags, or I'll be late. Before I go, though, how 'bout one little snog in your ear, for luck."

She shook her head and covered her ears with her hands. He shrugged and hurried off, grabbing his shirt and stuffing on his shoes. Her eyes softened, watching him. He was a very, very strange bloke.

But more than a little wonky, too. In the middle of last night, he'd woken her up with a shout, or a cry.

She got up and went to the door of her room. He came out of the spare, rubbing his face.

"Sorry," he said, sitting down on the arm of the couch, struggling for breath. "Didn't mean to scare you. Sometimes I wake up back in the war, and I can't get there in time to, to. . . ."

At the end of this sentence, his voice drifted off, but in her gut, she knew what he meant.

"To save them, you mean. You think," she said, "Jack felt like that?"

"No doubt. But every minute of it," he said, "he still had you. I can't tell you how that must've felt."

She stepped back and over to Jack's photograph. It was dark, but she knew it intimately. The tears flooded out.

"I can't," she said, or coughed, "live without him."

Ditch came immediately to her side, and put his arm around her. "I know," he said. "But you're just gonna fucking have to. You have his baby to think of now."

She wept against his shoulder for a while, until the shuddering stopped, and then he guided her back to bed, settled her and tucked her in. Then he bent down and kissed her, in the middle of her forehead, just the way Jack with his last kiss had done.

And alone at brekkie that morning, the sour taste of yogurt and the sweetness of blueberries on her tongue, she marveled over the similarity of those kisses, both on the spot that the Buddhists call "the third eye," the eye of the soul within. It flashed across her mind briefly, like a quark, that Jack might have sent her this strange Yank. Could that be true?

No, abso-not. She had a handle on her emotions. She loved Jack. He was the deepest reaching, most nourishing root of her tree. He held her fast in place. That's the way it was, and always would be. And Ditch? She didn't love him, not exactly, not even close to her bindings with Jack, though she did feel roused with him. But he would always be an aside, a mate who made you feel alright. She told herself this was true, abso-true.

CHAPTER 23

"ISN'T CHANTEL A surprise and a delight?" Louisa asked.

"She's unbelievable," Joe D. agreed. "They all are. Where do we get such fine people?"

He stood beside Louisa's rolling bed, or gurney, or whatever they're called, holding onto her left hand, the one without the needles and tubes in it, worried out of his skull, but trying not to show it.

"She found your vein, first shot. Oh, hi, Chantel," he said when she pulled the curtain and came back in. "We were just talking about what a wonderful, cheerful person you are."

Chantel smiled. Her teeth were very white against her plump black face. She now wore her blue surgery cap.

"Well, you two are just the loveliest couple ever, so nice."

"No," Joe D. said. "She's nice. I've been an asshole my whole life. But I'm improving, toward the end."

"That's the way to do it," Chantel laughed, then looked at Louisa. "You ready? You're gonna be the star of the show."

Louisa smiled, dreamily. "Yes, they'll all be dancing around me."

"As they should." Joe D. patted her hand. "I'll be in the waiting room with Dan and Moira and the Gypsy family."

133

"Yes, the Romani," Chantel said, starting to roll the bed. "They're Vlax clan, I think, very big in Houston. Survivors of the Nazi death camps in Poland. The matriarch is having a radical mastectomy."

"Oh, oh, oh," Joe D. said, visibly shaken as he followed. "No wonder that poor guy's so beside himself. He's completely unhinged. I better go talk to him."

Louisa watched Joe D. as she rolled away. Unbelievable, she thought. She should have come down with cancer twenty years ago. She waved at him, and then at all the staff in pre-op, and they waved back, calling out encouragements. In the matter of an hour, she'd charmed them all, but none loved her to the degree of Joe D. His heart tried to leap out and follow her, as she blew him a kiss, and rolled through the double doors.

Joe D. called after her, "You look like the Queen, on the float in the County Fair parade."

The double doors hissed shut. Joe D. turned and stepped back into the curtained cubicle, his eyes clenched, head bowed, hands together as if in prayer. He tried to think of the words to say, but then he thought, fuck the words. God, if He exists, already knew what his heart was pleading. No atheists in the foxhole, he thought, or in the Cancer Center either.

Down the hall, in the brightly lit operating theater, Louisa was introduced to what seemed the very large team who'd be opening her up soon, laparoscopically. Just snip, snip, and pull the uterus out of her vagina. No problem: they'd all done it before. But for the first-time participant, the equipment and the tables stacked with shiny instruments – all of them rolled up around her now – seemed incalculably mysterious, and somewhat ominous, until the drip began. Chantel bent down quickly and said, "Good night."

"When I wake up," Louisa slurred, "I wanna see your fa. . . ."

Before she fell off the precipice, she thought, if God has a face, it resembles Chantel's.

"Ditch," Dan said in the snack bar, "you're still here?"

"Yeah, I'm waiting to get the news before I fly back. Everybody's gonna want to know. Sit down. Take a load off."

Dan didn't particularly want to sit down, but he didn't want to go back to the waiting room either. It was filled with very emotional Gypsies, or Romani's, and his dad was hugging an old man, telling him it would be okay.

Also, Dan didn't want to sit down with Ditch in particular, because last night the guy's ex-wife had fucked him silly. He didn't normally act like that. He was a man of science, a science-monk, reasonably content in celibacy. But that Gully had blitzed him in a weak moment, as travel-dazed and worried about his mom as he was. Still, he probably ought to explain, and he also had a few questions for Ditch.

"Ahhh," he said, pulling out a chair, "about last night, I probably. . . ."

Ditch just laughed. "No worries, mate. You look like you've been rode hard and put up wet. Are you okay?"

Dan sat back in his plastic chair, and ran a hand through his hair.

"If you don't mind me saying, your ex-, she's a little extreme."

"A little?"

"Yeah, like. . . and I hope this doesn't offend you. . . ."

Ditch raised his hands: Go on.

"She should come with a User's Manual. Is she always so full of instructions? 'Down a little. Over to the right. Three short and one long.'"

Ditch laughed so violently, one of his ribs may have cracked.

135

"What's so funny?" Dan asked, a little offended himself.

"Believe me," Ditch said, "it's funnier from the outside. 'Three shorts and one long.' Boy, did I hear that a lot."

He went back to laughing, and Dan joined in.

"And why, after each time, did she do a shoulder stand? Was she trying to get pregnant, or what?"

"Bro, you do *not* want to know."

"Well, she's going to be disappointed. A low sperm count is hereditary. Oh, look, there's Moira."

Moira had spotted them across the room and came over, smiling at her brother.

"She's in Recovery. Daddy's with her. Let's join them."

"And. . ?" Dan stood up, tense. "How'd it go?"

"She's okay. They got it out. Stage One, they think, and it appears contained."

Dan sagged, relieved, and Moira hugged him. Ditch stood by.

"I'll carry the news back to the Gland Manse," he said. They both looked at him for an explanation. "Sorry, that's what the staff calls the Grand Manse."

"We," Moira put a finger on her brother's chest, "will not tell that to Daddy."

Then, after a moment's thought, they both had to laugh, because Gland Manse was pretty damned apt.

Meg and Stormy saw Beryl before she saw them, so they quickly re-traced their steps to their horse box parked on the ferry's car deck. But it was too late.

"I've been attempting to contact you for weeks," Beryl said, when she caught them up. "I've left dozens of messages on your new answer machine."

"Na yeah, that machine is defective," Meg said, pretending to reach into the cab of the horse box to fetch something she'd forgotten. "It deletes near everything."

"Then you should purchase another. Or answer the phone yourself."

Stormy Day did not like the disagreeable tone Beryl was using on his wife, and he would have spoken up, but he was a wee bit scared of the woman. She had a formidable personality, and a strong sense of entitled rank. Small wonder, he thought, Jack had fled the family embrace first chance. As Meg put it, he "was born with a silver spoon in his mouth, but soon as he could, he spit it out."

Meg spoke to Beryl in a conciliatory tone. "Let's talk now, shall we? We were just heading up to the café."

"Very well," Beryl said, turning toward the stairs to the top deck.

They were on the *Strait Feronia*, one of the ferries of the BlueBridge line, crossing Cook Straits from Picton, South Island, to Wellington on the North, a three-hour trip over calm seas on this pleasant, sunny late November Spring afternoon. Stormy and Meg were returning from a farm south of Christchurch where they'd delivered three Sporthorse yearlings to their buyer. And Beryl was returning home to Wellington from the Ellersllie International Flower Show. She had won two red ribbons, so she should have been in a better mood than she was, but this was due to that stubborn girl. While they drank coffee in the café, she spoke her piece.

"Someone needs to go up there, and talk some sense into her. You do see that, don't you?"

"For certain, Beryl, we do wish she were closer, but she's being quite well looked after, up and over. Besides Louisa Grand, there's her other mates, espesh one named Ditch."

Beryl reacted with several hard blinks. A person named Ditch? This only reinforced her notion of Texas, inhabited primarily by cowboys and the like.

"Someone must go," she repeated, "and I'll do it myself if – ."

"Matter fact," Meg interrupted, "Storm and I are considering a visit, before the next foaling season starts."

"We are?" Stormy said, then corrected it when Meg shot him a look. "We are. Definitely. Considering it."

Meg went on, "If we can book seats cheap enough."

Beryl smiled, very slightly, as she stirred cream into her coffee. "If it's a matter of finances, the Judge and I would – ."

"Yeah na, ta. We'll suss that part out."

"In the meantime, perhaps I can speak directly to her, if you give me her mobile number."

"So sorry, Beryl: don't have that with me now. But I wrote it down in our kitchen, so give me a buzz when you're home."

"And will I get that defective machine again?"

"No worries. Storm will fix it with a good whack. That's how he fixes most all our machines."

Sipping her coffee, Beryl took a quick glance at the large man's large hands. How had she become so embroiled with such people? Never mind that, she thought, this wasn't about them, or even the girl. This was about Jack, her only child, her son, their son, their heir, and his legacy. She would swallow whatever it took, to have that piece of him back with them again.

CHAPTER 24

HUGO SAT AT his cottage kitchen table finishing a letter to Nan, congratulating her on her months of sobriety. He promised at six months, if she kept attending meetings, they could try again. After sealing the letter, he started cleaning his Glock 9-mil.

Pierre sat on the floor beside him watching, ears, eyes, and nose intent. He whined a little, as Daphne had taught him, at the sight and smell of the pistol, the cartridges, and the cleaning solvent. Hugo always cleaned his weapons with Jim Beam, an excellent solvent he'd discovered as a drunk. To Pierre, the smell of whiskey set off alarm bells.

"Don't worry, buddy," Hugo told him. "I'm not gonna top myself, or take a drink. But I sure coulda used you after I got out of Ramstein, last time."

He put the piece down and scratched Pierre's ears. Pierre licked his hand. He loved smelly, farty Hugo with every atom. Hugo was pack; he was Alpha.

"Yeah, back then I was royally fucked up. Came close to eating my gun, but I couldn't pull the shot. I kept thinking, my buddies died, I lived, I owe them my life, so I have to live."

Pierre whined, with concerned sympathy.

"That's right, buddy," Hugo told him. "They were my pack."

At that moment, the door to his cottage swung open, and Daphne walked in without a knock.

"Hey, what the fuck? A little privacy, please," Hugo said. "I could've been jerking off."

"What?" Daphne laughed. "You're a thirty-something married man: you still do that?"

"Men," Hugo said, "always still do that. For a smart chicka, you're pretty dumb. You ready?"

Daphne held up her shooter's bag. "Let's go blow some shit up!"

"Hoo—ahh!" Hugo said, reassembling his piece. He'd suggested the firing range to cheer Daphne up, after her latest breakup with Sam. Shooting things always buoyed a warrior's mood.

Pierre watched both of them, tail wagging. Daphne was also pack. He would give his life for either of them. He'd never been so happy.

On the drive down the lane they saw Ditch maneuvering his canary yellow J-3 Cub into the hangar. He'd been away for the week, making up time for the Reserves. His formal letter resigning his commission had somehow, somewhere, gotten jammed up in the chain of command.

"Pull over," Hugo said. "Let's get the skinny."

"About what?"

"A private matter," Hugo said. He knew Ditch wouldn't want Daphne to learn about his possible deployment. She was Rainey's mate. "Just pull over, please."

Daphne swung the truck to a stop. Ditch walked toward them, wiping sweat off his face with a greasy rag, which left a smudge on his cheek. Daphne rolled the window down, and Hugo spoke across her and Pierre.

"News?"

"The worst," Ditch said. "Tell you about it later. I'm off to take Rainey to the OB/GYN."

"Her first sonogram," Daphne said. "How cool is that?"

In the waiting room, Ditch was so bloody annoying, yacking on and on about the mechanics of a transvaginal ultrasound. During his week away, he'd done heaps of research.

"It'll give a much clearer picture than the abdominal sonogram," he said. "The doc'll use a transducer that sends out sound waves. They bounce off the tissues and capture the waves sent back. Then the machine converts the waves into images."

"Will you shut your cakehole?" Rainey said, not too politely. "I'm trying to concentrate on this bleeding questionnaire."

With effort, she focused on the next line, something about twins in the family. She'd already answered that question, during her initial exam. Rainey squinted, to help herself knuckle down, and wrote yes, fraternal twin brothers. Then she added, to Ditch, "Sorry, mate. I know you're excited."

"To put it mildly," Ditch said. "Thanks for waiting till I got back to do this."

Rainey nodded, moving on to the next confusing question. "No," she wrote, "no longer constantly morning sick." Nevertheless, the hormone hurricane was still blowing strong, and she often thought she was losing her grip. Having Ditch with her did help heaps, although his presence in her life these last weeks made for a spaghetti bowl of complications, too. He couldn't be more lathered up if he were the father, which was a very remote possibility, true, but that shoe would never drop. She'd taken different path. He said he believed her, but she suspected some residue of doubts.

Meantime, he'd stood and was walking impatiently around the waiting room, looking at diagrams on the wall depicting fetal development. He stopped in front of one.

"You should be near twelve weeks by now, right? This is what the pepi looks like."

"Yes, but I'm sure there are many variables," she said. "And this pepi seems mountains larger than that." Then she added, peevishly, "You have grease on your face."

Later, in the examination room, Ditch turned his back while Rainey removed her moleskins, chambray shirt, and undergarments to put on a hospital gown. But when he went to the mirror to wipe off the grease, he caught a glimpse of her reflection. He knew he shouldn't feel it, but her plump-bellied naked body caused a spasm of wonder that clutched his throat. He couldn't help the words he next spoke.

"You mean the world to me, Kiwi."

She opened her mouth, a saucy rebuke on her tongue – a rebuke that included the word "unrequited" – but she couldn't say the words because he'd turned and was gazing at her with those honest green-brown eyes. She'd only been adored like that by one other man. Oh, for certain, randy boys and men around the barns had gawked, with lust, but not with a true heart. A true heart, something she didn't feel for Ditch, not exactly. Fact was, right now his feelings for her were quite irritating.

"Rack off," she said, holding the gown closed behind her. "You're embarrassing me."

At that moment, fortunately, the young smiling female OB/GYN came in, reviewing Rainey's chart. Dr. Lily had met Ditch, Rainey's "friend," during the initial exam. Or rather, he was introduced to her as "a mate," although Dr. Lily suspected something more, from the way they acted together. No judgements, no judgements: after all, this was the New Age. Patients could tell her what they wanted, including an in utero AI back in Auckland.

"We normally don't ultrasound this early, but I need to confirm my thoughts. So Rainey, Ditch, let's get started," she said, rolling up her stool. "This is going to be interesting, I think."

After the initial palpation, and when her patient was comfortably situated in the stirrups, Dr. Lily slid the lubricated transvaginal transducer into her body cavity gingerly, her attention divided between the transducer and the images flitting across the screen. She moved the "magic wand" – that's what Ditch called it – ever so gently to the left and then the right. Then she moved it again, and again, and a few more times to be absolutely certain.

"Ah-hah!" she said. "Yes!"

"Yes what?" Ditch said.

He and Rainey were scanning the screen, but all they could see were ghostly phantasms.

"I thought this might be the case," Dr. Lily said. "You've been feeling a lot of activity recently?"

"Heaps."

"Perfectly normal," Dr. Lily said, "for a mother carrying healthy twins."

Both Rainey and Ditch hissed in their breath.

"No!" Rainey shouted.

"But she's too small," Ditch protested.

"Well," Dr. Lily laughed, "in the second trimester, she's really going to expand."

Ditch reached for Rainey's hand. She pulled it away. Dr. Lily reflected that, statistically, parents of twins were much more likely to end up separated.

"Now, what questions do you have?"

A torrent flooded out from Ditch, and mostly about nutrition, exercise, and delivery options.

About the last, Dr. Lily said, "In America, seventy-five percent of twin births are by C-section."

Meantime, Rainey lay back, stunned. Twins? C-section? Could it get any more pakaru?

Ditch continued with the non-stop questions. "How soon before you can tell their sex?"

"Typically, after eighteen weeks we can get an accurate picture. Until then, on the screen a vagina looks pretty much like a penis."

"Excuse me," Rainey butted in. "But I *do* have a question myself. How likely are twins when you've had an in-utero insemination?"

"There's a higher percentage, significantly. And you were on fertility drugs?"

Rainey nodded that she was. But in her mind, the paternity issue was settled. She shot Ditch an I-told-you-so look, then said, "I have another question, and I need to ask it privately."

"Oh," Ditch said, "okay." He might have overstepped his bounds, as excited as he was. With some reluctance, he left the room. Dr. Lily watched him go.

"Okay, before your question, I need to add to what I just said. There's also a higher percentage when you have fraternal twins in the family line, which you do."

"Oh," Rainey said, wobbling before returning to the certainty that they were Jack's.

"Other questions?" Dr. Lily asked.

"Na yeah, one more, about bizarre pregnancy dreams." Rainey had one last night that was mostly responsible for her mare-ish mood today. "I dreamt I gave birth to an adult, a man with a moustache. Am I going completely barmy?"

"No," Dr. Lily smiled. "That's a fairly normal first trimester dream – adult births, journeys, water dreams. Second trimester dreams will be different. My favorites were the erotic ones. Who knew I had all that stuff inside me? So perhaps we need to dialog about pregnancy sex."

"No, there'll be none of that."

"Okay, but it's your loss," Dr. Lily said, sitting down next to Rainey on the examining bed. "The orgasms are off the charts. All thanks to progesterone and estrogen, not to mention the blood flow to the genitals and pelvic region. Your breasts are larger, too, the nipples more sensitive, and for me, multiple orgasms: Whoa! Let me tell you, hang on."

Rainey blushed, which she rarely did. "I did have to hang on, to the shower head the other day. I never had a spontaneous one before." She'd been shampooing, remembering Ditch's moustache in her ear.

Dr. Lily laughed. "Oxytocin is the purest bliss. I've had three kids myself. Sometimes I wonder if I get pregnant just for the sex. Now let me give you a few tips."

While Dr. Lily talked, Rainey stared at the examining room door. She and Ditch had been celibo-mates, nothing more, though she had just seen him squizzing her in the mirror. She smiled, suddenly warm.

"But why must *I* talk to her?" Meg said.

"Because," her husband said, "whenever I say something, she bows her back."

They were three hours into an eighteen-hour flight on Qantas, from Auckland to the States, in economy seats. Stormy Day's long legs stuck out in the aisle, a hazard to anyone passing. He wore his ill-fitting funeral suit, and his name fit his mood today. His demand that she do the talking ticked off Meg no end. Still, he persisted.

"And you *do* want her to come home, don't you?"

Meg thought about that. "I've never been as abso-sure about it as Beryl. Our girl's found a place there, with mates. Back home she'll just be a sad widow, through and through."

"Remind her of her responsibilities: Jack's family, Beryl and the Judge. The baby's part of their family, too."

"Yes, Beryl and the Judge," she said. "You've sure changed your tune there, luv."

Stormy sighed, or maybe it was more of a groan. "That woman calls every bloody day. She's worn me down. And mayhaps," he said, "it would be for the best."

Mayhaps, Meg thought, but coming home meant that the Gauges would dominate Rainey, molding her and turning her into a vessel for Jack. Rainey wouldn't be onboard for that.

She opened her mouth to speak, but then closed it. What was the use? Stormy was nothing if not strong-minded. Fortunately, Rainey was, too. Two peas in a pod, she often thought: no wonder they never got on. And privately, Meg felt enormous pride for her daughter. She'd struck out, at sixteen, and never looked back. She made her way in a competitive world of men – an emancipated young woman, they used to call them – and when she found Jack, she took him on her own terms and with the whole of her heart. And when disaster struck, twice, she'd struck out again, for a new life up and over. What a girl she was! And when Meg thought about her daughter like that, her eyes brimmed with loving tears. She covered them this morning by turning her face to the seat window.

To change the subject, she said, "I'm interested in this Ditch. He sounds a bit of all right."

Stormy Day stretched out his legs with a thoughtful grunt. "Hmmm," he said, then added, "But he's also a soldier, like Jack. Does it sound like a grand plan, for her to get involved with another of that lot?"

Meg sighed, seeing his point. She turned to look back out the seat window, very glad once again that she was not young.

CHAPTER 25

THEY ATE DINNER together, as they often did lately, at her kitchen table: Bangers and beans and fried tomatoes, her one specialty.

"Don't *ever* serve this to Hugo," he said.

She smiled. "I surely won't."

"But no wakas with me. I rarely toot, and when I do, the odor is sweet as."

She laughed, full tit in a better mood, all due to Ditch, of course. He was nothing if not unrelenting. "You are *so* full of shite," she said. "I've been to the dunny after you, mate."

Her hair had grown, maybe two, three inches, blonde. then back to black. It made her head look striped, like a tabby cat. It also looked thicker than it'd been, probably, Ditch thought, due to the hormones.

They ate and talked about everything but the twins: Louisa's amazing recovery, and Warbucks' looming legal troubles with the government, Moira and Rudy's romance, Hugo and his recovering alcoholic wife, Daphne's latest reconciliation with Sam.

When they finished, Ditch washed the pans and plates. While he sloshed about in the sink, she came over to watch.

"In my family, the men didn't do dishes."

"In mine, dad and I always washed up. That's when he'd give me his goofy advice, like 'warm sudsy water being good for the digestion.'" He paused, then added, "I miss that guy."

"Sorry, mate," Rainey said. "I know you do."

She turned and leaned back on the counter, fondly thinking about her own oldies. Funny how binding were family ties. Then she felt movement and looked down. She put her hands across her belly. They were tumbling inside her, two little people. How could that be? And what a responsibility. The thought of it over-swept her, and damn the progesterone and estrogen, she began to sniffle, bloody sook that she was. Before Ditch could see, she limped off, through the door to the living room.

Looking at her over his shoulder, he dried his hands and followed. She stopped in front of the couch. He came up behind her, took her by the shoulders, and turned her around. Then he wiped the tears off her cheeks with the damp dish-towel. Then he dried her eyes. But she was still preoccupied with the tumbling act inside.

"Twins,' she said, horrified.

"I know, babe. But it'll be okay."

This was the first time he'd used a term of endearment, and it embarrassed her. If she were thinking straight, she would set this right. No "babe," no "luv," none of "we're a couple" bull crap. But it also felt okay something strong, being cared about, being looked after. The feelings were a wee lopsided, too true, not reciprocated, not exactly – she'd never love any like Jack. And it was all probably hormonal, but Ditch did have those bloody green-brown eyes that were looking deeply into hers right now.

She took his hands and put them on her belly. His hands smelled of pomegranate, from the dishwashing liquid. Amazing, her sense of smell these days. Caused by progester-one and estrogen, no doubt, the same thing that caused her to rise on her toes to pash his lips. Then she stepped back, unexpectedly shy.

He stepped forward, kissing her again, not so hungrily as her, but tenderly, with reverence, and, okay, with passion. He bent over to make it easier to kiss on. And on.

You eat with your mouth, Ditch thought, you speak with your mouth, you make all kinds of facial expressions with it, but until you kiss someone you crave, you don't know what a mouth is really for. How many nerves must there be? How many glands got triggered? Kissing Rainey that night, Ditch thought the answer might be infinity.

Finally, she drew back. "I can't kiss you anymore," she said, "while I'm still wearing togs."

"I," Ditch confessed, "I'm not any kind of strange, or exotic, with sex. But when it comes to you, I'm too impulsive. So, did the doc say this is okay, and are you sure you really want to?"

"It's okay for the twins, and I'm abso-sure what I want and need." She finished her thought silently: I'm scared, and I need to be loved, and not have to fully love back yet.

"Very well," he said, with a dramatic sigh, "if you must. But do be patient with me, and go slow."

She smiled at him, and for Ditch, the sight of her smiling that way was so wonderful, it caused him pain. He undid the first button on her chambray shirt. Then another, and another. At the bottom, his hands came back up and lifted the shirt from her shoulders and let it slide off. Then, with a kind of awe in his eyes, he traced with his index finger the edges of her brassiere. She felt herself vibrate.

"You," he said, his voice hoarse, "are gonna need a much bigger bra. You're busting out of this."

"I'm busting," she said, her voice hoarse, too. "I know I am."

He unclasp the bra and let it fall, then immediately moved south. Her moleskins were already unbuttoned, for her belly, so he moved to the zip and let them fall to the floor.

"Oh, my God," he said. "I've never seen anything so beautiful before."

He slid his hands around to her bum and pulled her big belly tenderly to him. But when he leaned down to kiss her, she turned her face.

"No, not until you drop your gear, too."

He pulled his shirt off, stepped on the cuffs of his jeans, and shucked them and his skivvies. Then they began touching, exploring, rubbing, pulling, and shaking with excitement. Bloody hormones had them steamed.

"How," he croaked, "do we do this?"

"Dr. Lily gave me explicit instructions."

"Doctor's orders. Just lead: I'll follow along."

In the spare room, she lay him down on the bed, flagpole raised, and with a little difficulty (her munted left leg) she climbed on and guided him home.

"Oh," she said.

"Oh," he said. "Oooooh."

Every movement was memorable, until it passed away to the next, the sweet stroking, the kissing, the nibbling, the tongues, the moans, his nose in her ear. He remembered her grip on him, her curly hair, her breasts and nipples so tender, his admission of what she meant to him.

"I," he said, "love you, Kiwi. I love you, heart and soul."

"Na yeah," she said, "Me, too."

It was a heat of passion proclamation, normally not credible, but it was enough for him tonight. He thought, as he held out to give her more, that he'd never "made" love before. Sure, he'd had good sex, with Gully and a few women since, but never so totally, never this selflessly, this giving, because he'd never felt so palpably, a love this clear and clean.

"Go ahead, let yourself," she panted.

"No," he said. "Not yet."

Afterwards, they literally fell into oxytocin sleep, deep, bottomless, and if he dreamt, no dream included war. He and she were finally at peace, on an island, the lapping sea around them, with a gentle breeze that cooled them beneath the leaves of the macadamia trees.

In the morning, a little later than usual, he was up and finished shaving in the dunny, returning to the spare room shiny faced.

"Come back to bed," she said, lazily running her hand under the sheet. She'd rarely ever felt this grand.

"Sorry, luv, no can do. I've got to meet with Ingrid and the lawyers about the ranch. I'll get brekkie while you go wee."

When she came out of the dunny, she noted that the spare room bed was tightly made, and Ditch was in the kitchen, again barefooted and shirtless, frying eggs while he sang and danced to a tune on the Kerrville oldies station. The song was a particularly stupid one, with lyrics she already knew.

"'I took my troubles down to Madame Ruth, You know that gypsy, With the gold cap tooth,'" he sang, smiling as she came near. "'I told her that I was a flop with chicks, I been this way since 1956.'"

As she limped by him, he took her by the elbow and made her dance, too.

"'She looked at my palm, And she made a magic sign, She said whatya need is a bottle of Love Potion Number Nine."

Laughing, she danced along, with abandon, until the song ended and he let her sit down. He turned off the radio, but still hummed the tune as he handed her a plate of scrambled eggs, buttered wheat toast and half a Texas ruby red grapefruit. She started with the grapefruit while looking at Ditch.

"I say again, you are a very–" she was going to say her usual, "a very strange bloke," but that really wasn't quite right. She thought a mo, and said, "You are very out of the ordinary."

He nodded, gobbling up his feed. "With a soft spot for oddballs, like you."

She smiled. "So what's going to happen, with your family ranch?"

"Ingrid is selling it to developers – but I'm keeping a hundred acres along the river. And I'm deeding Daphne and Hugo twenty acres to build their service dog training facility."

"You're a right good mate," she said, realizing again it was true. "But wait, you really have to leave?"

Ditch had stood, checking his watch. "Got to, babe. But before I go, how 'bout one little snog in your ear?"

"Just this once," she said. "I don't want to get a rep for being easy."

He stuck his nose in her ear, inhaling her deep inner-fragrance, then kissed it, stuffed on his go-fasters, and danced out the door singing "'I didn't know if it was day or night, I started kissing everything in sight," while levering into his shirt.

Whatever she felt for Ditch – she'd just call it kinda-love, for now – it made her sit smiling stupidly at the table, scarfing eggs, glad to have her appetite back. After all, she was eating for three. When she heard a knock at the door, she went eagerly, thinking he'd come back for more.

When she opened it, her mum stood outside, along with her dad.

"A bloke just ran out of the barn singing," her mother said.

"Na yeah, that was just Ditch."

"Oh," her mum said.

All her dad said was, "Hmmm."

They'd intended the visit to be a pleasant surprise, and in The Land of the Long White Cloud, rellies often popped in and lingered for weeks at a time. And they were chuffed out the yin yang to hear the news about the twins.

"But they're gonna be work: you've no idea," her mum said. "So don't worry about us, luv. We'll be gone before Boxing Day, if you don't mind having us underfoot that long."

"No wakas, mum. The spare room's yours for as long as you want. I'll just need to change the bed linens."

"Hmmm," her dad said, squizzing the neatly made bed in that room, with his hands clasped behind his back.

"That'll do us fine," she said. "Now take your dad down and introduce him to the horses. Maybe he'll talk to them. He's hardly spoken since we had a squabble on the plane."

Rainey's towering, craggy-faced dad walked out, muttering a deep and thoughtful grunt. Rainey glanced at her mum, who held up her hands in a gesture of helplessness. Sighing, Rainey limped out and down the steps, remembering exactly why she'd left home at sixteen.

Meg Day watched them go, thinking again, two peas in a pod they were. Thank goodness she had her boys, Sunny and Happy, to counterbalance Stormy and Rainey. Thinking of her boys back home keeping the farm going in their absence, she smiled, patted her thighs, and went to roll her suitcase into the spare bedroom to unpack. Installing dresses on hangers, she realized again, how few feminine clothes Rainey had. Mostly moleskin jeans and chambray shirts, her barn uniform. They'd have to go shopping soon, for maternity clothes. What fun!

Later she heard her husband's heavy footsteps coming back up. She greeted him with a, "Sit down. I'll rustle you up a cuppa."

He sat, with his big hands flat upon the kitchen table. "She's gone off on a tramp, happy as you like, with a one footed girl and some other goofy blokes."

"They're right mates," Meg said, then added, "And you're worrying very loudly, luv."

"That's as may be, but I don't care how many mates she has," he said. "She can't stay here with twins, so far away. You tell her that."

Meg paused, filling the kettle. "Storm, let's kick that down the road a week or two. No sense having a barney straight off." To change the topic of conversation, Meg said, "I liked the look of that mate who ran out of the barn. He has lovely eyes, did you see?"

"What I saw was a soldier running out of our girl's apartment," Stormy Day said, "buttoning his shirt. Also, the bed in the spare needed new linens, and it was made up tight like a military bed."

Facing away at the sink, Meg Day smiled, her head buzzing with questions, the answers to which were not all bad.

CHAPTER 26

"EVERY CARD DEALT must be played," Joe D. explained as they walked.

"You're becoming quite cryptic," Louisa replied.

"I'm just saying, these are the cards I dealt myself, and I have to own them. It's what we 'Friends of Bill' call a 'fearless and searching moral inventory.'"

"So what'll happen with the plea agreement?"

"It turns out there's three kinds of bargains, but the Fact Agreement is the one I want. It stipulates to the admission of certain facts, in exchange for other evidence not being introduced. That'll protect Jonny and the others."

"But?" Louisa said.

"But the Judge could pitch it out. They often do."

Bundled in coats this chilly December morning, they were walking along the river path, holding gloved hands. They'd slowed their pace and drifted back because ahead of them, Jonny and Kohsoom were discussing their future, or their lack of one. Color had returned to Louisa's face – she was back to her daily yoga routine – and Joe D. looked positively ruddy. He'd worked out with dumbbells in the home gym that morning, to fight the effects of sarcopenia.

"So," Louisa said, "how are you going to handle it?"

"I'm gonna sell myself to the Judge. It's what I do. It's what I'm good at."

"And when will this happen?"

"Mid to late January. Wait. Stop. Is that Ditch's cow?"

They were walking past the far paddock, and the big, friendly animal was looking over a fence at them.

"Technically, Rowdy's a steer," Louisa said.

"And Ditch rides him?"

"So does Rainey now. He's very safe."

Joe D. laughed. "They're a very odd couple," he said.

"If," Louisa said, "a couple they are. Rainey's still holding tight to dead Jack."

They walked on, Joe D. putting his arm around his wife to warm her.

"Love," he said, "shouldn't be so complicated."

"Yes," Louisa said, "but it is."

Joe D. smiled as he walked. It was a much more pleasant expression than a scowl.

"Now," he said, "let's talk about funding some non-profits, starting with that Freedom Dogs facility. Also, we need to deed all the cottages over to the staff."

Ahead of them, Jonny was trying to understand Kohsoom's motivation. "And you're absolutely sure about this?"

"I have cousin," she nodded, "in Santa Fe need me to work at his spa. Beside, you still carry torch for wife."

Jonny didn't need to ask which one: he'd mentioned Elena a few too many times.

"I can't thank you enough," he said. "You've made my chi run free. And you don't need to worry about money."

"Jonny, you are generous man. I hope wife is generous, too."

"There's something I haven't told you," Ditch said, "and it's been eating at me."

This was near a month after their mates-who-bonk thing had begun. They were both insatiable, not just for sex, but because they got off on being together. He helped mucking and working the horses, she helped changing cylinders in his little airplane's engine, and when he took her up in it, he started teaching her to fly. They even enjoyed shopping together. Once, in the lingerie aisle at Walmart, when Ditch held a frilly, big-cupped brassiere to his chest and wiggled his eyebrows at her, she laughed so hard she peed herself.

Ditch cupped his hands like a megaphone and announced, "Spill on Aisle Three."

But today she was in a dreamier mood, having slipped away from the oldies for an afternoon yack and root – damn, this was bloody addictive. The oxytocin was like a drug. Still under its effects, she felt too muzzy to remember what he'd said.

"You're eating something?"

"No, something's eating me. I resigned my commission, but it didn't go through," Ditch said. "You know what FIGMO means?"

She shrugged, still feeling dreamy.

"Fuck It, Got My Orders," Ditch said, and after a pause, added, "The final word came last week: I'm activated and headed back."

Rainey blinked, hearing the words, but it took a moment to translate them into what they meant. As she stirred, the mental cobwebs began to clear: Ditch going off to that war.

Ditch went on. "Not a full can of worms. Three, maybe four months tops, to assist in the Spring Offensive. I should be back home for the births."

Rainey sat up, and looked across the room without seeing the far wall. All she could see was Jack's tail-lights going around the bend. Not that this should hold a candle Jack's departure, because of his dominance in her heart – but surprisingly it did anyway, and it cut her to the quick. Ditch was her lover, and her best mate ever, no pressure. He always tried to cheer her, and felt dismal about delivering this news. She tried to keep the fear and stress out of her voice when she spoke.

"How soon? When?"

"Late January. First some death-by-PowerPoint training in Twentynine Palms, then the 'Stan in February."

She lay back down and put her hands on her womb. The twins were active today. She had to think of them, and not her own life or that of her lover. But she wasn't ready to address this. She reached up and put a hand on his shoulder.

"Then near a month more," she said, trying to smile at him.

"And I'll be back."

"No worries, you will," she said, and she hugged onto him so he couldn't see her eyes. She was afraid he might note the mixed emotions in them. For certain there were alarming feelings for him, but more for certain, a jump of alarming fears. And she was brassed off, too, about being kept in the dark until now. So she was glad she'd always held back a little of her heart, not committing fully to Ditch. According to Daphne, her bullshit detecting mate, she was scared shitless of loving fully again. Once bitten, twice shy. Magnifying it even further, she had the twins to consider now, in every one of her life's equations. Of course, about them, she had held back vital information, too. She was confused by the blitz of emotions.

So, maybe better, him gone away. Let the dust clear. She could be just herself again, or be the horrible, inauthentic person she had become. How could she be that person, the one who said she loved, when she didn't with a whole heart, not completely? She broke off the hug, rolled, and climbed out of bed, suddenly filled with self-loathing.

"You really have to go right now?" he asked. "We're just starting to talk."

"Na yeah, a lesson with Moira at three. And no, you can't come and watch. My oldies will be there, and last time, dad shirtfronted you."

"He knows about us," Ditch said. "And he loves his daughter."

Rainey groaned. She never could fool her dad.

Ditch watched her depart with an ache in his chest that was becoming all too familiar. He knew she was holding back, and this deployment would give her more reason to push him farther away. But he'd hoped that he might become so large in her life, he'd cause an eclipse in her heart. Anyway, what choice did he have? It was like flying into a battle where the intel was bass-ackwards: you pressed on, hoping to sort things out. Nevertheless, he'd heard a slogan at one of the AA meetings he'd attended with Hugo: "Hope is not a plan." Well, he thought, it fucking well is, when that's all you got.

"I think he's known all along he'd get deployed, the blighter," Rainey said. "It's not right, doing me this way."

"Okay, look, he's not a blighter, whatever the fuck that means," Daphne said. "You're not thinking clearly, so I'm telling you, here's the way it is: He may be a lovey cream puff with you – but on the inside, he's still a warrior, and warriors follow orders and go fight." Then she added, "Jack was no different. You're obviously attracted to them, so suck it up and be there for him."

"Na yeah, but I'm preggers now with twins," Rainey said. "I can't go out on a skinny limb. And I'm not for certain what I really feel, anyroad. I'm at my limits, and confused."

"Bullshit. What's so confusing? Anyone can see, there's juice between the two of you. And don't give me another load of that 'I'll always love Jack' shit. I've told you before: you're scared shitless of taking another risk."

"Yeah na, now that's complete bullshit. And it's not about just me anymore."

They faced each other a moment, nostrils flaring. But by inches, it subsided. After all, they were mates, through and true. Rainey turned her attention back to Snorkel. She was lunging him in the arena, warming him up for the lesson that Moira was a half hour late for already. Irritating – as was Daphne's instinct for bullshit detection. Rainey felt as if she were being pushed on from without and from within.

Meantime, Daphne attended her stubborn friend. She decided to take some of Hugo's AA advice: Speak your truth, then walk away.

"I'll go up to Gland Manse and roust Moira," Daphne said, climbing down from the arena rail. "She probably forgot again."

"And ask how Louisa's latest screening went," Rainey called, "if you happen to see Sam."

Daphne flipped her the bird. Rainey was always ragging her about her mercurial romance with Sam. And Rainey smiled at her dig: turnabout is fair play among mates. Then she focused on guiding Snorkel closer to the cavelletti.

As Daphne walked up the lane, she passed Rainey's parents as they came down from the barn. It was late afternoon, and they'd been on the phone to down under. Daphne greeted them. Meg responded cheerily, but all Rainey's craggy-faced father did was grunt. To Daphne, he resembled one of those Easter Island Heads.

Stormy marched on, hands stuffed in his trouser pockets, studying the horse on the lunge line. Rainey was guiding him over the cavelletti, which he negotiated with ease. She did have an eye for the exceptional horse, and this gelding was one for certain. Stormy rested his big arms on the arena rail, watching, but also urging Meg on. They had to return to home tomorrow, to prepare for the January foaling season.

"No more putting it off," he said. "Time to drop the hammer."

Meg shifted on her feet, uncomfortable.

"Luv," she called out, "can we talk to you a mo?"

Rainey shook the lunge line and clucked. Snorkel halted, turned on his hindquarters, and walked toward her, head low and relaxed. Rainey smoothed his forelock, stroked his jaw, and led him over.

Stormy pretended to regard the gelding, forcing Meg take the lead.

"Luv, we just got off the phone to Jack's mum."

"Beryl? What did she want?"

"She's very antsy to see you. You won't believe how A over T they are about the twins."

In the House of Gauge, Jack's father, Sir Grey, was an uptight, judge-everyone sort of man, and Beryl, she came from a family of whom one was a founding member of the New Zealand Women's Christian Temperance Union. It was hard to imagine either of them ever getting arse over tits about anything. But maybe they were, sort of, at the thought of their only child's twins.

"Na yeah, I'm sure they have everything in the twins lives pre-planned."

At the stubbornness in his daughter's voice, Stormy thundered up.

"They got their rights, too. You have to give them their due. And you_don't know about this job here, neither. Warbucks is facing criminal charges, and who knows what that'll mean. You need to follow your head, not your heart."

"What? Go back and let them control my every move."

"No, no," Meg said, in an attempt to calm the waters, "but maybe a short visit, before you're too far along. By then, you'll know if there's still a job here for you."

Rainey thought about that a moment. A short visit down under presented a way to avoid the stress of seeing Ditch off to the war, and might make the transition easier. She looked down thoughtfully and studied the arena sand, nudging a dung beetle along with the toe of her paddock boot.

"I might," she said finally, "could manage that. Say, late January."

CHAPTER 27

JOE D. GRAND stood before the judge, one Aretha Jackson, a long time occupant of the Federal Bench. His six lawyers from Vinson and Elkins sat at a table to his left, their heads hung. In contrast, the federal prosecutor beamed: this would be a feather in his cap.

'Your Honor," Joe D. said, "I wish to say a few words before you consider the plea before you."

"Words of mitigation, Mr. Grand?"

"No, Your Honor. I'm guilty as charged. No, I want to say I alone am responsible. My partner and employees are guiltless, and if they're brought to trial, I'll testify under oath to that. It was me, and only me, who's guilty."

"But?" Judge Jackson waited for more.

"No buts, Your Honor. Naturally, I hope you accept this agreement, so I can start serving my time posthaste. When it's over, I want to spend every moment I have with my wife, my family, and my friends. But first, I need to make amends. Crime," he said, "and punishment."

Judge Aretha Jackson, known for being severe, rocked back in her chair, which squeaked. Two things struck her about his last words. First was his use of "amends." She herself was a "double winner," a member of both AA for alcohol, and Al-anon for codependency. Second was his reference to "crime and punishment."

"Mr. Grand," the Judge steepled her fingers, "have you been reading Dostoyevsky?"

Joe D.'s eyes brightened noticeably. "No, Your Honor, but he's one of the guys on my prison reading list."

The Judge couldn't help but smile. Here was an incorrigible but somehow charming man on a quest for redemption, something rarely seen in her court.

"Very well, Mr. Grand. I will review the agreement before me, and render my decision two days hence, at noon."

"High Noon," Joe D. said. "There was a movie with that title, wasn't there?"

Despite herself, the Judge smiled again as she stood. The Court Clerk called out, "All Rise," and the Judge departed, humming "Do Not Forsake Me, Oh My Darling" to herself. This was an interesting case, indeed, although the sentence of five years was altogether too light. As a rule, this meant only four years, three months actually served. That, she thought, would have to be adjudicated.

They said what they had to say to get away without a barney, which would put undue stress on the twins. Least said, soonest mended, what they both thought. He would go off, but be back by May. She would leave, only temporarily, a short visit to placate the House of Gauge. She'd return, he'd return, all would be okay, and whatever needed to be ironed out could wait until that later day.

Except that maybe it couldn't, Ditch thought at 32,000 feet over the Atlantic in a Hercules, bound for Germany and then Bagram. With this deployment, he'd added greatly to her troubles, rather than subtract, 180 degrees out from what he wanted. She had the twins to consider, too, in every decision she made. Further, he knew she was deeply hurt and angry at his lie of omission, though she denied it. Given his deception, it may have been wise of her not to open her whole heart to him.

They'd left it with promises – we'll email, call, and skype – and then they'd see what would happen. It would either maintain, or it would dry out with absence and time, until it withered and fell off the vine. And it wasn't like he had any choice in the matter: FIGMO.

His seatmate on the flight was a Marine Gunny, a POG in Supply, who like Ditch had suffered multiple deployments.

"Don't you fucking love it," he said, "embracing the suck another time?"

"BOHICA," Ditch replied: Bend Over, Here It Comes Again.

The Gunny laughed. "But after this one, I'll have my twenty in. And you know what I learned from all them years?"

"What, Gunny?"

"I love only two things in life: my fat wife, and fixing antique clocks. Everything else is shit. You got a wife, Captain?"

"Had one. Lost her. Might've had another, but I got a feeling I may lose that, too. She's already had one husband get smoked downrange."

"Shit. That's fucked up."

"Beyond all recognition," Ditch agreed.

"Well, not to be unsympathetic, but I gotta get some shut eye. The wife fucked me in half last night. Wake me up if I fall over and start drooling on you."

Ditch laughed, because over here you had to either laugh or go bugfuck.

He looked around the cabin at the other men and women, yanked out of their lives and headed to war. They read, they slept, they played cards, they watched downloaded movies on their laptops, or listened to music on earbuds. But some just stared forlornly at the seatback in front of them. What was that phrase? "Forlorn of hope." He knew what it meant now, viscerally: the phantom pain you felt in your chest from the part that had been removed.

But it occurred to him that he was only repeating a pattern: fuck up your life at home, then run off to war. Matter fact, war was far simpler than life.

Headed in the opposite direction, looking out her seat window at the Pacific, Rainey wrestled to understand how she felt. Anger, too true. He had omitted his possible redeployment to that bloody war, which might have been unforgiveable if it weren't for what she'd omitted, too: he was truly, remotely, possibly the father of the twins. Did two lies of omission cancel each other out, or only compound the blame?

Nevertheless, something sweet as had grown between the two of them. For sure, she had scary strong feelings for him, far more than she ever expected to, maybe even love. And for sure, she already missed him terrible, his steady good humor, the way he looked at her like she was a riot, the way he always buoyed her up. He made her laugh, and he made her say things that made him laugh, too – not to mention his lovely, adoring eyes and his tender hands. And she loved getting up at sparrow's farts to silly-dance with him to oldies before brekkie.

But she also knew that in their love affair she'd always kept one foot on the boat, and one foot back on the dock. Further, she knew the absence of full commitment was fatal. It was like the fall that shattered her leg. She'd been grieving for Jack with a numb heart, instead of telling the horse with her hands, feet, legs and seat, "We *are* going over this jump."

So, in her mind, the lack of full commitment would likely cock it up eventually, leaving both of them further gutted. But maybe, maybe when they both came back, they could work it all out. For now, though, she was doing the right thing going south, the only thing, not just for herself, but for the twins. However, with her hands on her belly, feeling them jockeying for room, she had to smile at a suggestion Ditch had made. He'd said if they were a boy and a girl, she ought to name them Jack and Jill. How ridiculous, she thought, but still the suggestion, and Ditch's earnest expression when he made it, caused her to continue to smile.

She patted her hands over the twins, and, leaning down, spoke to them.

"No worries, luvs. From now on, your mum will follow only her head."

"Beg pardon?" her seatmate said. She was a mid-fifties neo-natal nurse returning to Wellington, and she'd been reading a romance novel while listening to music on earbuds. She pulled one out now.

"Sorry, luv, didn't hear you."

"I was telling my twins that from now on I'm not listening to my heart, only my head."

"Oh, yes, dear," she said, "if you can. But the heart has a hard time keeping quiet."

Which, of course, was exactly what this woman would say. Obviously, she'd overdosed on romance novels. From her dangling earbud drifted up the sound of Harry Nielsen singing "As Time Goes By."

"It's still the same old story, A fight for love and glory, A case of do or die. . . ."

"Na yeah," Rainey countered. "But I don't have to listen."

"And when two lovers woo, They still say I love you. . . ."

Rainey couldn't bear that bullshit anymore. She stuffed in her own earbuds and thumbed her iPhone to iTunes, selecting a new musical Hugo had downloaded before she left. It was *The Book of Mormon,* and the song that played was "Turn It Off:"

"When you start to get confused because of thoughts in your head, Don't feel those feelings! Hold them in instead. Turn it off, like a light switch."

Listening, Rainey smiled, because that's exactly what she intended to do.

"Einstein wasn't all that smart," Hugo said. "When people repeat their mistakes, they know exactly what's going to happen. But if they try something new, even worse shit can pop up."

Daphne considered this as they drove along.

"And this explains Rainey going back to New Zealand exactly how?"

"Down there, she knows what to expect."

"Yeah, Jack's bossy family."

"The devil you know," Hugo explained.

After a pause, Daphne asked, "But she is coming back, isn't she?"

Hugo shrugged, and it caused him some discomfort. They'd made a very good pack, the bunch of them. Now it was falling apart: Joe D. sentenced to ten years at a white-collar prison, along with very massive fines. No more private jets and helicopters, a severe lifestyle change. Louisa even had to sell that horse, and the staff was being cut to the bone. Life was turning pear shaped for them all, but worst of all for Rainey.

"She's in a hard place," he said, "expecting twins, with likely no job back here."

Daphne rolled up the truck window with a sigh. She was driving Hugo and Pierre to town for groceries at Walmart. After that, they'd go look at the building site. Construction of Freedom Dogs would begin next week, and with luck, they all – including Nan, if she was still sober – would move there June 1st. But on this cold, late January morning the trees and fields glistened with frost.

"Yeah no," she said. "Your theory also explains why Ditch actually wanted to go downrange again."

"The devil you know," Hugo said.

"FUBAR," Daphne replied.

CHAPTER 28

HE WAS BACK where he belonged, or so he told himself. But Camp Leatherneck had changed since he'd fought here in the 2009 surge. Back then, the personnel slept in 100-man tents with dirt floors, and now there were choos and prefabricated housing for up to 20,000 Marines. There was no longer one gym, but four, each with different equipment. But the best improvement was the PX. A Marine no longer had a two hour wait in line, only to find the shelves stripped bare. The new PX was 10,000 square feet and amply stocked with sundries like toothpaste, Instant Tears, baby wipes, Red Bulls, and Monsters. Chow halls, known as D-FAC's (Dining Facilities) were more numerous, too, with varied menus, not to mention soup and sandwich stations in some living quarters. There was even a new place called The Coffee Bean where you could get a decent afternoon latte. Also, several Grand Wright Corp. shipping containers had been converted into Morale, Welfare and Recreation centers for phone calls and Internet access 24 hours a day.

So, overall, life wasn't too bad here, for the nine out of ten who stayed behind the wire – not too bad, that is, once you got used to the hammer of summer, the blade of winter, the mass of humanity walking or marching to and fro, the constant stream of clattering helicopters overhead, the thousand military vehicles churning up the brown sand (not tan here, not like in Al Anbar), and the baffling, whipping winds that coated your teeth and eyeballs with that sand (hence the need for toothpaste and Instant Tears), not to mention the stupid military protocol ("Captain, are you chewing gum? What kind of example are you setting for the enlisted men?") – once you got used to all that, life for the nine out of ten who stayed behind the wire wasn't too bad. Only occasional mortar and rocket attacks and assorted truck bombs – mixed, lately, with green on blue suicide attacks. Not too bad, for the nine out of the ten.

But for the one in ten like Ditch who went beyond the wire, it was the same old Whack-a-Mole war. When he arrived, the Marines had just retaken Marjah, house by house, and the brass was busy drawing up operational orders for a shockingly unversed Spring Offensive. It called for the old standby, a pincer movement up two parallel valleys to an overwhelming waiting force.

"Very clever," Ditch told Hugo on the phone. "They'll never expect the hammer and anvil."

"Yeah, that always works," Hugo said, and waited for Ditch to get to the real reason he'd called.

"Rainey's gone dark with me, bro. Have you heard how she's doing, and when she's coming back?"

Hugo took a deep breath. "Dude, she ain't coming back. She called Louisa last week to explain. With no job here, she's got herself set up down there."

Ditch went quiet on the other end. His lie of omission again: the worm in the apple, a betrayal of trust, a violation that could not be healed. He didn't blame her, though. She had to look after herself now, and Jack's twins. She couldn't count on a duplicitous asshole like him.

"You still there?" Hugo asked.

"Oh, yeah, still here where I belong." Ditch said. "Thanks for giving it to me straight, bro. I'll call you again when I can, but now I got to go. There are guys with wives waiting for the phone."

The phone line took a beat to go dead, the way it always did with those calls back home – just a beat, but long enough for a guy to understand he was an awful long way from the world.

At his end, Hugo punched off. He was glad Ditch hadn't asked for Rainey's number down under, because it was out of service now, as was her email account: she'd gone off the grid. And Ditch really didn't need this shit. He needed to tighten up and keep his head on a swivel. If Hugo knew anything, he knew the mindset needed in a war zone. And he loved his brother Ditch: he didn't want to see him home in a flag draped box.

"Dear Dan, I'm emailing you via TRULICS, the Bureau of Prisons system, and all correspondence here is monitored. Your mom suggested I write to tell you we managed to keep the house and land and a few assets, so we're not dead broke. As for me, I'm doing well, now that I'm over the learning curve. The Bastrop FCI (Federal Correction Institution) is so low-level security they call it a camp and not a prison. There's a high double fence but no guard towers, and dormitories called Units where I have my own room. There's no violence here, no gangs or drugs or any the stuff you see in the movies, but life is very regimented.

"The general wake-up call comes at 0600. I make my bed (they're very particular about hospital corners) and straighten my locker and my shelf before the breakfast and work calls. All movement around the camp is controlled by our Unit

Supervisors (don't call them guards). In the afternoon I work at the Education Complex where they have me teaching, of all things, Business Ethics. We all wear khaki, black boots, and a belt. Of course, there's no privacy – open showers, sinks and toilets – but you get used to that. In fact, this morning I was doing my duty next to a very funny embezzler named Matt, and he made me laugh so hard, I might get hemorrhoids.

"There's a lot of enjoyable guys in my Unit. We go to AA meetings, play cards, recommend books to read, and give each other nicknames. And no, I'm not known as Warbucks here. I'm called "Choo," because of the portable buildings your Uncle Jonny and I invented. About Jonny, your mom told me he and Elena got re-married and are building low-cost housing for the homeless in San Francisco. Good on him, as that Kiwi girl Rainey would say.

"As I'm writing this, it occurs to me that my Spartan daily life now is not much different than the monks in monasteries centuries ago. Actually, it's probably not that much different than the life of a modern science-monk in Antarctica. I never understood what you saw in it, but now I do. There's some-thing about the metronomic regularity (yes, I used a word like "metronomic" because I'm reading a hell of a lot) that's soothing, an ironing of the soul, a way to get the wrinkles out.

"At least, that's what I think when I'm in my best mind. But when the supervisor shines his light through the door for the 3:00 am headcount, I'm usually awake and missing your mother and you and Moira – and Hortensia, Harry, Pauline, Hugo, Ditch, Rainey, Daphne, and all them. And I've come to understand that prison isn't bars, or double fences, or toilets all in a row. Prison is being separated from the people you love. And I love you, son. I pray for you every day. Love, your only Dad."

At the bottom of the world, Dan read this email, and thoughtfully closed his laptop. He wished his dad had been sent to prison thirty years ago.

"How are you settling into the little house?"

"Fine, Beryl. Ta."

"Perhaps you should start calling me 'Mother.'"

"I don't think so, Beryl. One mum is more than enough for me."

"As you wish. Now, shall we talk about our shopping trip?"

While Beryl talked about the plans, Rainey pretended to listen, while looking out to the grounds and trees. They sat in the den of the House of Gauge, a dark paneled room lined with legal books on one side and ornamental horticulture books on the other. Beryl was an expert on that, and the grounds around the old colonial house bulged with the last flowering plants of the New Zealand summer. Winter would start in May, and Beryl's platoon of gardeners were already stripping and preparing the beds for their autumn color. It would be nice as to be outside with the gardeners, getting sweaty, instead of trying to sit with erect posture in this den dominated by the tomes and the tick-tock of the huge Howard Miller grandfather clock.

Tick. . . . Tock. . . . Tick. . . .Tock. Jack claimed that time actually slowed down in this room. An hour here could make sixty minutes feel like sixty years.

When Rainey tuned back in, Beryl was saying they needed to purchase several dresses for her to wear to "the Club." As she spoke, Beryl noted the pull-over print maternity dress and open-toed sandals Rainey wore today: the girl had very limited sense of decorum and good taste.

"Yeah na. No need. My mum bought me heaps of these togs in Texas."

"Yes, well," Beryl said, "Texas. And you're sure the little house will still do you, when the twins come? There's more than enough room here with us."

"Yeah na, Beryl. We'll be right. And I insist on paying the rent."

"And the stable, you still insist on working there?"

"Very much so. Have to earn my keep."

The stable was nearby, in Ohariu Valley, and offered horse trekking and riding lessons in the dressage and jumping arenas. Rainey planned, over Beryl's objections, to give lessons to the upper crust, and sell them horses, too. She had the creds, having ridden for Sir Mark Todd.

At that moment, the Henry Miller grandfather clock chimed, so loudly that Rainey jumped. Truth was, she was a wee bit afraid of that clock. It was large enough to hold a body, and loud enough to send out shock waves.

"Oh, my, look at the time," Beryl said, rising. "We need to complete the shopping to be early to the Club. The Judge likes to move through the buffet line first, when everything is still unblemished."

Rainey hurried to the door, casting an ugly look at that clock. She made a mental note to limit, as much as was humanly possible, visits with Beryl. She decided that in the future she would feign pregnancy pains, Braxton Hicks, or whatever. Beryl wouldn't question that. Nothing, abso-nothing was more important to her than Jack's twins.

Following along on clicking heels, Beryl shook her head at the way her burgeoning daughter-in-law limped – actually, it was a limp combined with a pregnancy waddle. But she would bring the girl to heel, of that much Beryl was certain, though she did wish Jack had chosen more wisely, say, a girl with more raw potential.

Ahead, Rainey was conscious of Beryl's clicking old lady shoes. She realized that she was a wee bit afraid of them, too. When she told her mum that, she'd get a laugh. But her mum seemed a long way off right now. And she was on her own, in the House of Gauge.

CHAPTER 29

"WHAT THE FUCK'S wrong with Captain Dietrick? He's got a massive cob up his ass. Three fucking fam-flights, and he never talks except to tell me what to do and when to do it."

The motor-mouth Fucking New Guy was talking across the D-FAC table to Captain Willie "Dubya" Bush, who wasn't listening. Dubya was looking across the crowded D-FAC to where Ditch and Colonel Glub were sitting, stirring their chow around, talking, no doubt, about Ditch's decision to pull his letter, go Regular, and make it a career. Dubya wished to hell he was sitting with them. But he'd been first in the chow line, and when the douchebag FNG Abbott sat down with him, his buddies had skirted their table. Everybody hated FNGs. Abbott was already known in the squadron as "Girl-Butt," because that's what his ass looked like in a flight suit.

"I mean, okay, he's a Major-select, and he knows everything – fuck, he's got a topo-map of Helmand in his head – but does he ever just ask, how's it hanging?"

"He's been bent over four times for this crap," Dubya explained. He could also have added that his girl had dumped him, but Ditch wouldn't want him sharing that shit with a FNG. Dubya hurried to finish his chicken fingers.

"Never-the-fucking-less!"

At Ditch's table, Colonel P. was passing on some intel: "Word on the vine has it some asshole guards at Parwan Detention found a bunch of Korans with notes written in the margins, thought they were terrorist shit, so they burned them. Our Afghan friends in green saw them do it, and now there are riots in Kabul. We're supposed to be on high alert here, but good luck with that. They rotated the MPs back last month."

"Same as it ever was," Ditch said, and glanced over at Dubya's table. The FNG was still talking a blue streak. Dubya caught Ditch's glance, and wiped a booger out of his eye with his middle finger. Ditch laughed and turned back to his food. "Do you think they could put any more salt on this chicken?"

Meantime, Dubya finished his feed and stood to make his getaway. But before he did, Girl-Butt wanted to know if he'd finally see some action tomorrow.

"Maybe," Dubya said. "But in the 'Stan, you can get your ass handed to you any time."

On his way to drop his paper plate and plastic utensils in the shit-can, Dubya stopped to yank Ditch's chain.

"Your boy over there is ultra-moto. Gonna win the war single-handed. Good job instilling esprit de corps."

Ditch laughed. "Fucking Butt doesn't quite get it yet."

"The Forever War," said Colonel Glub.

"Sorry about scraping him off on you," Ditch said, standing. "Here, I'll take all this crap to the shit-can."

And for that reason he was behind them, just passing through the outside door, when the vest bomb went off behind him. The blast picked him up and pitched him twenty feet to a Hesco barrier that he hit with his face. Partially conscious, he felt hands under his armpits, lifting and dragging him away from the flames and heat. After that he could hear only the weirdly distorted voices of the corpsmen attending him. They sounded like a Steven Hawkins' speech synthesizer.

"Facial lacerations."

"Whoa, I got an entry wound, his upper back."

"No sign of exit."

"Shit, it's still in there, close to his heart. We need to stabilize ASAP."

"I'm giving him two hits. That should do it."

And it did, because the lights went out for Ditch right then.

Rainey tried to get out of the hospital bed, with Meg holding one arm and Nurse Gates on the other, while Stormy pushed the walker closer. Still seated, Rainey took hold of the handrails, then wrenched forward in pain.

"I can give you Demerol," Nurse said.

"No," Rainey coughed. "Bloody stuff gets into the milk."

"Come on, luv, it's been near six hours since the table," Meg said. "Time to get you up on your pins. They won't bring the pepis to you again until you do. Let's just walk down to the viewing window and see them."

With that motivation, and some help, Rainey rocked forward and stood.

"Come on, luv," her dad encouraged. "Put one foot in front of the other. Nurse says after a C-section you have to move about to get the gas out."

Rainey shuffled slowly toward the door, letting out a string of explosive farts. "Crickey, now I'm turning into Hugo," she said.

Meg laughed. "Your sense of humor's coming back."

Shuffling down the corridor behind Nurse Gates, Rainey asked, "Where's Beryl? I thought she'd be hovering by now."

Meg and Stormy shared a look. Stormy nodded to her, to go ahead and tell Rainey.

"Luv, Beryl's in over her head. Yesterday the Judge fell off the bench, with a stroke."

"He's in hospital in Wellington," Stormy added. "Looks like he's gonna cark it."

"Very sensitively put, Storm."

Rainey stopped shuffling a moment, farted, and thought. "Poor Beryl. I can't for fuck's sake understand their marriage. Best you could say is they leaned against each other in a hard wind, like two old trees, except they never, ever touch."

"Nobody understands other people's marriages, luv. Oh, look, there they are! Aren't they beautiful?"

Rainey pressed her face to the window and wept, farted, and knocked on the glass. There they were, on the outside at last. And beautiful they were, one with a pink cap and one with a blue, both brown-vanilla haired with blue eyes, though that would likely change. Of course, she'd seen them before, had nursed them three times each already, but the sight of them still flushed her with amazement. Beside her, Meg wept, too, and Stormy wiped his eyes with a sleeve.

"They're so small," Rainey said. "They felt mountains larger inside."

"Near six pounds each," Meg said proudly, her face to the glass. "And they'll be bigger soon, the way they suck. Luv, you're dripping."

Rainey looked at the front of her gown, and laughed. "Every time I see them, I squirt," she said. "Is there a medical term for projectile lactation?"

"Meg-luv, you get her back. I'll speak with nurse and have them brought to the room." Stormy paused, looking in with his big hands on the glass. "It's a bloody miracle of nature, isn't it now. No matter how many times I see it, it knocks me flat." He wiped his eyes again with his sleeve.

"Dad, I've never seen you like this. You're turning into a bloody sook," Rainey said.

"Oh," Meg said, "around babies, he's a sook and a half. Come, luv. You're making a puddle on the floor."

"Spill on Aisle Three," Rainey said, then wished she hadn't. It made her think of Ditch. As she hurried dripping to her room, she looked down at her front, and commented, "How big can my knockers possibly get? I'm in a D cup already."

Meg laughed, following along. "I hope they stock a DD cup," she said. "About the pepis, luv, they're beautiful, but, don't mind me saying, they don't much favor Jack."

"Let's not go there straight away. They're scarce six hours old, and don't look like anyone yet."

"Only just saying, when I was at your house, fetching your things, I came across a stack of unposted letters in your dainties drawer, all to Ditch."

Rainey turned on her mum. "Don't I have *any* privacy anymore?"

"Luv, you're wearing a gown that's open in the back, and you're the mother of twins. Privacy is something you'll never have again."

Grumbling, Rainey pushed her way into her room, but her mood softened instantly when her dad came in with a pepi in each of his big hands.

"They let me carry them!" he said, his eyes glistening happily.

Meantime, Rainey pulled her gown down, baring her dripping breasts. No modesty in hospital. She took the pepis and put one on each teat. They rooted around a mo, little blind people, then latched on, greedily smacking. She looked from one to the other, each little face, their tiny, wrinkled hands, and she started weeping again. Sniffling, she looked at her mum.

"I truly don't know who they favor, mum. What am I gonna say to Beryl."

"Why bring it up, the state she's in?" Meg said. "You're not a bludger with them: you pull your own weight. Now, have you thought about their names yet, luv?"

"Yes, and I'm still thinking," she said. She lay her head back on the pillow, closed her eyes, and let the hormones of breast-feeding wash over her. Letting down, she thought, was almost as smoothing as sex.

Louisa sat in Dr. Eva Hoffsteader's office feeling very pleased.

"The screening came back clean?"

"Yes, no signs that it's spread, yet"

"Yet?"

Eva lay the latest results down. This was always the part she most dreaded, the explanation of the evil nature of cancer.

"When the cancer cells grew in your endometria, the lining of your uterus, they needed vast amounts of blood to multiply. It's always a possibility that some cells broke away and moved through the vascular system to land somewhere else. But the good news is, they haven't shown up again."

"Yet," Louisa thought. That's such an important adverb unspoken. No sense fretting over it, though. Prayer would help, and perhaps a little fuck-knuckle cussing, too. She stood up to leave, saying, "Okay, we'll test again in three months."

"Yes, and maybe lunch next week? You can tell me how the weekend went."

Eva walked her friend to the office door. She knew Louisa had a long drive to Bastrop this afternoon. Joe D. had an overnight furlough, and they were going to spend it together in an Austin hotel. If Louisa were younger and had a uterus, Eva might have advised her to take precautions not to get pregnant – which reminded her of something else.

"Your young New Zealand friend, have you heard if she's had the twins yet?"

Louisa stopped at the door, a sudden sadness in her eyes.

"No," she said. "We've lost all contact."

"Well, that's not surprising," Eva said, "for a single woman with twin newborns. It's
probably all she can do to keep her head above water. No doubt she'll get back to you when she can."

"Yes, no doubt," Louisa said, in a tone that indicated the opposite. The loss of contact with Rainey felt intentional and permanent, and Louisa would respect that. Rainey had a new life now, and couldn't look back. But it tightened the muscles in Louisa's chest, to lose touch with a much-loved friend.

On the way across the parking lot, she also thought about Ditch. Wonderful Ditch, she prayed, please don't give up hope. You're still young yet – and, heck, look at Joe D. and me. She smiled, starting her car. She very much looked forward to cuddling with him tonight in a hotel bed. It turned out he could be trained.

CHAPTER 30

NEAR RAMSTEIN, GERMANY, in Landstuhl Medical Center, the largest American hospital outside the U.S., he lay immobilized face down in his hospital bed, feeling – well, you don't feel anything, immobilized face down, and some part of you keeps whispering, Are you sure you're not dead? He certainly hoped not, because if this was the After-Life, it was extremely disappointing.

The surgeon came in to brief him. "A minor concussion, no problem. And the facial laceration, you'll have what they used to call a saber scar, very attractive, I hear, to women. But the shrapnel in your chest, that's a different story. It's lodged between your heart and aorta."

He held an X-ray in front of Ditch's face. "That's your heart." The doc pointed with a pencil tip. "And that's your aortic arch. And this is what appears to be a ball bearing wedged between the two. Pulling it out is going to be dicey."

"Just do what you have to do," Ditch said, turning away.

The doc waited a moment. He was accustomed to critically wounded patients who were quite downcast. "Isn't there anybody you want to call?"

"No," Ditch said. If he lived, he'd call Louisa, and Hugo, and maybe his spend-thrift sister. And if he died, well, they'd all be eventually notified.

"You should be grateful you have all of your limbs."

"At the top of my gratitude list, doc. Just tell me, if you don't kill me on the table, how soon can I get back to my squadron?"

"Oh, that's the good news," the doc said cheerily. "You could return to Leatherneck in a month or maybe two."

Strange to say, but to Ditch that was cheering news. The devil he knew had a need for him, and for better or worse, for the foreseeable future, he was married to the Corps.

Rainey had fallen asleep, nursing the twins on her bed, one on each of her quite bodacious knockers. She frequently fell asleep now, twice while she was standing, and even when she was awake, she felt she was sleepwalking. But she woke when her mum came in the bedroom, lifting each sleeping pepi very gently, and putting them each in their bassinette. Were they really three months old? Rainey scarce remembered the last ninety days.

She sat up and looked around the room, at a momentary loss as to where she was. Her mum came and sat down beside her, speaking in a whisper.

"How you keeping, luv?"

Rainey rubbed her face. "You know, mum. Had twins yourself."

Yes, Meg thought, but not all by myself. "You're going stir-crazy," she said. "Why don't you go out for a walk in the air? You need a fuck-it-break."

Rainey smiled. That phrase, "a fuck-it-break," was one of Ditch's, but she'd picked it up, and now her mum used it regularly. She stirred, and swung her legs out of bed, but

waited before she stood. She suddenly felt so lightheaded, she.
. . she couldn't complete the thought. She had no idea what
she'd just been thinking. Her mum stood and watched her
climb to her feet. Rainey flipped up the flaps of her nursing
bra over her nips, making sure the velcro was attached. Then
she buttoned her blouse. But what was she going to do next?

"You're going outside, luv, for a breath of fresh air. Here,
I'll get you two bottles of water, and you must drink them.
Your blood pressure's very low, for certain."

Rainey followed along limping to the kitchen. "Mum,
I'm usually better than this. It's just when you come, I finally
get to relax a nibble."

"I know," her mum said. "Come, I want to see you drink
this first bottle right now."

Rainey did as she was told, like a child and not the mother
of twins. By the time she finished and squeezed the bottle
flat with a pleasing crinkle, she felt herself again.

"Just you go out and walk around the block. Then sit on
the porch. Take in the sky and the trees."

Later, Meg joined her on the porch. The house was a pleasant little one in an older, sedate Wellington suburb. Very few
cars passed by, and the trees, planted by the original owners,
had grown quite large. Seated, Meg looked at her daughter.

"I'll talk to Beryl today, see if she can spare someone from
the big house to help you for the next month or two."

"Sounds grand, mum. You know, Beryl had a wet nurse
for Jack?"

"It doesn't surprise me she'd farm that one out."

"Yeah na, but that's not for me."

"Yes, but poor Beryl," Meg said, "she's coming apart at
the seams. She has a full plate now, taking care of the Judge,
even with James, the nurse."

The Judge had not carked it, as Storm had predicted,
but he was invalided to a wheelchair. Mostly he rolled his

eyes about and moved his mouth, like he was either trying to form words, or spit.

"Yeah na," Rainey said. "I'm coming to terms with Beryl, just not quite there yet. But a wet nurse, really? I wouldn't give up nursing the kids for anything. Best parts of every day."

Meg smiled. "For all three of you," she said. "You're producing an amazing quantity."

"Na yeah, I'm a Guernsey among nursing mums. Must be in my bloodlines."

"Speaking of bloodlines, luv, has Beryl said anything about the pepis?"

"Na yeah, she sees only Jack in them. No harm in it, I suppose, as it cheers her no end, at a time she's got little else. But I told her they were dusky because of some Maori back in our family."

"Oh, that must've thrilled her, for sure."

Rainey laughed. "I don't know, mum. I sometimes think I fucked everything up."

Her mum sat thoughtfully silent a mo.

"You still haven't posted any of those letters, have you, to Ditch?"

"No, and I'm not going to," she said. "I'm firm here now, and busy taking care of the kids and batty Beryl. If he's still alive, better he move on from me. He thinks he's an insensitive asshole, but really he's a one funny, staunch bloke. Women will be lining up for a prize like him."

"But you're at the head of that line, luv. I saw it in his eyes every time."

Rainey cocked her chin down, holding it in, the cold sweats she'd come to have, whenever she flashed on Ditch and that war – that bloody war which had already robbed her of Jack. If anything happened to Ditch, she'd never come to grips. Better to let him go, better not to forebode, better that she never know, better to have him in her life at least and if only through the kids.

Still, her mum persisted: "Send him a letter, luv."

"No, mum, I won't. But I'll keep writing them. It's almost like talking to him."

"The key word in that sentence," her mum said, "is 'almost.'"

Ditch called home regularly over the next months and then years, to touch base and give himself something else to think about besides war.

"Hiya, Louisa. Just letting you know I'm alive and well."

"Oh, Ditch, how wonderful to hear your voice! Where are you, can you say?"

"A beautiful place called Djibouti. It's next to the even more exotic Somalia. How you doing, and how's Joe D.?"

"He's better than ever," she said, "but still with a long stretch ahead. That's how we say it prison lingo."

"And you?"

She decided not to mention the possible fallopian tube cancer. He already had enough on his plate.

"All good," she said.

"Excellent!" Ditch said. "Tell Hugo I'll call next week." After a pause, he asked, "Any word from Rainey?"

"No," she said. "I'm sorry. Will you be back home soon?"

"No," Ditch said, "I don't think so. Listen, Louisa, I got to go. There're guys with wives waiting for the phone. I'll call you from my next duty station, in Salerno."

"Take care of yourself, wonderful Ditch."

"Copy that," Ditch said, but for a Marine Officer, taking care of yourself was the last priority. You had your people to take care of first, then your aircraft. Those were the important things, not your petty little fucked up life. That'd have to wait until the shooting stopped.

August 2015 Wellington, New Zealand

RAINEY SAT WITH her oldest mate on Adirondack chairs in the back garden of her little house, trying to have a conversation. The three-year-old twins were playing about, but Naomi was without her own kids, first time back to Godzone alone, which she could do, now that her youngest was seven. Both mums were accustomed to rarely having a sequential conversation.

"Twins: I don't know how you did it," Naomi said. "Is he supposed to be eating that?"

"Jack, take the plastic rake out of your mouth. Na yeah, I was sleep deprived and border-line mad," Rainey said. "So I don't remember a thing – spit out the sand, Jack – a pepi on each tit, doing the washing, feeding, burping, bathing, nappy changing – Ta, Jill. Now show the leaf to Aunt Naomi – mopping up, taking temperatures, wiping noses and bums, cooking, reading, tidying up."

"That's the prettiest leaf I've ever seen. I love your curly ranga hair – you'll let me brush it later, won't you? And what a lovely complexion. Na yeah, one pepi at a time was psycho enough."

"But mum was grand. Jill, dear, no pouring sand in your brother's ear. She knew what having twins was about. Jack, that's a sand shovel, not a hammer."

"She did, but with a hubby's help," Naomi said. "Jack, stop here. You're so handsome, so tall and dark, with such beautiful eyes," she said. "Do you ever think about him?"

Rainey knew who she was referring to. Naomi was one of the few people who knew.

"No, not atall." Rainey lied, tucking down her chin. "Kiddoes, you do know toys are meant to be shared."

Naomi watched the twins as they tugged on the plastic shovel until they both fell over. "Fred says the concept of private property must be shouted into kids." Then she changed the subject back again. "About that peelot, I just thought – ."

"Quit thinking. Turn it off, like a light switch. What I did," Rainey said. "If he's alive, he's surely moved on by now. I'm an old slipper: he needs a new pair of shoes."

For a moment they watched the kids, who were off playing happily at different ends of the garden. From an earlier conversational thread, Rainey knew Naomi disapproved of her relationship with Beryl. She even disapproved of Rainey's new staid wardrobe, which she said made her look frumpy and mature. How did she always come to have such bullshit detector friends? And so what if Beryl was giving the kids a leg up? Thanks to her, they'd been accepted into ECE next month, Queen Margaret College pre-school. Rainey mentioned that again.

"And once they start, I'll be back to the barn teaching lessons full time."

"A return to the world for you, then. But do you have to wear clothes like her, really?"

"Aye, mate, don't knock 'em. They're protective: keep the blokes off me bum. And Beryl's a loose cannon now. Progressive dementia. Started after her double knee replacement and the general anesthesia. If I dress this way, she doesn't get so aggro."

"You could always just walk away, couldn't you?"

"No." Rainey shook her head. "Not anymore. They need me: they've no one else."

In the quiet moment that followed, Naomi looked over at her mate, whose love for the twins so filled her heart. But, Naomi thought, there was also a gaping, empty spot. Back years ago, when Rainey had visited The Old Pile of Bricks, her eyes had sparked whenever she mentioned the pilot. They'd lost that spark now, sure enough – but on the good side, she hadn't talked at all about poor dead Jack. His death had become more a fact now than a factor. Good on that. But between caring for the twins, as well as ailing Beryl and the paralyzed Judge, did she have any time left for herself.

"And have you had any chance to move on then," Naomi asked, "with other men?"

"Na yeah, squeaked it out with exactly three."

"Tell me. I'm dying. I been married so long I forgot what it's like."

Rainey used her fingers to count the three. "First was a smoothy show jumper, I won't tell you his name, only that what he wanted in a woman was a woodpecker. And do they really think that gets us off? I mean, it's smashing when you doing it for a fella you love, but for some bloke off the shelf? Yeah na, fuck that."

"And then?"

"I went in a full different direction: a dull solicitor, specialized in real estate transactions. He took care of the work when I sold the Bream Bay farm. But if he had a sausage, he for certain didn't know how to use it. I shoulda known: bloke in his thirties living with his mum."

"And then?"

"A surfer body builder. Flash as all shit, with muscles out the yin-yang, but a complete wankstain. I mean, he spent yonks squizzing himself in the mirror, turning this way and that, asking if I fancied his trapezius. Fucking narcissist. That's when I settled on being a mum-nun."

Rainey paused and took a deep breath that ended with a sigh. "For certain, the two blokes in my life," she said, "they ruined me. They were Romeo Mikes, through and true."

Naomi was about to point out that only one of them should be referred to in past tense, when Rainey jumped up and hurried limping across the back garden. Jill had tripped over a garden hose and lay on the turf crying. But Jack beat his mum there, and was trying to cheer his sister as he gave her a hand up. Jack was always like that, the best mate ever, like his dad. He also had green-brown eyes.

CHAPTER 31

April 2013 – January 2018

ALWAYS BEFORE, DITCH'S deployments lasted eight, nine months, then he returned to the world. The result was a bit unsettling, a mental whiplash. But it was different when you kept stepping up as a confirmed-bachelor Officer, always volunteering to take the place of Marines with loving families who wanted them home. And you, you didn't have anything like that. In fact, going home seemed pretty bleak. As Rainey had said, "Sometimes you can't stay where the memories are."

But in time you got used to it, the tempo, the seasonal rhythms of war, in Helmand, Djibouti, Somalia, Yemen, Libya, Niger, Salerno, Romania, Syria, and Al Anbar. It became your new-normal, no big spikes of adrenalin, just a slow, steady drip that carried you through one mission to the next.

And you thought you were doing some good, in a world that was pakaru. Like on that sortie to central Somalia, bringing medical help to a village decimated overnight by a feuding warlord. From your vantage protectively circling above, you watched the medical teams fan out from the delivery bird, to the villagers gunned down when they'd fled. A good number of them were still flopping around. The corpsmen had to chase away the white-backed buzzards who were hopping closer each minute, impatient for their meals to die.

"Shit, Major," your new co-pilot observed, "that's extreme."

"Roger that," you came back. "Over here, life is nasty, brutish, and fucked."

But you did what you could. You told yourself that your life was here now, looking after your people, and it would be until the wars ended (yeah, right), or until you could retire, or were RIFed out of uniform. And as year after year ticked by, you thought the memories might fade, the memories of something better, something shining, something blessed, someone loved. But, no, they didn't fade in the least.

And it's not like you didn't try to fill the hole by finding, like dad said, "a replacement woman." For example, in Salerno, with tall, stylish Lucia, whose legs looked so lovely in Italian high heels. An assistant bank manager and investment advisor, she'd helped with some stock transactions, then you had coffee and became friends, and eventually lovers. To her you never mentioned Rainey, but she apparently knew, somehow, because when you told her you were pushing off to the next duty station, she hugged you goodbye, but did not ask you to call.

And at Kogalniceanu Air Base near Constanta, Romania, there was Ruxandra, the athletic, raven-haired Romanian beauty who held national records in the 100 and 200 meter butterfly. At London 2012, however, she had not done well, due to a touch of what she called "the Olympic crud." You met her while distance swimming in the Black Sea and hit it off, despite the slight language barrier. It lasted only a month before she broke it off. When you asked why, the look she gave you said, you really are quite dense.

"In your eyes, I see the woman broke your heart into the many pieces. You are honest in the eyes, always."

"No," you said, "not always. And I didn't deserve her. I let her down."

So okay, okay, just admit it, asshole. You still thought about her every single day, many times, but especially at night when you swung into the rack, and in the morning when your feet hit the deck. You even heard her voice in your head. Oh, yes, you deed.

"Hey, bro. Just calling to let you know I'm back in Al Anbar again," Ditch said.

"Fuck," Hugo said. "I saw it on the news, those assholes are beheading Yazidis."

"Where are you?" Ditch said. "What was that sound?"

"I'm in the can, and I just flushed the shitter. Got to make Nan think I'm busy."

"You're hiding from your wife in the head?"

"Dude, do you know the most terrifying sentence a husband can ever hear?" When Ditch said nothing, Hugo answered his own question. "It's 'Honey, I'm ovulating.' It means the rest of your day is shot."

Ditch laughed. He knew they were trying to get pregnant.

"It's not funny, asshole. I'm being treated like a stud. Three times today, already. I had to leave Daph to do all the work herself. I feel so, so used."

Ditch laughed again, which irritated Hugo. But he did have something to tell Ditch.

"So I been sitting in here so long my legs have gone to sleep, and there's nothing to read but Nan's women magazines. But I hit on this article wrote just for you. It's about lost love partners. Did you know, studies have shown that when they get back together, they have, and I quote, 'the strongest sexual experience of their lives.' It goes on to say, somewhere here – ."

Ditch could hear him flipping magazine pages, searching for the line.

"It says, their renewed romance is the most trusting and comfortable of their lives. Dude, this is an *a*ctual study."

"Oh," Ditch said. "Well, then." After a pause, he added, "When I hang up, I'm calling Nan and telling her you're hiding in there faking a shit."

"You better not, you bastard," Hugo said. But when Ditch broke the connection, he stood up, shook some feeling back into his legs, and hurried out.

He called, "I'm coming, cher," pronouncing it the Cajun way, "sha" with a short "a."

"I'm in here," she sang from their bed. "Did you take those vitamins like I told you?"

At the door, Hugo took a deep, sustaining breath, before he went in. "You know I did."

"And you're not wearing those tighty-whiteys anymore. From now on, loose boxers."

"Yes, cher," Hugo said, climbing into bed.

When Rainey and the kids came in the front door, Ngiao looked instantly relieved. She was the middle-aged Maori maid at the House of Gauge, and a good friend and ally of Rainey's.

"Oh, *Hauaua*," she said, hugging Rainey, "you came so quick. Ta. We couldn't stop her this time. You know how aggro she gets. She made James and me load the Judge in her car, and off she drove."

"Crickey-dick! Did she hurt you again?"

"Tried to, but James took a conk on his nose."

Lately, Beryl's mental decline had reached the stage where frustration about her limitations sometimes led to violent angry fits. But this would pass, according to Dr. Maynard, their gerontologist, once she became too demented to know what was going on. "After that, she could cruise on for years, on autopilot," he said, basically the same condition the Judge was in. Nobody knew how much, if anything, he comprehended. He sat all day helpless in his wheelchair, rolling his eyes about and moving his mouth.

"Should we call the police?" Ngiao asked.

"No, not yet. Let me think," Rainey said. Where would Beryl be taking the Judge?

Meantime, Jack and Jill, near five now, took advantage of the distraction to run around. This big dark house fascinated and frightened them, as chocka as it was with knickknacks from the Orient. When the Gauges were much younger, they travelled frequently. But while Rainey thought about Beryl's destination, her mum-eye still kept watch on the kids.

"Jack, don't touch that jade thingamabob. Remember, if you spill or break here, you'll never live it down. And Jill, don't stick that up your nose, like you did with the Barbie shoe."

She looked back at Ngiao. "Can you look after them for a bit? I know where she might be headed."

Despite her worry, Ngiao smiled. She loved taking care of these kids. They always brightened this dark house. She bent down, saying, "Come here, my *manhanga*. Let's go to kitchen. I'm sure cook can find something sweet for you to eat."

This delighted the kids. Their mum was very strict with sweets. While they ran ahead, with Ngiao hurrying to follow, Rainey found her car keys and limped back out. Driving, she rolled down the windows so she could hear any honking or sirens. Even at her best, Beryl had not been a good driver – she felt entitled to do whatever she wanted, even if it meant making a right turn from the far-left lane – so she often left honking drivers in her wake.

At the Royal Wellington Golf Club, Rainey spotted Beryl's gold Lexus sedan, and parked her Corolla hatchback beside it. Good, she thought, almost run to ground. Behind the clubhouse, she found a greenskeeper taking a smoko.

"Mrs. Gauge, you seen her, mate?"

"Bloody hell," the bloke said. "That banshee made me carry the old man from her car to their golf cart."

Rainey looked around the golf course. A light rain, *hau-aua*, was beginning to fall, and the wind was gusting from the south.

"Which way'd she go?"

"The back nine. The water hazard on twelve, best guess. Made me load a bucket of pellets in the cart, for the ducks."

"Can I trouble you for a bottle of water and a cart?"

"Only if you promise me something," he said, stepping inside to the caddy room for the water. "Promise she'll never, ever come back."

"Oh, mate, she's not coming back, that's for sure."

Beryl thought – no, there were no thoughts in her mind anymore – she just felt that if she and the Judge were on the course they loved, they'd be themselves again. And bumping along in their cart, she did feel almost unafraid, as she ramble-talked, commenting randomly on the vegetation, the weather, and anything else popped into her head. The fall evening that late May had cooled considerably, and a light, slanting rain fell. The Judge sat beside her with his head drooping the way it did now, his eyes rolling and lips moving.

"We'll go, the ducks, feeding. Comfortable?" she asked. "Cool this eve."

She reached to pull his scarf around his neck, which brought her in contact with the crepey skin on his neck. How strange it felt. Experimentally, she pushed the crepe down with her thumb, then watched it spring back again. Surprised, she repeated the process, and smiled when it bounced back again. Ahead she maybe saw the water hazard on the twelfth. She may even have tried to stop short of it, but the cart's floor pedals, so confusing. On the edge of the pond, the ducks flapped and quacked and waddled toward them, hoping for a treat. She ran over a few of them. Beside her, the Judge rolled his eyes, possibly seeing the water rushing toward them. He moved his mouth.

The impact of going down the slope into the water knocked him forward, and he banged his head on the windscreen. Beryl must have banged her head, too, because the next thing she knew a young woman in a nice dress was picking her up from the half-submerged cart and carrying her to a cart on the shore.

Rainey deposited her on the seat, and returned for the Judge, a heavier dead-weight load, for sure. Her old lady shoes got sucked off in the pond muck. At her cart, she slid the Judge in, reached back for the bottled water, and handed it to Beryl.

"Drink it, all of it, right now," she said. "You're not thinking straight: you're dehydrated."

With shaking hands, Beryl did as she was told, resentful she was being spoken to like this by a woman she didn't know. But a minute after she drank, she was thinking nearly as clearly as she ever did now.

"I don't know," she said. "The Judge's scarf, his neck, and out of no, the. I wasn't. . . ."

"Trying to harm yourself? No, Beryl, I'm sure."

Back at the House of Gauge, Rainey left James to carry the Judge into his chair, while she supported an indignant, wet Beryl in through the kitchen door. Out and in, she was, but at the sight of the kids at the kitchen table, she brightened.

"Oh, children," she said. "The children!" She turned and looked around the room, searching for something, her mind muzzy again. Her eyes passed over Rainey, then returned.

"The children's mother, that horse-girl? Where is she, what's become of her?"

"Sometimes I wonder," Rainey replied. She handed Ngiao the Lexus keys, whispering, "After you drive us to the Club for our car, come back and hide these."

"Good on that," Ngiao said.

"And I'll talk to Dr. Maynard tonight about finding them spots in a Home."

"You take such care of them, *Hauaua*. They're lucky devils to have you."

Rainey smiled wryly, watching Beryl stump indignantly out of the kitchen without a word of thanks. It reminded her of a proverb: "Eaten bread is soon forgotten."

CHAPTER 32

February 1, 2018 South Pacific

DITCH, NEWLY RELEASED from the Marine Corps, was sent to New Zealand at the request of a dying friend. Not that Louisa was dying immediately, but the end would arrive soon enough, and before it reached her, she asked to see again some of the people she most loved.

Otherwise, Ditch wouldn't have been on that Qantas flight. He'd briefly considered a covert visit, just to check that Rainey and the twins were okay, but by now she'd probably remarried, and the twins didn't know him from Adam anyway. Nevertheless, he still thought about them every day. Nobody back home had heard from her in over six years.

So, as he sat there, in First Class at Louisa's insistence, waiting to douse himself with a second glass of Pinot Noir, he thought about the things Louisa had said. She told him that dying by inches had given her time to think, and an insight beyond any she'd formerly had. And she'd come to understand that above all things, she believed in the transformative power of love.

"Because when the right two people unite in love, each becomes more than they are."

After a moment, she added, "By giving, they gain. By risking, they reap. And by surrendering themselves to one another, their souls travel God's path."

When she told him this, she was at home in bed, and he sat close, holding her thin hand. Her head was covered with a slip-on slinky-cap favored by women with chemo cancer hair loss. She'd finished the course of an experimental chemo the week before, and was depleted, but it didn't stop her from talking about true love, a miracle which she'd both experienced and seen.

"Believe it when they say," she said, "God *is* Love."

She closed her eyes, and just when Ditch thought she'd slipped into sleep, she opened them again and looked directly into his. She reached out and touched the scar on his face.

"Wonderful Ditch," she said, her voice firmer now. "Rainey would say I'm mucking about in other people's lives, but for me, please go to Godzone. Go find that girl and her twins, and bring them back for me to see."

When he nodded that he'd try, she smiled at him. Oh, yes, she was happily mucking about, meddling, intruding, and sticking her nose in again where it didn't belong. She couldn't help it, though: that was her nature.

"Excuse me."

A voice broke into Ditch's thoughts. It was the flight attendant, handing him the Pinot Noir.

"Thank you," he said. "Chur."

Wanda, the flight attendant, smiled at Ditch. She'd been squizzing him since he stepped onboard and stopped at the cockpit to rag the crew about not getting lost. And as was her habit, she began constructing a story about the dusky bloke in 7 B. He had a quiet ease about him, a sense of humor, a short haircut, a saucy moustache, no wedding ring, and a scar on his cheekbone that spoke of the cannon's mouth. There was something wistful about him, too, a pensive melancholy, when his gaze drifted out the seat window. But, of course, at uni Wanda had read a lot of Shelley, Keats, and Byron, which tinted her impressions of handsome men.

"If you don't mind me saying, you're a pilot, aren't you? Former military, I'd guess?"

Ditch admitted that he was.

"Fine now," she said. "You just give me a jingle, anything you need."

He smiled his thanks, then sipped wine and looked out the window, thoughtful again.

After he'd left Louisa sleeping, he and Hortensia stepped out of the room. Hortensia was a wise soul who'd suffered a lot, so he asked, "What do you think about all that, Ten, true love and God's path?"

Hortensia smiled. "Heavy stuff," she said, "but back in the day, you were pretty keen on true love yourself. Has life turned you into a skeptic?"

"Maybe," Ditch admitted. "I just know, windows of opportunity tend to close."

Hortensia moved off down the hall, to prepare Louisa's afternoon tea, but over her shoulder she asked, "How do you know a window's closed, until you try to climb through?"

And so here he was on the plane, with the attendant chatting him up.

"Have you been to New Zealand before?"

"I feel like I have, but no."

"And your reason for visiting us now?"

"Making contact," he said, "with an old friend, to deliver some news."

The way he said this was embedded with emotions, so she made a guess and asked, "How long since you've seen her?"

"Yonks," he said. "Six years."

"What's her name? Maybe I know her. Godzone isn't very large."

Ditch sat silent a moment, flooded by memories – her gray eyes, her broken nose, her lips and the sound of her laugh, the fragrance of her ear, and the feel of the twins tumbling within her – memories that triggered a sharp, familiar, and somehow pleasant pang. But still it was difficult to say her name.

"Rainey," he said, straightening himself up in the seat. "Rainey Gauge."

The flight attendant blinked in recognition.

"Mrs. Gauge? I do bloody know her, or I know her by sight. She's a prominent equestrian judge, and the chair of the National Equestrian Centre."

"Is she?"

"And you know, they're having the big National Show Jumping, Show Hunters Championship next week. You're sure to see her there."

"Oh," Ditch said. "Thanks for the tip."

But the way he said it made Wanda think he'd known this all along. He was a dark horse himself. He'd probably done his research, or collected intel, or whatever a soldier would say.

"I'll fetch you another wine, shall I?"

"Sweet as," Ditch said. "Ta."

But when Wanda returned, he'd fully reclined and put on his sleep mask. She set the wine cup down. A handsome bloke, genuine, salt of the earth, and a bit of a dag. She wondered about him and Mrs. Gauge. She could not imagine them being old friends: it didn't fit into her story of him. The Mrs. Gauge she knew looked and acted like the stiff, proper family she'd married into. Was widowed, the rumors said, with twins by the dead husband. But maybe she'd been different, back when. Whatever, because since then she'd taken a different path, for certain.

And it occurred to Wanda, as she went about her duties in the cabin, how complex life could become, how each turn took you some place new, until you'd forgot where you'd begun and where you were headed to. She herself would never make that mistake, of course: she merely noted it in others.

Joe D. was getting sprung. The new President had commuted his sentence to time served at Bastrop FIC. He tidied up his room in the Unit, dropped his large collection of paperbacks at the library, and on his way out, stopped at the Education Complex to say so long to his pals.

"We'll be praying for your wife, Choo." Charlie Reynolds shook his hand. Charlie had introduced Joe D. to C. S. Lewis with *Mere Christianity*. From there he'd gone on to read all of "Jack" Lewis' writings, particularly those concerning his conversion from atheist to Christian apologist. In fact, he could quote whole passages from *A Grief Observed*, when Jack's faith is shaken by the death of his beloved wife Helen. She sounded a lot like Louisa:

"For a good wife contains so many persons in herself. What was H. not to me? She was my daughter and my mother, my pupil and my teacher, my subject and my sovereign; and always, holding all these in solution, my trusty comrade, friend, shipmate, fellow-soldier."

"When they open the gates for you," Joe D. told Charlie, "come by the house and see us. Until then, God bless."

Outside, he stood in the parking lot sunlight, looking for his ride. Hugo waved him over and tried to take his bag, but Joe D. wouldn't stand for it.

"I carry my own water," he said. "Now, let's get driving, and fill me in on Louisa. The last visit she didn't look good."

"Chemo," Hugo said, "kicks the stuffing out of you."

As he drove on, Hugo thought Joe D. was in for a shock. Louisa had kept the seriousness of her condition from him.

All he knew was that the cancer had re-occurred, and not that it had spread. Dan was back from Antarctica, and Moira, Rudy, and their baby girl were down from DC where they now lived. And for the last several weeks, friends had flown in from everywhere, which tired Louisa out. From now on, she requested, visits by only family and loving staff.

"Hugo," Joe D. said, leaning forward in his seat, "can you get that dog to stop licking my ear?"

Hugo glanced to the back seat, where Pierre was still trying to give Joe D. a sniff.

"He's just welcoming you to the pack. Daph and I trained a support dog for you and Louisa."

"I don't really," Joe D. said, still leaning forward, "like dogs."

"You will this one. He's an Irish Terrier, and Louisa says he reminds her of you. She calls him Badger."

"Badger?" Joe D. liked the sound of that. He straightened up and looked down the long road ahead. "Could you drive any faster?" he asked. "And tell me about your daughter. Do you have a picture?"

Hugo thumbed his phone and passed it to Joe D. The photo showed two-year-old, dimpled Lyla at her recent birthday party tapping on her favorite present, a xylophone.

"God, she's amazing," Joe D. said. "How could a little person that beautiful come from you?"

"It's a mystery," Hugo beamed. "She looks like Nan, and she's already musical like her, too."

CHAPTER 33

RAINEY WOKE AT 0630 and lay in bed for ten minutes listening to the sounds of the house and feeling quite alone. When she went to the dunny and sat, she was aware of the smells, or the lack of them, or the lack of one of them, from back in Texas. That had been a time in her life, or what she thought of as "her other life." And a happy time, despite all of her stubborn attempts to continue to grieve, but that was down to Ditch. He was – what was the word? Indefatigable – cheering her up constantly. That last month before they parted, before brekkie every morning, they'd silly-danced together to the oldies. And on the toilet that morning she laughed, remembering the way it had started with "Love Potion Number Nine."

Then she got up, washed her face, brushed her teeth, and went to shake the kids. When they got to the kitchen, she put in front of them their plates.

"Bulgarian yogurt, prunes, blueberries, and macadamia nuts," she said. "Impaction should not be taken lightly."

Jack and Jill shared a look, and a giggle. They loved mum when she acted goofy like this. They actually thought they had two mums. This rare one – fun, a little wild, with color in her cheeks and a mischievous look in her gray eyes – and the other, in public and espesh around Grandmother and the crippled Judge, very strict, straight-laced, upright, and somewhat frightening.

"What are you humming, mummy?" Jill asked.

"Nothing. Just a stupid tune got stuck in my head. Now finish up and get ready. Queen Margaret school doesn't tolerate tardiness."

The strict mum was back.

"And remember, the Show is day after tomorrow, and I want you on your best behavior."

After she dropped the kids, she returned home and re-dressed: an ivory dress, pearls, and high heels. She checked her watch. Due to visit Beryl and the Judge at the Home. Beryl still had moments when she was her old condescending, judging self, and she'd continued her program of indoctrinating the kids into the House of Gauge. The Jack she described to them was a fictitious version of her son: a sober, virtuous young man who upheld the highest traditions of the family, and not the wild, fun, risk-taker he'd really been. And Rainey worried about the effect this was having on the kids. Fortunately, however, more often lately than not, Beryl was off the deep end. Last week she'd held her arm out to Rainey, staring strangely at it, and asked, "What *is* this?"

After the Home, she had an afternoon slew of meetings about the Show, including one to design the show jumping course with that smooth jumper she'd briefly dated. He was still strong on her, and, she admitted, she was a wee bit tempted.

After that, the kids would need picking up, and she looked forward to an evening eating, reading, doing homework, and watching telly with them. She told herself she had a busy, good life. Precocious six-year-olds, a home, a decent car, and work with horses. But as she drove, she found herself humming that old, incredibly stupid, perfectly goofy song. It made her inexplicably happy.

"Hey, bro. Just calling to let you know I made it to Wellington," Ditch said.

"And?" Hugo said.

"And nothing. I haven't seen her yet. I'm still scouting the terrain. Where are you? What was that?"

"Oh, that's just Nan retching. She got herself up the duff again."

Ditch laughed. "You Cajun hound," he said. "How's Daph? I didn't get to see her when I was there."

"Working hard. She's sworn entirely off men after Sam. Turned into a work-nun."

"And Louisa since I left?"

"Bro, she's actually looking a skosh better. And Joe D. dotes on her. Did you know, Moira and Rudy had a little baby girl, too?"

"Shit, you assholes back home are proliferating."

"Families: something for you to think about, dumbass. Got to punch off now, bro," Hugo said, "and make Nan some chamomile tea."

The line went dead, but Ditch kept the phone to his ear, thinking how much he envied Hugo.

At the Show she thought she'd glimpsed a face in the large crowd, but no, when she looked again, the glimpse was gone. And this wasn't the first time she'd imagined him in crowds. She briefly searched the sea of faces again. No, all she saw was her towering dad, climbing down the bleachers and headed to the rear. And she couldn't stop to indulge in this shite right now. She was the big noise at the Show, and the Show must go on. She put on her mask and went back to work.

She tallied the scores, determined the results, made the announcements, presented the trophies, and mediated disputes, not to mention introducing the dignitaries in the flagged and bannered section to her rear. Even the Prime Minister, The Right Honorable Jacinda Ardern, had appeared. Also among the group were Beryl and the Judge, sedated in their wheelchairs, and Beryl seemed almost *compos mentis*. She even smiled once at Rainey. For her, this might be Rainey's finest hour. She was commanding and exceedingly presentable, curly hair coifed, in a dark beige suit skirt, maroon scarf, and sensible shoes – what Rainey privately thought of as her "House of Gauge disguise." Underneath it, she told herself, she was the same as she ever was.

But in the wee hours of the morning she did sometimes wake with worry: could faces grow to fit the masks they wear? No, stuff that. Needs must; necessity compels. And it was only natural that as you mature, you learn to compromise. But could you also be compromised? That was the question that opened her eyes at night. She knew how to deal with it, though.

"'When you start to get confused because of thoughts in your head, Don't feel those feelings! Hold them in instead. Turn it off, like a light switch.'"

But it occurred to her that maybe she hadn't turned that light switch off. Maybe she'd only put it on to dim, because why, so often, did she still think of him.

Meantime, that show jumper sidled close past her on the dais again. Last few times, he'd dipped his head, giving her a smooth wink, and once he'd even touched her on the shoulder. Enough of that, she thought, turning brusquely away. Like bloody hell she'd ever give that wanker another go!

Behind the stands, with his daughter's voice echoing in the loudspeaker, Stormy Day caught up and put a big hand on the shoulder of the bloke he'd been following.

"You there," he said. "Mind: I'll have a word with you."

The man turned, and it was him. He now had a scar on his cheekbone, and a look in his eye like, if it's a shirtfront you want, bring it on. But Stormy had only a question to ask.

"You're come to take my girl away, have you?"

The directness of the question took Ditch aback. "No Sir. I've come, but not like that. I'm here on a simple errand, to personally deliver some news from Texas."

"An errand?" Stormy Day asked. Flummoxed and disappointed, he raised his shoulders high, then released them with a sigh – and the wind that came out of him was like the gust front from a spent thunderstorm. Embarrassed now, he hung his big, Easter Island Head.

Ditch continued, "Maybe I can give you the news to pass on. I don't want to disturb her life."

"You wouldn't be disturbing that much," Stormy said.

"That's not what it looks like. She appears to have it nailed."

That's the way Ditch had seen it from the stands. Rainey wasn't Rainey anymore. Gone was the down to earth, plucky girl working the barn in moleskins and sweaty chambray – gone and replaced by a proper, official woman in a dark beige dress, sensible shoes, and makeup on her face. She seemed completely settled into this life, and there was clearly something between her and that jumper dude, from the knowing way he'd touched her shoulder on the dais. The window of opportunity had closed, and she was gone, albeit not forgotten, but a stranger to him now.

But Stormy protested. "Got it nailed, has she? That's as may be, if you don't dig deep. Honest, mate, I was wrong about you years back. And about her. Meg was abso-right. She says our girl's been soul-sick something desperate ever since. And it's sorry about that, I truly am."

The heart-broken quality in his voice got Ditch's attention, and something inside him slightly loosened.

"No apology needed," he said. "But you're right: I would like to see her, privately."

"It wouldn't be private," Stormy said, "not with Jack and Jill."

This was the first time Ditch had heard the names of the twins. The remainder of something collapsed within him, the last reserves of his resident bitter regret, for his lie of omission that had so let her down. He'd always kept a supply of it on hand, as salve for the scar tissue of having loved so poorly again. But she'd apparently forgiven him enough that she'd taken his suggestion for the kids' names.

Stormy Day noted the change in Ditch's face, the softening, and he felt more hopeful than he had.

"Where you staying?" he asked, and Ditch told him, that old nut farm up north, on Bream Bay beach in Waipu. It had recently been converted by the new owner into an air B&B.

"You're pulling my tits," Stormy said. "Parfect! Now come with me, mate. There's something you need to see."

CHAPTER 34

HER MUM AND dad didn't tell her a thing but that she abso-needed to go off with the kids for a drive-about. A fuck-it-break, her mum said.

"Start with where you left off," Meg said, "at the old macadamia farm at Bream Bay you sold. Spend the night there, why don't you? It's an air B&B now."

"But I can't – ."

"No questions, luv. It's already reserved. Just," her dad said, "please, please go."

He sounded serious something awful. And he didn't use his usual bossy tone. This sounded more like a plea.

But in the rear seat of the Corolla the next morning, the kids had heaps of questions. This was unusual behavior for their mum. Like all six-year-olds, even precocious ones, they valued stability above all else. This didn't seem like that. They questioned her about this sudden trip.

"What's so special about this nut farm, mum?"

"It's the farm where your dad-Jack and I planned to live, our escape hatch – but we never got to stay there one night."

"Because he was killed?"

She nodded. Crickey, that seemed so long ago, she sometimes wasn't even sure it was real. But Jack's death had started a series of events, like a ripple sent through a garden hose. And now here they were, the three of them. She'd told the kids to pack light and dress "rough," as Beryl would say. And she'd even dug out her old moleskins and chambray. Felt sweet as to be in them again.

"Will we be there soon?"

"I dunno. I'm a little bit lost."

"When we were young, Grandmother always told us Gauges never get lost. Gauges always stand up straight and do the family proud."

"Na yeah, there's Gauge rules for most everything. And by the bye, you two are still quite young."

"And she said we are their ambassadors."

Rainey checked her kids in the rear-view mirror. Is that what they thought they were? Ambassadors for the House of Gauge? Small wonder that Jack had run. Not for the first time she thought, what the fuck have I done?

"When will we be going back?" Jack asked.

"I'm not," Rainey said, "I'm not sure that we will straight away. Maybe the three of us need to be on our own a while, to suss out the rules *we* want to live by."

This stunned them into silence. Jack looked out his window; Jill looked out hers.

"But if we're on our own," Jill turned and asked, "who will we be?"

"And what'll happen to us?" Jack asked. He was always the long-range planner.

Rainey sought to put their fears at rest. "Jack, you're the kindest, smartest, funniest boy I ever knew, bar your dad. And Jill, you're stroppy, fearless, and accident prone."

"Like you, mummy?"

Rainey laughed. "Yes, like your mum. And both of you have hearts so large, I'm surprised they fit in your chests. The day you were born, I never felt so blessed. I just wish your dad could see you now. But every time I look at you, I see a slice of him."

She wasn't thinking of Jack, of course, but of Ditch – of what might have been, and of what she'd kept from him.

"Mummy, you're crying," Jack said. "And you never do."

"Na yeah, but once upon a time I cried buckets, and at the drop of a hat."

"Why?" Jill asked. "I mean, why now?"

Rainey took a deep breath between sobs. The words that came out had been a long time stuffed down.

"Because years back, I did something I shouldn't have done, passed up a chance I shouldn't have missed. And I tried to fix it by becoming something I'm not. I," she said, "I fucked it all up."

Jack and Jill looked at each other, and despite their mum's weeping, they grinned. They loved it when mummy cussed. She only did it when there were just the three of them. It was a shared secret from Grandmother and the Judge, who never uttered foul words. Still, it worried them she was crying.

"But mummy," Jack said, reaching forward to touch her shaking shoulder, "you always tell us if we fuck up, we can still put things right."

"Na yeah," Jill said, "and I'm real glad about that, because I fuck up all the time."

Rainey laughed, and dabbed her eyes.

"You okay now, mummy?" Jack asked.

"Fine as feathers," she said. "A box of budgies. Oh, look, I think I know where I am."

How do you tell someone who's become a stranger that you know you're the father of her kids?

Do you just pop up and say, hey, thanks for the twins, here's a little cash in case you're strapped, and, oh, by the bye, why the fuck didn't you tell me, and what the fuck have you become?

No, better not that. Truth was, Ditch didn't know what to say. He didn't do well with emotions, those angry, stinging hornets that poured out once you lifted the lid. Better to keep it screwed down tight: a good trait for an aircraft commander. Nobody wanted an emotional pilot at the controls. But this situation, the emotions, they went way over the top.

So that afternoon, to take the edge off the joy, anger, sorrow, and guilt roiling inside of him, he distance-swam the salty waters of Bream Bay. As he stroked far away from the shore, he rehearsed several soliloquies to a matronly Rainey Gauge, none of them worth a rat's ass.

While her kids explored the old farmhouse, Rainey picked up the note left for her on the kitchen table. The handwriting was his, so before she read it, she had to sit down.

"Rainey, I'm here, and didn't want to come at you out of the blue. But no wakas, I didn't come to kick-start us. I saw at the Show, your ship's already sailed. I just have some news from Texas, which can wait.

"Stormy took me to squiz the kids at the Show. Even from a distance, I knew. We need to suss out what to do.

"I'm down at the beach taking a swim. You can come down, or not.

"Before I sign off, I need to formally admit, I did wrong to you. And I'll regret it, as you'd say, until the end of me days."

After she read it, she sat for a while thinking: he's alive, and he's here. Her heart beat hard as she called to the kids to put on their bathers. They were all going to the beach for a swim.

When he'd turned and headed back to the shore, he saw them topping the dunes, one short female figure, and two shorter ones chasing crabs. A few minutes later he splashed out of the bay. Rainey was squizzing him, shading her eyes with her hand. Her hand fell, then raised back up, to check again what she'd seen.

He couldn't help his grin: she'd smiled instantly when she recognized his face. That broad smile, he remembered it so clearly, and the joy it always shot through him. And she didn't look matronly anymore, not in a swimsuit, her curly blonde hair blowing in the wind. His heart drummed in his chest. But then he reminded himself, that was all in the past, something he'd fucked up and lost: you can't step into the same river twice.

Rainey seemed cautious and reserved, too, crossing her arms and tucking her chin down. Ditch lowered his gaze to the kids as he slip-walked up the dunes toward them. The kids were all that mattered now.

Jack and Jill were lost in the crab chase until they saw him, a tall, dark man advancing on their mum. They moved closer to her to stand. She put a hand on each of their shoulders.

"Ditch," she said, "really, what're you doing here? And what's this news from Texas?"

The twins relaxed a nibble, since mum seemed to know this mustached man.

He didn't answer her questions, focused as he was on the twins. He squatted down like a kid, eye-level with them.

"You're Jack, I bet," he said to Jill.

"I'm not! Are you daft? I'm a girl."

"So you are. But I bet you're a tom-boy, like your mum. I bet you have a pony, too."

"I do," she said. "His name is Thunder, and he's as gray as mummy's eyes. You should see me ride him."

"I'd like to someday." Then he turned his attention to Jack, who'd suddenly become quite shy. He overcame it by saying something bold.

"How'd you get that scar on your face?"

Ditch smiled. "I bumped into something hard."

"Got any others?"

"Just this." Ditch swiveled so Jack could see the shrapnel scar on his upper back. "Got hit by a piece of flying metal," he said. "Missed my heart by a centimeter."

Above them, Rainey hissed in her breath. "The same distance," she said. "A centimeter?"

Ditch glanced up briefly and nodded. "I was luckier than Jack," he said. "But now, let's all go down to the beach. I'll give you numpties five dollars for every shorebird you catch."

"Five dollars?" they said at once, looking at each other wide-eyed. "Mummy, come on!"

"You run ahead. But stay out of the water till I'm there."

Ditch remained squatting, watching the kids running in circles, without a hope in hell of catching a shorebird. The impossibility of it didn't diminish their fun.

"Jill," he said at length, "has your mom's hair, and my mom's eyes."

"And Jack has yours," Rainey said, folding her arms as she watched them. "They both have your complexion, too. . . . I should've, I did, only I wrote it in a letter, never posted. I wouldn't blame you for cracking the shits with me right now."

He smiled. "If that means angry, I'm not. Right now," he said, "with you, I'm just in awe. Those smart, spunky kids. . . . You're a bonza mum, and I admire the hell out of you."

"Ta," she said, deeply touched. Those simple words, from him, meant mountains.

"Truth is," she said, "I didn't raise them: they raised me."

He stood up, still watching them. "And you were always so sure they were Jack's."

"I was, for certain, and I wanted them to be, as a way for Jack to come home from the war." At the mention of the war, she asked, "So you really did near get killed over there?"

When he nodded, Rainey bit her lip, and looked away.

Ditch knew what she was feeling. "But when my life hung in the balance, I was glad that you didn't know. It was wrong to think I could put you through that again, and I'll regret – ."

"– until the end of your days," she said. "But I have regrets, too, mate."

They turned to face each other, the temperature between them warming a bit. After all, they were old friends. They were both a little amazed: they didn't look all that much older – okay, maybe a little worn around the edges, but better in other ways. Rainey had grown into a full woman, and he into a man seasoned by years of command.

"Been yonks," Ditch said.

"Donkey's ears," she agreed.

"But," Ditch added, "I thought about you a lot. I even talked to you, in my head."

"Na yeah, I deed that, too."

"I hoped you deed."

"Quit poking me accent." She slapped his arm with a smile, and then paused before she asked, "Question is, mate, where we going with this?"

She looked down, waiting for him to speak. They seemed poised, at the brink of something, until Ditch backed away. She had her life here, and he wouldn't interfere.

"I want to help with the kids, of course – financially, I mean. You obviously don't need me otherwise."

She looked up sharply. "You want to throw money at it, then scarper? Got someone waiting in the wings?"

"No," he said. "But I saw you did, at the Show. I mean, that show jumper and you."

"You saw shite," she said. She threw up her hands, exasperated, and limped off down the dunes to the beach. Over her shoulder she hurled back, "You don't know your arse from your elbow, do you? You don't know my heart. And we don't need your bloody bickies. We do well enough on our own. I'll collect my kids, and go."

At those words, Ditch's heart clenched. He tried to speak, but couldn't. His life ahead, bereft of Rainey? There'd always been a tiny seed of hope tucked away, a hope for a life with that girl. And now he'd fucked it up again. He watched her leaving him.

Rainey marched on, at a loss for what more to say. Something in her chest was burning. The farther down the dune she went, the more certain she became. It was all too bloody complicated. Best move was to turn around and drive back now, return to the life they had. She opened her mouth to call to the kids, who'd stopped playing and looked toward her. Their mum was in a blistering mood. But then she halted, stared at them for a long moment, and pivoted. She'd missed this boat once before: she wasn't missing it again, not if that boat could still float. Time to find out. Still fuming, she started marching up the dune again.

Seeing the determined fury in her face, Ditch took a half step back, his hands up defensively. "Look, I'm sorry. I really insulted you. Can we at least talk some more?"

"Yeah na, I'll have no more of that. About you and me, I've thought about it heaps since I left. Only back then, I wasn't ready. I was scared of losing the last half of my heart in that bloody war. But that was then."

She took his hand – hers was still amazingly muscular – and drew him to her. With her free hand, she put a finger to his lips.

"No more bloody talk," she said. "Let's find out what we need to know another way."

She cupped her hand behind his head, and pulled him down to her. They kissed for the first time in six years, very tentatively at first, to test if anything was still truly there. And it was. The kiss quickly became more intense, more heated.

And the way a liquid evaporates at its boiling point, the years between them turned to gas and floated away. She was who she was, he was who he was, and something in each of them enfolded around a familiar piece of the other.

Breathless, she finally pulled back, but he followed with his hand, running it through her bushy, curly blonde hair. She looked up into his eyes, those bloody green-brown honest, loving eyes.

"Jack and Jill are watching us," he said.

"They'll be gobsmacked, for sure. And chocka with questions."

"Why don't you talk to them, while I'll go make some sammies," he said, turning.

"Yeah na." She pulled him back. "That's not the way it's gonna happen. We'll not separate. From here on out, luv, we do everything together. Now," she added, "pash me again."

"If you insist, but I'm getting dizzy. If they were filming us for a movie – and believe me, I've seen a lot of shitty movies overseas – the camera would be swirling around us."

"I'm swirling," she said, "in me head."

But before their lips met again, Ditch whispered a warning, "This time I won't stop."

"Na yeah, and I won't let you, ever."

And they experienced, as Louisa would say, the sweet release of a total surrender.

CHAPTER 35

THAT AFTERNOON THEY spent in the water, Ditch teaching the kids something called "the combat sidestroke," and then after sammies on the front porch of the old farmhouse, they went down to the beach to start a bonfire. Ditch taught the kids how to add sticks to the crackling flames without burning their hands. Rainey watched him. There was a natural ease about him with them. And they were comfortable with him, she could tell. They thought he was smart, and funny, and there was something about him they recognized. As Ditch would say, they clicked.

While the kids kept the fire blazing, Ditch sat back on a log with Rainey. He put his hand on her knee and squeezed it. "Take that walk down the beach, luv, and make your calls," he told her. "We'll be okay."

The first call was the most difficult, to the Home, to make sure Beryl and the Judge would be well cared for while she was gone away. They were like babies now, her charges, her responsibility. The second call, to her oldies, was easier. Her mum was too thrilled to be able to form words. Her dad spoke up from the extension phone.

"No worries, luv," he said. "We'll drive your passports to the airport, and see you on the plane."

"But that's very grievous news," her mum said, "about Louisa."

"Not another like her," Rainey said, "not in this hemisphere or the other."

On her way back to the fire, she stopped for a beach-wee, and from that position, she watched the kids pelting Ditch with personal questions, not like six year olds, but more like parents grilling a potential suitor.

"And exactly where'd you meet our mum?" Jack asked.

"In Texas, a couple of days after she arrived."

"Wasn't she already pregnant with us then?" Jill asked. That's the way the family story went. She turned to carefully watch him answer.

"Well, she thought so, yes. She'd been artificially inseminated. You know what that is?"

They paused, poking the fire with sticks, and shot him a you're-such-a-numpty look.

"We help inseminate the broodmares on Nan and Pop's farm," said Jack.

"I hand them the semen straws," Jill added, quite proud of that.

Ditch laughed. "Are you guys sure you're just six?"

"Mum says we're too clever by half," Jack explained. "And we're trying to suss out you and her. We saw you pashing her on the dunes."

"That's because I love her," Ditch said. "And I have for years."

"Then why haven't you done anything about it, before now?" Jill asked.

Ditch took a breath. "You know what a lie of omission is?"

Jack and Jill looked to each other for the answer. At that moment, Rainey limped back into the firelight to explain.

"It's when you tell someone a story, but leave out the most important bits."

"Oh," Jack said, but before he could go on, Jill completed his thought.

"Like when we were keeping care of Cindy's prize bitch?"

Cindy was their next-door neighbor, a breeder of champion Basset Hounds.

"And you told Cindy she never left the back garden," Jack said. "But you didn't mention the gate came open."

"And the randy Dalmatian from down the street got in."

"Exactly," Rainey said. "A lie of omission, for sure. And if you want to know about Ditch and me, we both lied by omission about some important things, and because of that, we lost years. We'll have an important conversation about that, laters."

"Why not now?" Jack said.

"No need, anyhow," Jill said. "I just sussed out what's what." When her mum didn't appear to believe her, Jill went on, "Honest, mum. Look at us, look at Ditch, look at the snap of dad-Jack on the wall, and look at you, the way you look at him."

Jack nodded. "It's as clear as the spots on Cindy's puppies, who Ditch really is."

Nonplused, Rainey lowered herself onto the log beside Ditch. She looked over at him, and he shrugged.

"That came out a little faster than I thought," he said. "You've raised detective kids."

But Jack wasn't finished with the grilling yet. "We're just saying, how well do you really know her now? After all, you haven't seen her in years. She could've changed heaps."

"Fair enough," Ditch said. "But I bet she still loves to dance."

"Mum dance?"

"She never."

"She ever." Ditch took the Samsung from Rainey's hand and thumbed it until he found what he wanted. "Just you watch," he told the kids.

The Searchers came on:

"I took my troubles down to Madame Ruth
You know that gypsy with the gold cap tooth"

Rainey shook her head when Ditch took her hand, but she couldn't say no for long. He was relentless, indefatigable. And the way he looked at her made her feel like who she really was. Within seconds, she was silly-dancing barefoot in the sand with abandon, and the kids, after a hesitant moment, gave in to the merriment and joined in, marveling at their mum. She didn't limp when she danced, and she had moves like the people on telly. She even knew the words.

"I didn't know if it was day or night," she sang. "I started kissing everything in sight."

While they danced about wildly laughing, goofy-mum ruled, and strict, straight-laced mum was nowhere to be seen. No cautioning them about the fire, no warnings to settle down, no worries about them getting covered in sand. They also watched this man with the funny name Ditch, who their mum looked at with such softness in her gray eyes. This could be the beginning of something, they sensed. Of course, they'd seen dads many times before, in crowds, and they'd both wondered what it must be like to have a real one of them.

Later that night, when Ditch tucked them into their beds and kissed them on the center of their foreheads, Jack couldn't stop himself. He threw his arms around Ditch's neck, and Jill jumped out of bed to hug him, too. And their mum, the funny one, was standing in the doorway weeping buckets.

"Mum, you okay?" Jack asked.

"A box of budgies," she sniffed. "Go to sleep now. We've got a long flight tomorrow afternoon."

As Ditch rose to leave, and Rainey came to kiss them, Jill climbed back into her bed singing, "I didn't know if it was day or night."

Jack joined in, "I started kissing everything in sight."

At the door, Ditch looked back at them and smiled. "Your mum," he told them, "is the secret ingredient, in Love Potion Number Nine."

Did they make love that night? Na yeah, they did, but in very slow motion, the way gourmands savor their favorite meal. Slowly, tenderly, intimately re-exploring favored territory. It was all the same. Okay, maybe Rainey had stitch scars from the C-section, and maybe Ditch wasn't as limber as once he'd been – but the rest of it was satisfying something extreme. But no, it was not like the spontaneous ignition in Hotel Manche, or the trembling passion after the first sonogram: something better, more long lasting, they felt, as they reconnoitered the familiar lands and grooves. And the lips – it was always the lips – and for Rainey the moustache, too. It really drove her a little mad. Like Naomi had said years ago, "Thank you, God, for the gift of sex."

When they reluctantly finished, and they lay on opposite pillows looking into each other's eyes, Ditch's mind returned to the twins.

"Do you think they're really okay with this?"

"Things will bubble up, for sure. But they're smart and tough, and they'll adjust. Only go slow: they never had a real dad, just a picture on the wall and Beryl's glorified stories."

She paused, and thought, then reached over to touch the scar on his cheekbone.

"You're worried about something," Ditch said.

"A bit, about Beryl and the Judge."

"There's no reason they should have to know. No sense upsetting the applecart. Sometimes a lie of omission is a simple kindness."

"Ta," she said, touched by his understanding. She didn't want to shatter Beryl and the Judge. They were very strange people, but in the last sentient moments of their lives, they didn't deserve that. Let them live out their lives believing the kids belonged to the House of Gauge.

"But we'll be on our own from now on," Ditch said, "as a family. And it's not your fault: you got swept away by a Texan of more than moderate means."

"Yeah na, but wait a tick," she said, drawing back to squiz him better. "You really do have bickies?"

Ditch nodded. First, the money from the sale of the ranch, then living with no overhead for six years, eating in chow halls or out of MRE packets, collecting and wisely investing his base, flight, combat, and per diem pay in a rising market, he wasn't Joe D. rich, but he had enough to launch their future.

"All my bickies," he said, "are yours."

They moved in, taking each other in their arms, preparing for the drift into sleep. But before they drifted very far, Rainey said, "If we wake early enough, we might have time to root again."

Ditch smiled. "Then my flag's going up at reveille. And, oh, one last thing: if you want more kids, I wouldn't object to Jack's swimmers."

"Too late on that," she said. "I sent them to Gully, after her disappointment with Dan."

Ditch rocked back with a snort of surprise. He'd gotten word somewhere, maybe in Libya, that Gully had given birth to a boy.

"You mean, she's now raising a stroppy little Jack?" he said. "God help her."

"Aye, luv. Too true that."

Before they fell smiling into sleep, he kissed her one last time, on the center of her forehead like Jack. It crossed her mind again, that Jack may have sent her this man. It could be true, because who the fuck really knew. So before she fell asleep, she murmured in her mind, "Thank you, Jack."

In the morning over brekkie – Bulgarian yogurt, blueberries, prunes, and macadamia nuts, of course – Ditch suggested a slight change in plans.

"Let's spend the morning walking around this old farm. It might be a fit for us. And on the drive to big smoke, maybe a stop at Jack's grave. I've got a few things I need to say to him."

Rainey blinked back tears. "Aye, luv, that's right with me. What'd you think?" she asked the kids.

"Na yeah," Jill said, a slight sob in her voice, "let's go visit dad-Jack, let's do."

Jack nodded emotionally. "We have some things we need to tell him, too. We talked about it last night. We want to keep dad-Jack, as our adopted dad."

"He should never, ever feel alone," Jill swallowed, "because he'll be in our hearts forever."

Rainey bowed her head at that. Always in her heart, too.

Ditch started weeping right then, for poor dead Jack and all the others lost in the wars, and for their families, the ones that were, and the ones that might have been. Ditch first, but Rainey quickly joined in, followed by the kids. They joined hands and sobbed together, and Rainey thought, as she looked at their faces around the table, that this was the first thing they'd done together as a family. And it was good, it was good for all of them.

And in a cosmic, Danny Boy sort of way, a visit to the grave would also be good for Jack.

You'll come and find the place where I am lying,
And kneel and say an Ave there for me.
And I shall hear, though soft you tread above me,
And all my grave will warmer, sweeter be

CHAPTER 36

EVA HOFFSTEADER SMILED at them as she sat down. She'd come to their house to deliver the news personally. They sat on the palazzo facing down the hill to the river, and the early February morning was hopeful and warm. Louisa looked more hopeful, too, with color in her cheeks. Joe D. sat beside her, leaning forward on his elbows to hear the news.

"It's a good report," Eva told them. "The targeted chemo appears to have had positive results."

"Remission?" Joe D. asked eagerly.

"Too early to say that. But likely containment."

"So," Louisa asked, "to be clear, I'm not out of the woods yet?"

"No, but for the first time, you can see much farther ahead through the trees. And for now, we just wait and see."

For a moment, she let the news sink in. The two of them held hands. A dog sat between their chairs, looking from one to the other. Joe D.'s eyes were damp. Louisa nodded at him.

"Thank you, Eva. We'll take whatever we've got," she said.

"We sure as hell will." Joe D. leaned over and kissed her. "Like we say in AA, One day at a time."

"And," Louisa said, turning back to Eva, "we have a Valentine's Day wedding to plan. You're invited, of course. You've met the bride: she's the mother of the twins."

Joe D. broke in with a sudden thought. "Let's make it a double wedding," he said. "Let's reaffirm our vows."

Louisa looked over. "Are you serious?"

"As a heart attack," he laughed, "Please marry me again. I'm begging you. I couldn't love you any more than I do right now."

"Keep trying," she said.

He smiled so much it hurt.

Eva Hoffsteader watched this playful exchange with a kind of envy. She remembered feeling that way once, but it hadn't turned out well: a piercing divorce, and an only daughter who wouldn't speak to her father. She felt a little guilty about encouraging that. But maybe it was time for another form of remission, a pardon, a forgiveness, a release to start moving on.

Later, walking out to her car, fumbling for the keys in her purse, she thought she might bump into that new cardio-vascular surgeon making rounds today. He was former Army, and his own marriage had not stood the many deployments to Germany, Iraq, and Afghanistan. Maybe he'd like to attend a Valentine's Day wedding. Thinking about that, she pushed the key-fob. Her headlights flashed, and her car let out a happy chirp.

The wedding on the palazzo was small, attended by family, staff, former staff, and friends. Daphne and Hugo were maid of honor and best man for them, while Moira and Dan stood for Louisa and Joe D. Their ring bearers were Jack and Jill and also Badger, who carried the rings on his collar. During the procession, Nan played Mendelssohn's "Wedding March" on her cello, a sound so deep and pure, it seemed to come from the center of the earth.

Harold, a deacon in Mount Olive Baptist Church, read the old-fashioned wedding vows: "To have and to hold, from this day forward, for better, for worse, for richer, for poorer, in sickness and in health, forsaking all others, to love and to cherish until death us do part."

And it all went very properly, until they were pronounced man and wife, and the four lovers kissed. That's when the DJ for the reception, Harold's great-grandson Charlie, played the first song. He'd chosen the Fontella Bass version, because he was a purist:

Come on and take my heart
Take your love and conquer every part
'Cause I'm lonely
And I'm blue
I need you
And your love too
Come on and rescue me

The jolt of music took everyone by surprise. Harold shot a dark look at his great-grandson, who just laughed and turned up the volume. Charlie had always been a bit of a prankster, but this time his instincts were right on. Fontella Bass's voice lifted everyone up, espesh Jack and Jill, for whom the formal occasion was abso no fun, until they started to dance.

Then, laughing, Rainey and Ditch joined in, and from there the contagion spread. Within a minute, everyone was swaying and dancing, even ninety-five-year-old Harold, who held The Good Book over his head. Pauline joined him, and they danced like they were twenty again. Louisa's two-year-old grand-daughter, Abby, toddle-danced out to join Nanny and Poppy, who each took one of her little hands. She didn't know exactly what was happening, but it was extremely fun.

The only one not dancing was Daphne, who'd moved off. Dan noticed her departure, and tried to coax her back. Embarrassed, she was forced to explain that she'd put on the wrong prosthetic foot for dancing. Dan was curious.

"How many feet do you have?" he asked.

"Five," Daph said. "And I should've worn an articulated one today."

"But even with the wrong foot, you can still slow dance, right?"

She nodded that she could, and he led her back to the dancing, where he took her in his arms. Her long brown hair tickled his nose. The next song played was Elvis, "Can't Help Falling."

"You probably noticed," Dan said as they danced, "I've been staring at you for days."

"Yes, Rainey pointed that out. But I prefer the company of dogs," she replied. Since her final breakup with Sam, two years ago, all she wanted was a manless peace. But Dan persisted.

"Yeah," he said, "I used to think I preferred the company of wingless midges."

She pulled back and looked at him. "Wingless midges?" she said. "Jeez, you're even more fucked up than me."

He laughed. "Probably true," he admitted. "But like Rainey says, if you fuck up, you can still put things right."

"Na yeah. Rainey talks a lot of shit. Have you noticed, people in love are always trying to push you into love, too?"

"Yes." Dan shook his head with fake sadness. "That's a terrible, terrible thing they do."

Daph smiled at that, and leaned back a little to look at his face.

"You know, you're impossibly handsome," she said, "not to mention intelligent and funny – everything I hate in a man."

"I make up for it by being a melancholy loner, with a low sperm count."

She smiled again, and she felt a knot loosen inside. She moved in a little closer, and put her chin on his shoulder. This wasn't so bad, she thought.

Across the dancers, Louisa watched this, and nudged Joe D. to point it out. He smiled and put his lips to her ear.

"You're meddling again," he whispered.

She kissed him on the cheek, and said, "Sweetheart, I'm just a small-time meddler. But, fortunately, there's a Bigger Meddler at work."

And as she danced, Louisa looked out on those whom she loved: Rainey and Ditch, Aunt Hortensia twirling the twins, Moira and Rudy, Jonny and Elena, Hugo and Nan and Lyla, Daph and Dan, and all of them. With these wonderful people in her vision, and many more in her memory, she felt that she was so close to them, she couldn't tell for certain where she ended and where they began.

"Why are you smiling?" Joe D. asked.

"Because," she said, "I've already lived such a surprising life."

"It *will* be longer," Joe D. said.

"Ha, ha, ha," she said. She wrapped her arms around him and hugged onto him tightly as they danced. He put his lips to her ear.

"When you hold me like this," he said, "my heart beats so hard, sometimes I think I'm dying."

"We all are, dear."

"Ha, ha, ha," he said.

Taking a time out on the sidelines across the palazzo, Ditch watched a happy Aunt Hortensia dance with the twins, while he talked to Eva Hoffsteader's date, the former Army doctor. Ditch had recognized the man instantly. He was the cardio-vascular surgeon who'd taken the shrapnel out of his chest back in Ramstein.

"I'm glad you didn't fuck up that operation, doc."

"You and me both," he said. "If I'd nicked your aorta, I wouldn't be here with Eva."

He kept glancing impatiently over Ditch's should toward Gland Manse, where Eva and Rainey had gone to the dunny. The poor fucker was obviously smitten.

"Funny how things work out," Ditch said. "A wise, goofy man once told me, 'Whatever you think is gonna happen, you're probably wrong.'"

But the surgeon wasn't listening. Eva and Rainey had just come into view. He stepped around Ditch to go to her. She smiled to see him so eager.

Rainey, however, didn't seem very happy. She came up to Ditch and hit him on the arm.

"You bastard," she said. "Eva thinks I'm already up the duff again."

"I blame it entirely on the moustache," he said.

She hit him again, but not very hard. He took her in his arms and twirled her.

"Why are you smiling like that?" she asked.

"Oh," Ditch said, "I'm just remembering pregnancy sex."

And Rainey, despite herself, smiled, too. Like Naomi said, Thank you, God, for the gift of sex. But the memory of raising babies caused her to add, "You're changing *all* of the nappies this time."

"I will, cher," Ditch said. "I surely will."